"Lisa Selin Davis's character Belly O'Leary is a captivating train wreck. It's impossible to look away from the glittering horror of a personality so twisted by alcohol, bad decisions, and tough luck. Davis's powerful prose and dark wit enthrall and entangle her readers in a world where men are men and life is like a sock in the jaw." — Samantha Hunt, author of *The Seas*

"If the way to a reader's heart is through his stomach, then *Belly*, with its gut-jiggling humor and its sucker-punch sadness, will find a fast track to your ticker. A remarkably honest, and honestly remarkable, debut."
— Michael Lowenthal, author of *Avoidance*

"*Belly* is a stunner — at once tough and gorgeous, hip and deeply insightful. Davis's novel follows the self-propelled downfall and redemption of Belly, but it could very well describe our own worst moments and how we find our way out. *Belly* is essential reading for anyone who looks around and sees not home but an alien landscape, which is to say most of us."
— Amy Benson, author of *The Sparkling-Eyed Boy*

"Lisa Selin Davis writes with the verve and skill of a seasoned novelist. With wry, energetic prose and a range of insight both astonishing and entertaining, she creates, in the character of Belly O'Leary, a new addition to American literature's panoply of unforgettable antiheroes, whose contradictions, absurdities, tragedies, and resiliencies make him a vibrant, roguish, quicksilver commentary on modern times."

— Melissa Pritchard, author of
Disappearing Ingenue and *Late Bloomer*

"In the character of Belly O'Leary, Lisa Selin Davis has performed that most mysterious of literary feats: she makes us care deeply about a man so flawed that he seems irredeemable. But nothing is irredeemable in Davis's world — not the memory-haunted streets of her beloved Saratoga, or the man who seems to love the thrills of money and liquor more than his four daughters; not even the idea of redemption itself, which gleams in these pages like a jewel waiting at the farthest extent of an old man's grasp."

— Rachel Pastan, author of *This Side of Married*

"This is an impressive first novel, one that beguiles and surprises at every turn. Lisa Selin Davis has written an amazing tale of family life and the consequences of love, a story revolving around a most unlikely and compelling figure, the eponymous Belly. She has caught contemporary life on the fly, and missed none of its poignance, its absurdity, its rich comic extravagance. A wonderful debut!"

— Jay Parini, author of *The Apprentice Lover*

Belly

Belly

A Novel

Lisa Selin Davis

Little, Brown and Company
New York   Boston

Little, Brown and Company
Time Warner Book Group
1271 Avenue of the Americas, New York, NY 10020
Visit our Web site at www.twbookmark.com

First Edition: July 2005

Library of Congress Cataloging-in-Publication Data

Davis, Lisa Selin.
    Belly : a novel / Lisa Selin Davis. — 1st ed.
        p. cm.
    ISBN 0-316-15880-1
    1. Ex-convicts — Fiction.   2. Children — Death — Fiction.   3. Fathers and daughters —
Fiction.   4. Parent and adult child — Fiction.   5. Saratoga Springs (N.Y.) — Fiction.
6. Self-destructive behavior — Fiction.   7. Accident victims — Family relationships —
Fiction.   I. Title.

PS3604.A9725B45   2005
813'.6 — dc22   2004016753

10   9   8   7   6   5   4   3   2   1

Q-FF

Book design by Bernard Klein

Printed in the United States of America

To my mother and brother

Belly

SARATOGA SPRINGS was stoic as the Statue of Liberty with Grace Kelly's face and the body of Bettie Page. That's the way Belly O'Leary thought of his town, like she was a woman in a Greek robe, to be revered. He stared out the big tinted front window of the Greyhound bus as it hobbled north on Route 9, down the long line of motels that sat hungry all winter and grew fat with tourists in the summer. They were fat now. August. Cars streamed out the little roundabouts and bled onto the highway.

August changed the face of Saratoga, from Grace Kelly to something a little brassier. Kim Novak, maybe, or any of the girls on the Alberto Vargas cards his father used to keep hidden in his sock drawer. For one month a year, she was a woman with a bad dye job and too much makeup, and this was the town he was coming home to in 2001; this was the lady welcoming him back.

Only he didn't recognize her. Where once green fields graced the sides of the highway, glass-box office buildings now rose like the great pyramids. Traffic and strip malls and smog choked the last promising stretches of hillside that used to hug the town.

The closer he got to home, the sicker he felt. A moan rumbled in his solar plexus. He recognized it as heartache. He was returning two years early to his hometown, four instead of six, his sentence commuted for good behavior — something he'd never been accused of in his life. He worried now he was back too soon. The town wasn't ready for him. He'd walk in on her with another man. He'd catch her in a lie.

For four years he'd kept quiet in a cinder-block cell, waiting to hear from his old mistress, Loretta, waiting for word from their colleagues at the New York Racing Association. They'd advised him not to talk. They'd sent Loretta to the courtroom to remind him, quietly, with a hand pressing gently on his shoulder, that two of his three remaining daughters still lived in this town. Loretta with her lips twisted into that sideways life-threatening smile, walking off with his unmarked $172,000 stashed in her fake Hermès Kelly bag.

He half imagined her waiting for him, his midwestern princess, at the bus station now, opening her arms to him, opening the sack of cash, pulling out from her cleavage a shiny gold key to a small office at the back of City Hall, where the NYRA boys and the Republican chairman would offer him cigars and checks bubbling with zeroes and shake his hand for not giving up their names. But he only wanted to see Loretta in his fantasies.

The bus pulled up to Springway Diner and squeaked to a stop. He sat there, in seat 3C, the other passengers milling about, collecting their things, getting up to stretch as the driver turned off the engine and announced a twenty-minute rest before continuing on to Montreal. He sat there and thought about what the prison doctor had told him after his release physical: no salt or cigarettes or alcohol, nothing that might raise his blood pressure. He wanted all of those things now, anything to calm the erratic beating of his heart, to lengthen his short breath. His hands shook. Only two other times in his life had he been this nervous, so nervous it burned, it was something that had to be doused: at his wedding and then, twenty years later, at his third daughter's funeral. Both those times, and now, he just wanted the moment to melt away, to have already happened. He wanted to turn around and see the hard times behind him.

He stepped off the bus into a blast of heat that surrounded him like an embrace. He'd left a dewy, cool Pennsylvania that morning for this: a thick stew of atmosphere, the air heavy and wet, and he was at that moment so very tired. Across the street from the bus stop were new stores and crummy old motels with new paint jobs and the road sparkled with new, dark tar. His oldest daughter, Nora, was not waiting for him. No one was. He looked at the strangers and tourists loitering on the concrete outside: *Who the hell are all you people and what have you done with my town?*

This used to be a twenty-four-day town, Belly thought. He remembered the queer quiet just before the racetrack opened each summer, the whole town preparing for the rain, the reign, of tourists to descend. It was like that every year: upscale specialty shops selling fancy linens and New Age chachkas and glossy horse paintings bloomed on Broadway, only to wither once track season ended. But now, since he'd been away, the racetrack stayed open almost twice as long, reaching back into July and stretching all the way to Labor Day. A season of horse racing straddled the town, scarring it up for the rest of the year, just like what they used to say in AA: one foot in tomorrow, one foot in yesterday, and you're pissing all over today.

He pushed the door open and stepped into the air-conditioned paradise of the perfectly preserved Springway Diner, to wait for Nora. The same greasy red booths, the same metallic wallpaper with flowers of orange and brown. The walls were plastered with black-and-white photographs of the grumpy old Greek who owned the place standing with celebrities — Liza Minnelli, Bob Dylan, some short guy with huge glasses Belly recognized but could not recall — who passed through on their way to SPAC, the performing arts center in the state park. In every picture, they held up a big white cake with strawberries dotting the top, the Greek's smile wide and white as the frosting. In every picture, the same Greek and the same white cake, and it seemed like this was the only thing in Saratoga that had not changed: cake.

He realized now this would not be easy. The whole time he was in, he just wanted to be out; the whole time he was away, he just wanted to be home, but now he stood on the horrible bridge between his two worlds, stretching like a big grin between his old town and what it had become. He stepped into the bathroom and checked himself in the mirror. A face returned his gaze, a countenance surprisingly unchanged, just grayer, somehow, the skin looser around the curve of his jaws.

Someday, he realized, jowls would swing at his neck, but for
now, for now, he could pass. The fifteen-hundred-some nights
spent in a cell with two other men, in a pod with three other
cells — the stress of all that time hadn't surfaced. He put his
hands in his pockets and did something he hadn't done since
the days of high school dances: he winked at himself. He
watched the lid close over one icy-blue eye, watched his right
side grow dark, then lifted the lid and let the light back in. He
decided he could pass for forty-five of his fifty-nine years, and
he nodded at himself and stepped out.

He made his way back toward the door, looking over the
counter at the desserts for the big white cake, but he saw only
the same sorry pies they'd always carried. They looked like
home, those crushed-in tops and browned meringue, and he
decided to buy one for Nora and the kids, if they ever showed
up to retrieve him. That seemed like the right thing to do in a
situation like this. He had no one to ask.

The waitress met him at the counter. "Can I get one of those
pies?" he asked her. She was a fine-looking woman, or girl;
he couldn't remember what you were supposed to call them
anymore.

"Which?" she said, and he didn't know one from the other
so he just said, "Lemon," and she took it down from the display and wrapped it in a pink box.

"It's eight seventy-five," she said, not looking at him.

He had one crisp twenty-dollar bill and a couple of ones
crumpled in his pocket: all his money in the world. He would
buy something for his family first, then he would get himself
something he'd been waiting four years to wrap his fingers
around. "Give me that lighter," he said. He'd been scrounging
for matches for four years, and with the power of lightning in

his hand, the weight of change in his pocket, he was half Thor, half Donald Trump, sans combover. "And some Newports," he added. It would be great to even have a box top after all those smuggled-in soft packs with the cigarettes smooshed.

"What color?" she asked, and he pointed to the red lighter.

He flicked and flicked, but he could not light the thing.

"Hey, miss, I think this lighter's broken."

The waitress turned around from the society section of the *Saratogian* and took the lighter from him. She pushed a microscopic lever on the back and rolled the gear till it lit. "Childproof," she said, handing it back to him.

Belly took it from her, but he just stood there holding it in his hand.

"You just get off the bus?" she asked, finally looking straight at him as she rolled a penny between her fingers. Her nails were an inch long, painted with palm trees, and she'd written "cat food" on the back of her hand with a ballpoint pen.

Belly nodded.

"Where you from?"

She was staring at him now, all the youth of her taking in his age.

"I'm from here. I've been gone four years. I just came back from Pennsylvania."

"What's there?"

"Prison," he said, watching her. She didn't even flinch.

A little flash erupted in the general area of her eyes, some curl around her brows and raising of the lids that made him think he'd been recognized. "Well, since you've been in, they made these new childproof lighters with these little buttons and stuff you have to push." She took the lighter back, her nails lightly scratching his fingers, showed him the tiny piece of metal. "But you can get rid of it." She pressed her thumb against it, and off popped the lever. She handed it back to him, circumcised.

He looked at her. She might still be in her twenties if he was lucky. Her name tag said "Maybelline."

"Named after the Chuck Berry song?" he asked her.

She shook her head. "The makeup company."

Maybelline didn't look too bad. Lots of orange hair, curled up and shiny, like copper. And her skin was kind of coppery, too, all metallic with goop. He looked at all that orange on her and thought about the business Nora used to have on Caroline Street, Everything Pumpkin, that sold food and clothes and anything orange. Maybelline could have been a mannequin there.

"You work here long?" he asked, shuffling his feet a little. He'd been wearing jail shoes — Velcro-and-canvas sneakers — these four years, and his cowboy boots weighed about a million pounds, mashing up his toes at the pointy fronts.

"Not too long." She took out a straw, unwrapped its white paper shroud. "I used to work at the Stewart's on Route 50 but things got kind of slow, so I came to work here." Then she took the straw between her lips, blew air through it, nibbled on it with her teeth.

She smiled and he turned to look behind him, but no one was there.

"I'm Belly."

She said, "That's what I thought," and she reached out to shake his hand, wrapped her soft fingers around his callused knuckles, and let them remain just a second too long. Her fingertips were cold and the rest of her hand was warm and kind of clammy: he could incubate there. Something could grow.

How do you know, he wondered, how do you tell if the woman wants you or is just playing with you or if that's just how she is? He was so out of practice, all his flirting skills dormant and foreign, but he kept looking at her, and she kept looking back at him, and he thought, Maybe, maybe. He looked at her orange-tinted lips and thought, Maybe.

He packed the Newports, peeled open the wrapper, and popped open the top and offered her one, and when she took it, he said, "You want to go out sometime?"

She nodded. "Sure."

"You want to go out tonight, maybe?"

"Okay."

Finally, that stinging feeling of nervousness began to float away.

"What time do you get off?"

"Six," she said, tossing the straw in the wastebasket.

He asked her if Ruffian's was still open and held his breath while she rolled her eyes back to search her memory, and when she said, "I guess it's there," he exhaled.

"Maybelline," he said, "I will meet you there at six." She handed him her phone number on the back of a Springway Diner business card. He tried not to smile, but a big dumb grin erupted on his face. He thought of that one dead tooth, that brown bicuspid poking from the side of his mouth, and he hoped she couldn't see it. She sashayed back to work, and he watched her ass move in acid-wash jeans, and he changed his mind: everything would be fine, easy as pie.

He stood at the window, smoking and staring into the sun. How many years since he'd whiled away an afternoon at

Springway Diner? Of his four daughters, only the third one ever wanted to come here, the one who was not with him anymore. Sometimes he'd take a break from the bar and walk down to meet her here, him and the kid in her favorite old-lady pink cardigan with the Izod alligator, slurping a cup of hot chocolate while she showed him her plans for the science fair: The Secret Life of Tornadoes.

He flinched when he saw Nora pull up alongside the diner, the tires of his sweet black Bronco squealing to a stop. It was a great truck, the best he'd ever had, with rock-stomper rods and 230 horses, tinted windows and chrome rims and a thin red pinstripe clinging to the sides. He could see two small dents like vampire bites by the rear left fender as he went out to meet her.

"I thought you quit," was the first thing Nora said when she saw him drag on his Newport, though she had an unlit cigarette poking from between her first two fingers. Her three boys in the backseat kept quiet.

"I did," Belly said, "but only 'cause it was so freaking hard to get cigarettes." He tossed the cigarette to the ground and swiveled his foot over it.

She didn't get out of the Bronco, just let her cigaretted hand hang out the open window, so he stood by the door and put his free hand on her shoulder, making a right angle. There was so much space between them.

"Nice to see you," he said.

She said, "Get in."

The burning feeling was back. He walked around to the back of the truck, his shirt sticking to him in the heat, and threw his duffel bag in, continued around till he got to the passenger door, and climbed inside. His license had run out almost two years before, and he knew his near future included a trip to the dreaded DMV, but not yet, not right away. He lowered himself into the seat and thought how he'd never been on the right side of his own truck. It was only five years old. He'd bought it just a few months before they locked him up.

Nora put the truck in reverse.

He turned to his grandsons. "How you boys doing?"

They just stared at him: a teenager, a little kid, a baby in a car seat. He noticed a slight tremor in his hands, like his fingers were saying hello without his consent. He placed one hand on top of the other to still them.

"You guys remember me?"

"It's only been four years, Belly," said the middle boy.

"That's Grampa to you," and he turned back around. This, he thought, is what it feels like on the first day of a new job you didn't want to do, standing there waiting for someone to direct you through a series of meaningless tasks, waiting for the day to end.

"Isn't it funny," he said, slipping the cigarette from Nora's hand and lighting it. "I think the only other time you drove me around was right after you got your permit. You must have been sixteen."

"You let me drive when I was twelve."

"Did I?"

"You made me drive even when I didn't want to, when you were too drunk." She rolled down her window to let the smoke escape and pressed the button to open Belly's. "You mean Eliza. You made Eliza wait till she was the right age."

"Oh."

"Yeah."

Four daughters and three grandchildren and their names circled above him like a fly he couldn't catch. Their differences eluded him.

"Well," he said, turning back to the boys. "Which one is which now?"

"See the one who's not even a year old, Belly?"

Why couldn't she call him Daddy?

"That's King. You haven't met him before."

"I've seen your picture, though," he said to the baby, who drooled on a plastic bib around his neck. "Who's this one named after?" he asked the oldest boy, the one who had turned into a teenager, pimples beginning to surface on his pale Irish skin.

The oldest boy turned his attention out the window and the middle boy said, "B. B. King." He looked down at his lap, then raised his eyes to his grandfather. "I'm Jimi," he said. "That's Stevie Ray."

"I know that," said Belly. "Stevie Ray with the big birthmark on his knee." He looked at the stretched-out teenage boy and could not believe he was the same little kid he said goodbye to four years ago. "How old are you now?"

The boy said nothing. "Stevie, your grandfather is talking to you," Nora said. "You know, when somebody talks to you, it's polite to say something back."

The boy shrugged.

"Don't roll your eyes at me, young man."

"I didn't," Stevie Ray said in a small voice, a voice far too delicate for a boy with O'Leary blood.

"It's all right, Nora. Jesus, give the kid a break. Sometimes a man just feels like keeping quiet." He nodded at the boy, but the boy's face was stone. Belly cleared his throat.

"So it's dead guitarists for all three of you, then?" he asked.

"B. B. King is alive and well," Nora said. She put a hand on her round stomach. "And number four is on the way."

"You're kidding."

"Don't say anything, Belly."

"Am I saying anything?" He looked at his grandsons. "Did I say anything?" The oldest one still wouldn't look at him. Nora took another cigarette from the pack on the dashboard and put it to her lips. "Aren't you supposed to give that up?" he asked her, and she turned and glared at him, let the car move down the street without even watching where it rolled.

"Do you see me smoking it?" she growled. "Dr. Pearson said this is the best way to quit." She nodded toward the ashes leaping from the tip of his cigarette. "You're the one infecting us with the secondhand smoke. I'm just holding the thing."

Belly cleared his throat. "Well, how's it going, then? Getting a girl this time around?"

Nora turned her eyes back to the road. "I don't know yet."

"Well, you better hope it's a girl. Girls are so much easier." He turned and winked at the boys in the backseat, but they didn't even blink.

"How are you doing, Belly?" Nora asked him. "That's the million-dollar question."

"Hot."

"Me, too, Mom," Jimi called. "Can you turn up the air-conditioning?"

"When Belly's done smoking." She turned to him. "There's a heat wave on. Supposed to last all week." They were still on Broadway, inching down with racetrack traffic, and he noticed now just where they were.

"Don't you want to turn down Spring Street?"

"We may as well just go on by there now," she said. "Get it over with."

He nodded, adjusted the seatbelt that hugged the hollow of his stomach. There it was, the corner of Washington and Broadway, the large glass doors on the street level, his old apartment teetering on top. It used to be his Man-o-War Bar, though everyone called it War Bar for short. He threw his cigarette butt on the sidewalk.

"What is it?" he asked.

"Café Newton," she said. She pulled up alongside it, put the truck in park. "I'm running in. You want something? A cappuccino?"

Belly shook his head.

"Be right back." Nora climbed out the door. He could see now that she was pregnant, her stomach starting to pop out, leading her like a divining rod.

He watched tourists mill in and out of his old bar, women in broad-brimmed hats and too much makeup and their toupeed husbands with diamond cufflinks glittering; he could almost see the clouds of perfume and cologne punctuating the air. These were people who never would have stepped foot in War Bar, and here they were surrounding it, squeezing the last bit of life out of its memory.

Jimi scooched forward in the seat, his hands grabbing Belly's headrest.

"Stevie Ray's getting confirmed on Sunday," Jimi said.

"That right?"

The oldest boy looked at his hands.

"I thought they did it older."

"They let you do it whenever you want to," said Jimi.

"Who's your patron saint?" Belly asked his oldest grandson. The boy didn't answer.

"Do you talk?"

"He talks when he feels like it," said Jimi.

"Now tell me your ages again. I haven't seen you boys since you were this big." He pinched his thumb and forefinger together.

"You can't see a baby when it's that big," said Stevie Ray. "Except on the ultrasound."

"Thirteen, eight, and eleven months," Jimi informed him. "I'm the eight."

Nora came back with a large coffee. "Sure you don't want some?" she asked. "It's decaf."

He raised one eyebrow at her. "Are you trying to make this hard?"

"It's just a latte," she said, but she was smiling, as if she'd won something.

She started the car and lifted another unlit cigarette, and he leaned over and eased it out of her hands, and he thought how they were old enough now to share all their bad habits.

"Belly," Nora said, and he said, "What?" and she said, "Can you hand me another cigarette if you're going to keep that one yourself?"

He handed her one, and they continued down Broadway. "What happened to that old building by the Y? It's got stars on it."

"It's the Jewish Community Center. They restored it. That's how it looked once upon a time and that's how it looks again."

"They don't have Christmas," said Jimi in the back.

"That's right, honey, they're different than us."

"I didn't know we had so many they'd need a whole center," said Belly.

"There are more now," Nora said, taking a long drag of her cigarette and ducking her head out the window to exhale. "One's the mayor now."

"Don't tell me it's a Democrat."

Nora nodded.

"Jesus, you're gone five minutes and the whole place goes to pot." He let this information sink in, tried to smooth out all its wrinkly meanings. He had nothing against the Democrats, not in theory, but without a Republican administration, all of Belly's plans would change. Those were his friends in office, or if not his friends, then his contacts, the people who owed him. How would he collect now? Who would see to it that he was repaid? There hadn't been a Democratic administration since before Belly was born. He wasn't even sure he knew any.

"They're all gone now," Nora said, looking at him sideways.

"Did they call you? Any of them?" He turned and looked at his grandsons, but their eyes were glazed over in the heat and they were glaring out the window. "Did they say anything to you about me coming back?"

Nora shook her head. "If you mean Loretta, no, I haven't heard from her. Or anybody. They've left us alone and that's just how I want it. That was your business, not mine."

He nodded, he bounced his head up and down, but he couldn't shake this new information into submission.

They kept driving, past where their favorite fast-food restaurant, the Red Barn, used to be, now some big chain bookstore, and the art supply store where his youngest daughter, Eliza, still worked, as far as he knew, past his old haunt Jatski's Diner and the big town clock that never, until now, kept good time.

"Looks like we got ourselves a makeover." He motioned at the white picket fences and mums that circled the big oak trees, yellow ribbons panting from lampposts.

"Those are the same decorations they put up every August. It's track season, remember?"

He remembered everything about track season. War Bar was his for more than thirty years, and the first twenty, the racetrack barely seeped inside. They might put the harness races up on the TV for a laugh, or take a glance at the Whitney, or some tourists might sit up at the counter on Dark Tuesdays and study up the tip sheets purchased from street vendors milling around the side gates. That's how it was before his mistress, Loretta, wandered sideways into War Bar in the hot August afternoon, not a week after the accident, fixed herself a Cuba Libre behind the counter, and turned on the TV to catch the tail end of the Travers. He remembered that foggy light in her eyes, the realization that even after she'd analyzed the Pink Sheet all morning she forgot to place the bet, her saying, "Put one in for me, would you? I've got Tsunami to place, Nada, Nada, Nada to show, and Ivanhoe to win." He remembered the soggy fifty-dollar bill that started the whole mess, that turned him from barkeep to bookie. It was all her idea. It was all her. He remembered this clearly while everything that went before, his real wife and daughters and their whole life together, remained a blur.

They passed Furness House, the old brown Queen Anne mansion on Union where the Down Syndrome kids used to live. It was pink now, or peach or salmon or one of those food names for pink, and it was a bed-and-breakfast with a fat, pastel "No Vacancy" sign out front.

"Where did all the retards go?" he asked.

"We have no idea," said Nora. "We've been wondering that ourselves."

Belly shifted back and forth in his seat, massaging his new titanium hips, looking at the new face on his old town. Saratoga was as strange and cold now as his metallic body parts, and August, he thought, was like any woman you couldn't live with or without. He thought of his grandmother in that last stage of her life, her dyed-rust pixie cut showing gray-white underneath, a marshmallow alcoholic smile continually pasted on her perfectly round face. Every time she looked up, it was as if she'd never seen you before. Right now, Belly felt just like that, like his grandmother, looking up and seeing Saratoga and her summer inhabitants as if for the first time, looking up and saying, again, *Who the hell are all you people and what have you done with my town?*

They turned down Circular and drove past Congress Park, the site of everything that ever happened to him — first kiss, first fuck, first coke cigarette. "Thing about this town is, you could have your whole life in a six-block radius, you know?" Belly asked.

His daughter nodded.

"Every mistake you made's in walking distance."

Finally they turned onto Spring Street, down one block and into the driveway. It seemed like the car ride took longer than the bus, and Belly just wanted to sit in the truck and take a nap, to wake and have his life be settled the way it was before. They all sat in the truck for a minute, Belly and Nora and the three kids, all quiet.

"The house looks good," said Belly. He was lying. An Erector set of scaffolding held up the front porch, and blobs of white paint dotted the soggy cedar siding. The houses all around looked pristine, straight out of a magazine, but their house seemed to belong on a long-gone block.

"It's getting there," Nora said, getting out and unstrapping the baby from his car seat. "Gene's been working on it for us."

"Gene, huh? He's still around? What about your husband?"

Nora pulled the baby up her hip and the boys ran ahead inside and she said, "Don't start."

They walked up the creaking side porch steps. "No one's fixed these yet, I see."

"It's next on Gene's list," she said, throwing her purse on the kitchen table and setting her Café Newton coffee cup down on the counter. "You can work on the dining room table if you need something to fix."

"What's wrong with it?"

"It wobbles."

Belly put his lemon meringue pie in the fridge and sat down at the table, fiddling with the leather straps of Nora's purse. He threaded one inside the other till they knotted up and held. "Any messages on that answering machine for me?"

"You just got here."

"People know I'm back."

Nora set the baby down in his walker. Belly heard the TV go on in the room behind him and the boys flopping on the couch, fighting over the remote. "What people?" asked Nora.

"People."

The baby waddled by him, banging plastic keys on the white rim of his walker.

"What people?" Nora said again, and he said nothing. "Belly, you just leave them alone, and they'll leave you alone. They let you rot down there, so just stay away from them. Especially that Loretta woman."

He unknotted the straps of her purse, tried to keep his hands busy so he wouldn't slam them down on the table. "You don't know what you're talking about," he said.

"Sure, I don't. Let's just pretend I don't know what I'm talking about. That sounds fine."

Belly pressed on the kitchen table to raise himself up. His hips were killing him. "Where do you want me?" He picked up the duffel bag.

"Jesus, I forgot. You're in the attic. There's a girl staying in your room."

"That was very kind of you," he said, but she didn't smile.

"Ann's friend is here for the week." Nora looked at him carefully when she said the name of his second daughter. "She's staying with us."

"She is?" He let the bag slide off his shoulders to the floor.

"Not Ann. Her friend."

"Oh."

"Bonnie."

"Okay, then."

"I gave her the guest room because she's our guest, and you're, you know . . ."

They looked at each other.

"What?" he said.

"Belly, can I just ask you one thing, one favor?"

"What?"

Nora opened the dishwasher and set in a couple of dirty plates. Then she picked up a greasy saucer and held on to it for a moment and she said, "I want you to be at Stevie's confirmation on Sunday."

"Why wouldn't I be?"

"Lower your voice."

"Why wouldn't I be?" he asked in a loud whisper.

"I'm just telling you now so you know. It's going to be a big affair." She set the saucer in the dishwasher, rinsed her hands, and called to the boys, "Kids, get your suits." Then she turned back to Belly. "We're going around the corner to swim. To Mrs. Radcliffe's. We do it every afternoon. Join us if you want."

Belly stood there with his duffel bag slumped around his feet and said, "I hate water," and Nora said, "I know," and she collected the baby and the boys like she was gathering dirty laundry in her arms. She said, "Make yourself at home," and they were gone and the house was hollow and echoey and hot.

He looked at the phone, but the phone did not ring. He picked it up, he cradled the receiver in his hand. He put it back. He lit a cigarette with his Maybelline lighter and he looked at her phone number scrawled in junior high school bubble letters on the card, and when he reached for the phone again, he could not remember Loretta's number. Fifteen years of calling that number, and all of a sudden it was gone. He took it as a sign. He should clean up some before he saw her. He should wait for her to contact him.

Belly sat down at the kitchen table in his son-in-law Phil's house, the house that used to belong to Phil's father and Belly's ex–best buddy, Phillip Sr. He was Belly's first friend to die, though they hadn't been friendly for a long time when he passed; the man did not approve of Belly's extracurricular activities. When Phillip Sr. used to live here, every house on the street had a menacing look, threatening to collapse. They'd sit on the sagging front porch and drink beer and joke about their kids hooking up and getting married, how the kids would steal their houses from them and banish them to nursing homes. By the time that prophecy half came true, Phillip Sr. wasn't speaking to him anymore, and the bank had taken Belly's own house around the corner. Just after their kids got married, Phillip had a heart attack one day while repaving the driveway. There was still that one darker strip of tar, as far as he'd gotten before he keeled over and died, right there by his car.

In the corner of the kitchen a computer in a shocking shade of green sat atop a plastic desk. The kids' drawings covered both doors of the fridge, and a printed-out picture from a sonogram was taped on top. Affixed to the left door was a long list of home repairs, almost half of them checked off, and then the ones left blank: the dining-room table, the front porch floor, the side porch steps, the two kitchen cabinets above the dishwasher, the leaky faucet, the stone walkway leading to the kitchen door. A silver medal from field day at the Lake Avenue School was looped around the refrigerator door. He remembered his mother telling him the only reason to have children was to have grandchildren, but already he couldn't recall their ages. His mother had scolded him for not giving her a grandson. "Four daughters, four daughters. Belly, you're doomed to a life of women," she'd said when Eliza, his fourth and final daughter, was born.

Belly inspected the cupboards. Fluff. Jif. Doritos. Not a real thing to eat in the house. But he opened the fridge door to find a six-pack of Piels, his old watery favorite. What a good daughter, he thought, as he checked his watch to make sure it was after noon. It was. It was 12:05, and he popped open the can, and that crisp sound called every cell in his body to attention and once it was in his mouth, the hops and barley and the suds and the cold, he thought, I have never been so happy. I have never been this happy in my life. He held the liquid on his tongue for a moment till the carbonation dissolved, and then he swallowed.

One beer sat stranded in the plastic loop when the side door burst open and Jimi ran inside, his wet suit dripping on the linoleum.

Jimi came right up to him, then he stopped and looked carefully at Belly's eyes.

"Hiya, kid," Belly said. He felt the whites of his eyes burning red; he felt the pure redemptive power of drunkenness.

Jimi whispered, "Grampa," and then climbed onto Belly's lap. He was wet, the boy was wet, and he made dark circles on Belly's jeans, his wet hair stuck to Belly's stubble, and the feel of cold and wet burned on his skin but the boy put his arms around Belly and this was his first embrace in four years. He pressed the child to him.

"Ow," said Jimi. He climbed off Belly's lap and scampered into the TV room.

"The kid has my eyes," he said to Nora, who leaned against the counter with the baby on her hip. Stevie Ray stood next to her, holding on to the baby's foot and glaring at his grandfather. Nora hoisted the baby up higher and then Stevie Ray's hand hung limp at his side.

"What's with you?" Belly asked him.

"Were you really in jail?" he asked.

"How old are you, again?"

"Thirteen," he said.

"Shit," said Belly. "That's almost old enough to drive."

"Were you?" Stevie Ray asked again.

"You bet," he said. "Four years of it."

"All right, enough." Nora gave Stevie Ray a light shove. "Upstairs, change, downstairs, dinner."

"I don't want to change," he said.

"Stevie, goddammit, go up and change, I said."

The boy's eyes widened, and he started to walk away slowly, shaking his head and whispering absolutions to himself.

"I'm sorry," Nora called after him. "Sorry I took the Lord's name in vain. Jesus," she said. "You can't say anything around him these days."

Nora plopped the baby in his high chair, cooing softly, wiping strands of dark hair away from the baby's blue eyes. "My little angel," she said to him. "My perfect little angel." There was something strange yet familiar about this image, something that made him feel just the tiniest bit sick, trapped in a scene from the past.

Belly realized he had not yet left the kitchen. Nora told him the time when he asked and then he knew he'd had two beers for every hour. That was nothing, normally that was nothing, but after four years with no alcohol — well, with some alcohol when they smuggled it in but almost none, some but not much — after all that time, those few beers in half as many hours had his brain cells sprained. He looked at the baby and the baby looked back at him.

"Nora, this was your high chair. Where'd you come up with this? I remember this."

"Mom had it."

"Oh. Your mother." How could he have gone so long, so many days stretched into weeks and then months, without thinking of his wife, Myrna? Guilt crawled up the back of his spine. "How is she, anyway?"

"We're not talking about her."

"Okay."

Nora sat down at the table with her now cold cup of fancy coffee. "Belly," she said. "You are welcome to stay here. Stay here for as long as you want. Stay here till you get a job, at least. But my kids are not driving until they're old enough to drive, and they're not drinking until, well, until high school, when everybody else drinks." She slid her fingers over his. "Is that okay?"

He withdrew his hand. "What did I say? Did I say anything?"

"You have to follow the rules."

"Nora, honey, I have been obeying the rules for four years." He heard his own voice break. "I am your father and not one of your children, so don't you go and —"

"Belly, are you drunk already?"

He said, "No." He said, "Give me a cigarette."

"You have to smoke outside."

"No I don't."

"Yes, you do. You can smoke on either of the porches but not in the house," she said.

"You're going to make an old man with two bad hips get up and go outside every time I have to have a cigarette?"

"It's not that much to ask, to get your ass up and walk ten feet to the porch to smoke."

He stood in the doorway, one foot inside and one foot out, fished a cigarette from the pack in his pocket, and lit it with his new lighter.

"Out," Nora said. "I mean it. Let's not get off to a bad start." He didn't budge. She raised her voice. "Move your ass outside, Belly."

He swayed in the doorway.

"Oh my god, you're totally drunk."

He lifted his hands in an overplayed shrug and smiled, and he exhaled smoke into the still heat of the kitchen.

"I won't be able to, I can't do this." She stopped, took a breath, started again. "I don't have room for trouble," she said.

All the beer circled inside him, it rose up his spine and into his brain and it made the words come out. "Trouble? Trouble? You were the most trying of the bunch, nothing but trouble your whole life, and who looked out for you? Your mother? You think because she saved your high chair she cares about you? She was the one who called you a mistake."

He was aware of the children standing in the doorway. Nora laid her head down on the table, and the baby pounded his fists on the high chair and gurgled with his spit.

All the day's nervousness had burned down to a fine dust inside him, and he felt calm and sedated and, even at this early hour, ready to find his bed.

Nora stood up and wiped her hands on her jeans. She opened and closed the cabinets gently, taking out cans and a package of pasta, ignoring him as the boys slumped back into the TV room, and the digital music of video games filled the air.

"Nora," he said, and she said, "No."

He stepped outside to the porch, put his cigarette out between the sagging and splintered wooden planks and carefully placed the lighter in the pocket of his jeans, the lighter Maybelline had fixed up just for him, and he knew he would see her soon and that she would save him from this house.

He waited on the porch. He waited for Nora to coax him back in, to ask him what he wanted to eat on his first night as a free man, but she kept her head bent over the boiling water and the half-open cans and the spine of a glossy magazine. He stepped off the porch, cowboy boots hitting macadam, and that was the moment when he finally and for the first time felt free.

The stillness of late-afternoon heat made his town look hazy in a movie sort of way. A slight breeze blew through the tall pines across from School Four, where all of his daughters had gone to elementary school before it became a center for vocational training. He walked down the hill and started up, traversing the great fault on which the city was built. Congress Park on his left, Hawthorne Spring on his right, the wide slide of Spring Street between them.

Long ago, the day after Nora was married, he'd walked down Spring Street, alone, early in the morning, 6:00, 6:30. He'd stayed up all night partying; those were the days when people still laid the coke out in little volcanoes on streaky mirrors in back rooms. The wedding was at St. Peter's and the reception at War Bar. It was one of those times when Loretta wasn't speaking to him, so he'd taken another girl, a girl whose name was long forgotten, but he could remember the spiderweb scars from a breast reduction reaching across her chest. At some point in the night, he'd screwed her in the bathroom; she'd been pounding Greyhounds, and right after he finished, she leaned over and vomited grapefruit and vodka into the sink. He sent her home in a cab, closed the place up himself, headed east, carrying the girl's long coat in his arms as the sun rose. Nora had married in December, amid all the gray gloom.

He was headed up the hill that morning when a car pulled over, a long, green station wagon with fake wood paneling on the side. It was Mrs. Radcliffe, the hot across-the-street neighbor from when the whole family lived on Phila Street, the one with the pool where his grandchildren now swam. "Can I give you a lift?" she'd asked, her big, wet, half-Mexican eyes taunting him.

"Why the hell not?"

He'd climbed into the passenger seat, watched her maneuver her big boat of a Ford through the empty street. He'd never once seen this woman without makeup, hair spray, the whole thing, never seen her in curlers or with her lipstick smudged. She came out every morning, afternoon, evening, like a perfectly done-up sex goddess, teasing him from across Phila Street.

"What are you doing out at this hour?" she'd asked.

"Nora got hitched last night. It was an all-night affair."

"I see," she'd said, pursing her lips, her perfect lips, in a half-moon of disapproval. He'd forgotten for a moment what a strict Catholic she was, that the few times he'd made it to church, hungover and disheveled, she'd always been up in the front pews with her perfect frilly dresses and her perfect husband in his pressed suit, like caricatures of good Christians.

They'd turned onto Circular Street, and she'd asked him, "Where are you headed? Where can I drop you?"

"Home," he'd said, like an accusation.

"Where do you live now? I don't even know."

He'd forgotten. Everything. That he lived above the bar by then with Ann and Eliza, daughters two and four, that his third daughter was taken too soon, and then his wife had left him. He'd thought she was taking him back to Phila Street, to his old life, that she'd drop him in front of the old place and he'd open the door to find everything, his former family all intact.

"Just let me out here," he'd said, and she pulled up against the curb, and he'd slammed the door without so much as a thank-you, as if she were responsible for the fact that his home was a cramped apartment above the bar where only two of the five women in his life still remained.

He stood now on that very corner, it must be fifteen years later. The house that stood before him that day — a crumbling brick Greek Revival — had loomed like a joke, a magnificent structure rotting from the inside out. Now that same house was whitewashed, remodeled, with two Mercedes tucked neatly in the multicolored gravel driveway where Volkswagen campers used to park. He never thought he'd hear himself say it, but he missed the hippies now. At least they let his poor lady-town rest in her stately disrepair and didn't dress her up with million-dollar cars and doodled driveways.

"There's the man himself," he heard a woman say, and next to him was Margie, Eliza's husband's sister. He supposed that made her some sort of long-lost daughter-in-law, and she had so much hair on her face she was almost like the son he'd never had. She was a big woman with wild brown hair and gray eyes that had too much white below the eyelid, giving her a startled look. She never wore makeup or even shaved her legs. He had often wondered how she'd found a husband.

"What are you doing out in the middle of the day, Margie? Don't you have a job?"

"Do you?" she asked.

He looked up toward his hairline and then at the clouds that held no promise of rain.

"I just walked home for a late lunch, heading back to the office now." Margie patted her briefcase. It looked like it was made of straw. "Prison did wonders for you. You look strangely good. Just your hair turned gray."

"Thanks, I guess."

"I thought you'd come back bald and fat or something. You look like you've been summering in the Hamptons."

"We did have golf," he said.

"Well, how the hell are you?"

"Fine. You?"

"Oh, come on. Really. How are you?"

"What do you want me to say? I'm tired. It's hot. I'm unemployed. I'm out of jail. I'm fine."

Margie switched her weight from one thick ankle to the other. "Well, in a strange sort of way we missed you. They cleaned out all the local criminal color and installed law-abiding yuppies."

"I heard you got one of your own in City Hall now."

"Yes, a Democrat, finally, after sixty years of Republican rule, not to mention a hundred years of racetrack corruption."

"I meant a Jew."

"Oh, that," she said.

"Your people have surmounted the final frontier."

"Jesus, Belly, leave my people alone. I do."

"I've got nothing against your people, Margie. I just believe in the Bible, and the Bible's got nothing to do with the Jews."

That burning feeling was beginning to resurface, here in the late-afternoon sun with Margie and the whitewashed mansion, and the beer was evaporating and the sweat beaded at his forehead.

"I am talking to Archie Bunker live and in person," Margie said.

He turned his head away from her, smiling with one side of his mouth, and when he saw her face turn red, saw her clench her teeth and force herself not to yell at him, he felt calm again.

"Tell you what, Belly. Why don't we go downtown and get

a cup of coffee? I know a nice place down there on the corner. They call it Café Newton, I believe."

"You go ahead. Just contribute to the downfall of Saratoga with your four-dollar coffee. Join Nora."

Margie stepped into the shade of a mulberry tree. "Hey, don't blame me. I'm on your side. I'm Mrs. Small Business Association. I'm the whole town planning office. I'd rather have a locally owned bookie joint than a big chain coffee store."

"It was a bar, not a bookie joint." He scraped his cowboy boot along the cracked sidewalk, wiped his palms on his jeans.

"They don't send you to prison for four years for running a bar in this town. We've got more bars per square foot than any other town in New York State."

"Thanks for the statistics."

"It's my job." She moved her briefcase to the other hand. "All I'm saying is, I'm on your side."

"No thanks, kid." He fanned his collar. "I don't need your help."

"Did I offer you any?" Margie looked down at her shoes and said, "Shit." Squashed mulberries stained the bottoms. "Goddammit, I have to go to my meeting with berry juice on my soles."

Belly laughed at her, two sharp ha's erupting from the back of his throat.

Margie brushed a sweaty clump of hair from her face. "Lord God, you're a misanthrope."

"I don't know what that means, but don't take the Lord's name in vain."

Margie started to cross the street, calling behind her, "Okay, Belly. Nice to run into you. Not really, but congratulations on getting out and I hope you turn into a nice person."

She was already halfway down Spring Street when he thought to yell back at her, "Fuck you and your ancestors!"

Maybelline the Springway waitress was a mighty step down from his normal harem. He'd been out with hostesses and a couple of sous-chefs; he'd even been out with girls who danced at the Bunk House down Route 9 in Half Moon, but most of those girls were putting themselves through law school on tips. That's what they said, anyway.

He'd never had a problem getting women. He could dance, that was one thing. He could lead any woman through the tango, like his grandfather taught him, twist her up till she collapsed in his arms. He could dance, and he had all his hair, and aside from a few extra moles sprouting on his back, age had mostly forgotten him. The older he got, the younger his girlfriends became, and it was this more than anything else in his life that made him feel his place was safe at the top of the food chain.

He walked into Ruffian's, trying to keep his head down and his eyes up at the same time, trying to hide himself and hoping to be recognized. This was a place he never came: the competition. Just a narrow, dark room painted billiard green, with a good jukebox. He fantasized for a split second that this bar was Loretta's new hangout, that she would see him here with his orange-gooped-up ladyfriend. There would be a fight, Loretta and Maybelline tearing at each other's hair, at each other's clothes, Belly between them playing referee, and he would get to go home with both of them, briefly, and then, after, send the younger girl on her way, and it would be just him and Loretta, alone and back together.

But he would never have the energy for that kind of

evening. He sat at a plastic table with the girl and ordered JD neat from the short, dark waitress who didn't know his name.

Maybelline had done herself up in a variety of animal prints. Cheetah, leopard, tiger — he couldn't remember the difference. He hated cats. But he had not touched a woman in four years, and here was this pretty, young girl before him, warm to him for some reason he couldn't determine, and he was in no mood to be choosy.

"What were you in jail for?" Maybelline asked him, doing that same stupid trick with the straw: blowing air through it and nibbling on the end. Then she dunked it in her whiskey sour, slurping drops of alcohol from the gnarled tip.

"Oh, you know," he started, but he could see he'd have to confess before she'd sleep with him. "Nothing bad, don't worry. Just gambling."

She giggled. "I know. I know all about it. It was in the papers."

"You read the papers?"

She stuck out her tongue. "I'm just saying, it was in the news."

"Just now it was?" he asked. "That I was out?"

"No, before," she said. "Whenever that was, five years ago. The trial and everything." She sipped from her tumbler and nibbled on the waxy maraschino stem. "You were famous."

"Only for three weeks," he said. He looked at the orange sparkling above her eyelid. He wanted her, but he wanted her to be someone else. She smiled at him, a little fleck of orangish lipstick wedded to her front tooth, and when he smiled back, his lips were lying.

"Will you open up your bar again?" she asked him.

He didn't tell her that he couldn't. "I have to get my own place first. I'm staying with my daughter for now."

She looked disappointed, kind of green like all that copper

had oxidized. He figured it was over, no chance to win this one, so he reached out to touch her hand, her small hand with thick fingers and long nails and too many fake gold rings. He rubbed the soft fleshy pad under her thumb and thought, if this was the only contact he had with a woman, maybe that would be enough. If he closed his eyes and held her hand, he could pretend something bigger had happened.

"I have roommates," Maybelline said. "But we can go to my place."

Belly looked up. She wasn't joking. He wondered if perhaps his daughters had pooled their resources and rented her for the night, if the New York Racing Association was sending him a sign, if Maybelline was a present offered him from some beneficent bystander waiting to reveal himself from behind the bar at Ruffian's. But it was just this girl, a girl who'd heard of him in his glory days, willing to give herself to him. Who was he to say no?

All he could think before, during, and after: It's so good to fuck.

They drove from Saratoga to her apartment in Ballston Spa, which was pretty much like living on Central Park West and driving out to Queens to get laid. He sat in the passenger seat of her puttering Hyundai while she drove him to her small, carpeted apartment in a sliced-up old Stick-style mansion. She had a tiny room with a tiny window and a tiny bed and two teddy bears in the corner: thirty-two years old with teddy bears. Two ugly calico cats circled them wherever they walked.

Belly lay on Maybelline's frilly dollhouse bed and let her wait on him. She couldn't cook anything. Burned the Pop-Tarts that were their dinner. Mixed too much water in the OJ. Heated up frozen mini-quiches in the oven till the crusts caught on fire and set off the smoke detectors so they belted out their songs like opera stars. It got so he was used to the taste of tar. "Inured" was the fancy word. And he lay there, inured, chewing on his burned-up food, his first meal out of prison, while Maybelline rested her head on the gray fuzz of his stomach, listening to his gastric juices stir and the smoke detectors sing till there was a whole orchestra in her house, in her bed, in her arms, every instrument off-key or broken, until she stood on her painted-pink step stool and silenced them, silenced even what was inside him.

If he closed his eyes, if he kept his eyes closed, yes, it wasn't Maybelline, it was Loretta. It was Loretta, it was the first time, it was War Bar in its heyday, there was music, there was the music of murmuring and bass beat and that reassuring scent of stale beer. He had cheated before, yes, of course, many times he had stepped out on Myrna, whose breasts drooped and swung like pendulums after nursing four babies, whose stomach turned to a rippling ocean of flesh, everything fallen on her, even her spirit, a body given up on, a body gone to bed.

All the times he'd strayed it had been easy. Easy. The first time — what was her name? A young girl, some folkie type, who'd come to the dais at the back of the bar and asked if she could play her lame Bob Dylan covers on a shiny acoustic guitar two sizes too big for her, that she barely knew how to strum. Such a sweet little thing all the way up from Half Moon in her daddy's Chevy Celebrity. How could he resist? Yes, he did think about Myrna, for a minute, thought about her the way she used to be, the way she was in their first six months together, before the accident of Nora sealed them up. Myrna, who was too smart for him, really, too sharp, she had something he'd never even touched, what his mother called Ambition.

And how she'd dulled over the years, and rounded, and grayed, so much more malleable than he ever would have guessed.

When he met Myrna, that last year of high school, she was an innocent. That's what he loved about her. She was shockable. His potty mouth, his chain-smoking, his binge drinking, his belt-wielding father, all of it caused her to gasp, to rub her soft hand on his thigh and say, "You poor dear." She had barely tasted alcohol, other than the sips of wine at Communion, and the first time he plied her with beer — the old Genny Cream Ale, he remembered, the thick dark bottle with the green label — her face lit up, her cheeks with round patches of red like a baby doll, and she twirled around him, his private dancer, his Catholic virgin. He adored her, and he wanted more than anything to fuck the innocence right out of her. And he did.

How long was it before she changed? How long before the alcohol took hold of her, so she had to fight her own hands to keep from pouring the wine or whiskey during four pregnancies? How long before her body changed from tight and thin and athletic to soft and heavy and inert? And then how could he resist, who would even want him to resist the cream puff from Half Moon with her big guitar and her small breasts? And then Nora's little friend from summer camp, his second — he never told Nora, of course — and then that woman from the track who kept her white straw hat on so she wouldn't mess up her hair. There were so many, and never did he think twice about it until Loretta. He thought twice about Loretta. Three times. Over and over, from the moment he saw her, he thought about Loretta, he mulled it over. Because just from looking at her he could tell that it wouldn't be just once, not with a woman like that.

And even though Loretta was so beautiful, so vital, so much the anti-Myrna, oozing with confidence, all painted and perfumed and well preserved, that first time, in the back room, he had to keep his eyes closed. In the self-imposed darkness he put his lips to hers, like two rows of zipper teeth meeting, metal on metal, yes, sparks, enamel on enamel, and he felt so guilty. He opened his eyes, he looked at Loretta pressed to the wall with her leg up and her shirt off and he said, "I'm in trouble now."

But Loretta was not here. It was Maybelline.

It was Maybelline who held him too tight and too long. "Time to take the convict home," he said, swinging one leg over the bed.

"Can't you stay here?"

She lay back on the lacy pillows in her red bra and granny underwear. A long black treasure trail ran from her navel, all those hairs pointing down there like arrows.

He was so bored he didn't even want to say no.

"I gotta go," he said. He stood and slipped on his jeans and buttoned them, stepped into his cowboy boots.

She tossed a teddy bear at his head and he thought, What is the bare minimum I have to do to get with this girl again, maybe just once more?

She scooched over in her little bed to make room for him, and he curled himself around her, and he knew right then there would be nothing between them, the way her hips pressed into his thighs instead of his stomach; their bodies just did not fit. But he closed his eyes and pretended that he held someone else, anyone else, any of the women he had loved or lusted after, he held her tight to him and ran his old-man hands along the soft skin of her inner arms until she was satisfied.

She put on the classic rock station as she drove him back to town. It was only 10:30 according to Maybelline's Hello Kitty watch, but he was so tired. He wondered what it would be like to come home at night with his fingertips stained from espresso, smelling of coffee grounds instead of booze. There were things he missed about the bar business: his pockets stuffed with wads of cash, smoky memories lingering on his shirt collar, meeting the sunrise most nights. He missed the mixing-in of vermouth and bitters, the satisfaction of pouring a perfect head on a Guinness. He missed that moment when he had a specialty drink ready and waiting for a regular: Loretta's Cuba Libre, Phillip Sr.'s god-awful Miller High Life — the Champagne of beers — Carlson's boilermaker, and a Shirley Temple for his never-ending supply of much-older lady friends, a Black Russian for Clem the sign painter, Stoli vanilla to start for Huck and Harmony the hippie couple, who made their way by the end of the night to prune liqueur, Rob Roys for the Knippenbergs, and always a Manhattan for Mad Martha, the cleanest bum ever known to man. In the winter sometimes, the graveyard shift guys from the Ball plant would stop in for a Bass.

He did not miss the vomit and the occasional brawl, the Skidmore students with sorry excuses for fake IDs indignant and threatening to sue when the bouncer turned them away, his wife Myrna's constant whining at the hours he kept, the impossible task of taxes in a cash-based business, the regulars whose skin sagged perceptibly from week to week, the effects of alcohol visible as they stumbled out to empty homes every night. August was the time he hated and cherished the most: fresh blood in the bar, bets rolling in and then away, trying to keep afloat in the sea of crisp bills. Every August, he longed for

September to come and save him, and as soon as September arrived, he wished the summer would return. For twenty-four days a year, back then, he owned the world.

Maybelline dropped him off and chirped, "Call me!" before she drove away. He had the card with her phone number and the lighter and the too-sweet scent of her perfume stuck to his collar, and he thought then that he might sidestep all the unpleasantness of starting over and just move in with her out there in Ballston Spa. Get free meals at Springway Diner. Split the gas for her Hyundai. Three blow jobs a week and cheap rent. He'd be all right.

Outside, in the tiny backyard, a girl swayed in the white rope hammock with a laptop computer on her legs. He couldn't see her face at first, just her long legs in tight jeans hugging her behind, long hair in a wild knot. All memories of Maybelline were murdered by that body. He thought, I want to pull on that hair. He cleared his throat.

"You Ann's friend?"

She turned.

What a dog. Her face really looked like a dog, like a basset hound, every feature too long, too sad. Her smile was a teardrop of lips.

"So you're Belly." She dropped a foot out of the hammock to make it swing. She wore big black boots, shit kickers almost. They made a dent in the soft ground and dry grass. "You're awfully thin for your nickname."

"I lost twenty pounds in prison," he lied.

"The food was that bad?" she asked, her question hooking up and then falling at the end, as if she were a Brit.

"Better than you'd think. And a state-of-the-art gym." He tried to flex his biceps, but they seemed to have shrunk on the way home.

The Basset Hound stared at him. He dug his foot in the dirt.

"Thanks for letting me stay in your room."

"It's not my house," he said. Then, "No problem." He took out a cigarette and held the pack out to her, but she shook her head. He was down to sixteen cigarettes, and they were now more than five bucks a pack. It was miserable math.

"I'm only here for three more days," she said.

"Okay."

"I'm at Skidmore for this journalism conference."

"It's fine," he said.

"But I'd love to talk to you about your experience of the last four years before I leave." She sounded so formal and faraway, like a telemarketer.

"Sure."

She stared at him a minute, as if she were waiting for him to ask her a question.

"I'm a journalist," she said, as if that answered it.

She sat straight up in the hammock then, and he could see she was too tall for him, all stretched out like taffy. "Do you think we could meet tomorrow for a cup of coffee? I'm buying."

Her questions kept pulling on him. He took a long drag of his cigarette, blew a line of smoke straight toward her midriff, toward her big silver belt buckle engraved with a hammer and sickle. "That depends," and he gave her his famous half-turned smile. "Will sex be involved?"

She didn't laugh.

"So tomorrow," she said, and she stood up, the whole giraffe of her with the basset hound head, and leaned in to shake his hand. "Okay, then," she said, and she shook his hand hard, like a man.

"You smell good," he said. "You smell like vegetable soup."

The Basset Hound went in and up to her room, and he looked at the three-story Queen Anne Victorian with the sloping side porch and the attic lit up like a fiery heaven and he knew he'd never make it to the top.

Even before he left they were working on this ailing, aging house, tearing out the saggy oak slabs and setting down new pine floorboards. They'd once painted it in what Nora termed "historically accurate colors," a jarring pink with darker-pink shutters, off-white windows, and teal trim, but now all the paint had faded, and the house craved cover for the patches of joint compound and scarred-up siding. It looked like a candy house after a thunderstorm, what Hansel and Gretel found deep in the woods. Tacked to the front, along the street, was a long front porch that nobody used anymore, not since he and Phillip Sr. had occupied it two decades before. Their two chairs sat lonely next to the railing, waiting for ghosts to roost.

He climbed up the little side porch and pushed open the screen door.

"You missed dinner," Nora said as he came into the kitchen. "Jesus, you reek. I can smell you from here. Go wash your mouth out."

"I love beer," he said. "I love it." Nora sat at the table with the baby asleep against her chest, leafing through a gardening catalog.

"Drink all you want now, but you better be sober on Sunday."

He opened the fridge and took out the last Piels. "No problem," he said. "Anybody call?"

"Not for you."

"Where is everybody?"

"Asleep, Belly, it's eleven o'clock."

"Jesus, you know, this is about the latest I've been up in years. We had lights out at ten."

Nora said, "I'm sorry." She squeezed his hand.

"Where's the husband?"

"The restaurant."

"He ever show up here?"

"He lives here."

"I'm just saying, when is he home?"

Nora turned the pages of the catalog. "He gets home between three and four, sleeps till noon, and does it all over again the next day. He works his ass off for us."

"I see."

"What? What do you see?"

"I just see, is all."

"Oh, Jesus, Belly." She slammed the catalog shut, and the baby made a low moan. She lowered her voice to say, "He keeps the same hours you did. The restaurant business, remember? Remember what it's like to work for a living?"

"I remember I stayed out much later than I had to," Belly said, watching Nora's tough face thaw just a little, a tiny tremor at the corner of her mouth. He smiled at her.

"Good night, darling Nora," he said.

She said, "Brush your goddamned teeth."

The house was quiet. He grabbed his duffel bag and crept through the kitchen to the TV room, through the TV room to the dining room, and up the stairs where the boys' rooms were, and Nora's bedroom, and the dark room where the Basset Hound was now undressing, then up another creaky flight of stairs to the attic. The whole Schuylkill FCI was one floor, and he hadn't climbed steps in four years. His hips, legs, lower back all ached from the long bus ride, from walking, from fucking, from mounting these crooked steps.

From the attic rose the old summer camp scent of mildew and musk. A twin bed was squeezed into the corner, under the rafters and next to the eyebrow windows. How could he sleep here, he'd never be able to sleep here, it was too much like a cell. He inspected all the items hiding in the tiny alcoves of the attic, the caves: an old spinning wheel, property of his great-grandmother who once owned a sheep farm in Ireland; ugly pressed-wood furniture that must be left over from Phil's bachelor days; a broken lava lamp; a pile of canvases pressed against the wall. He leafed through them, big blobs of institutional green-gray with little specks of red, his youngest daughter Eliza's initials at the bottom. There were a few more realistic paintings, and he recognized some from her high school career. Nude figures, which he lingered over for a moment, a portrait of his wife, Myrna, in her younger days, against a black and glittering sky. He stopped at the last one. He recognized the face, the eyes, her mother's eyes, the wavy blond hair, Eliza's sister, his lost daughter, no date. He turned it back to face the wall.

If he knew anything, he knew you were not supposed to have favorites, or if you did, you weren't supposed to admit it. But there were so many reasons to love the third one best. Nora was born with a glare, all her early words five letters with *w*'s — scowl and frown and growl. And after her came Ann, with those gray eyes, huge gray woman eyes in a four-and-a-half-year-old blond head, gazing at her father with total indifference. And Eliza, the baby, a colicky baby at that, up and crying all the time, eyes and nose and ears and mouth all running with waterfalls of want. They came into the world with their personalities already formed — the angry one, the apathetic one, the sad one, and the one who seemed to feel nothing but joy. His perfect little angel.

The third girl was born with her mother's green eyes, open and sallow as a sickened sea. But she was all his, even as a baby, a toddler, a little and then bigger kid, as a seven-year-old trailing six inches behind him at the track, twenty-four days in August made just for the two of them, her begging him to bet only on the gray horses, him explaining to her day after day how the odds worked, the higher the odds, the more the bet would pay. And he lost her like that, like a bet on the high odds, his beautiful sixteen-year-old girl in her thrift-store dresses and the shabby pink grandma cardigan around her shoulders. He shook his head and breathed through his mouth, fluttering his lips like a horse to expunge thoughts of her from his memory.

He pressed back behind the piles of junk, and there lay hidden the contents of his old above-the-bar apartment. His favorite brown recliner. His neon Piels sign. The wall-sized poster of a white sandy beach with a palm tree. He had never owned much. Even after his third daughter was gone and then Myrna left him and he and Ann and Eliza all crammed into the cramped two-bedroom apartment, they had not collected *stuff*. Nora surely made up for it now, overflowing her house with toys and books and videos and those ridiculous little porcelain figurines that sat in his mother's old hutch in the dining room.

He unpacked his duffel bag and placed the contents into his grandfather's old scuffed dresser. Humidity had seeped into the wood, expanding it, and the drawers resisted as he pulled them out. One by one he unloaded his clothes, jeans and jeans and jeans and white button-down shirts that he hung in the makeshift closet Nora had fixed — a metal bar wedged between two rafters. His thick white socks and his collection of plaid boxer shorts. Always the same clothes, every day. His two good pairs of trousers he put on a hanger, vowing never to wear them. He had honed his fashion style back when Loretta told him how sorry he looked in dress pants, how they hung off him and made him look old. He thought of his style as vaguely rock star — the jeans and cowboy boots and white shirts — but a fogey rock star, Rick Springfield maybe. Jackson Browne. Somebody over the hill, but somebody who looked good over there, on his way down. He finished unpacking, and as he pressed the drawers shut, they squeaked, and the sound echoed off the wooden beams and made him feel too small and too alone in this high, dark cave of a space.

He could not sleep here. The rain when it came would seep in through the cracking rafters, and he could not stand that feeling of water on his skin. His mother used to joke he must have had a traumatic baptism.

He crept back down all forty-eight steps, grabbed a blanket from the living room, and laid himself down on the TV room couch, waiting for morning to save him.

HE WAS dreaming of his wife and his truck, the beloved Bronco. He was dreaming of the brilliance of chrome rims and the fillings glinting from the back of Myrna's mouth, of choosing between them, and he loved the truck, he had always loved the truck, and he never knew if he loved his wife or not. He opened his eyes.

Every time Belly woke, the thought, the fact, that he had four daughters appeared to him like a preview before the real movie of his life recommenced. Nora, his eldest, and Ann, the lesbian, and Eliza, the baby, with the look of a newborn panda, some skeevy little mammal whose skull you could crush in the palm of one hand. Those three, plus the other one. The third one. Before he could call up her name, those little sleep bugs would wander off his stubble and dried saliva, and he would remember all over again that the third one was gone, there were still four, but one was a hole and the other three were just hills to be traversed.

He sat up and saw morning just beginning to creep into the room. He was hollowed out; someone, something, had just reached in and scooped out his organs, and hot air blew through him. Once he'd lost the crown off his right incisor, and each time he ate or drank, each time he breathed, a sharp, angry ache ripped into his gums. He had that same feeling, only now it focused in his heart, it beat against him.

Maybe I'm having a heart attack, he thought. But he knew what it was and how to cure it.

He did not turn the light on in the kitchen, just felt his way to the counter, rubbed his fingers along the liquor cabinet until he found the handle, and fumbled through the bottles. It didn't matter which one. He pulled one down and unscrewed the cap and tilted his head back and poured. Cheap tequila burned the back of his throat and melted the ache away.

He shuffled back to the couch and laid himself down, dizzy now as light filled the room, and he closed his eyes for a few more moments of sleep. He vowed that today he would be kind and keep sober, not lose his temper or his mind. He would start anew and do better this time.

When he opened his eyes again, his youngest daughter peered down at him. His first night's sleep as a free man in four years, and he'd spent it on the old plaid couch that once hugged the dirty walls above War Bar. For just a moment, he felt he

was back there, in the old place, Eliza waking him before
school to get a permission slip signed or tell him she'd be sleeping at Margie's that night. But now his new hips pressed into
the nubby fabric and he knew how much time had passed.

"Hi, Daddy."

The word softened him, his bones. He thought all the flesh
would just melt off his body. Nobody called him Daddy anymore.

Eliza sat down on the couch and he sat up. She wrapped her
arms around him, her pale, freckled forearms clasping one another around his neck. She was still so skinny. He didn't want
to hug her for fear of cracking her.

"Are you okay? Are you adjusting okay? I brought you a
hemp bar." She handed him a hard block of what looked like
wood coated in Saran Wrap.

"Are you still doing that health-food thing? Jesus, kid, you
need to eat a steak."

He saw her mouth twist a little, her nose twitch.

"What?"

She withdrew from him. "Your breath."

"I just woke up."

She stroked his hand and stared so hard into his eyes that he
felt her pupils pressing against him, some unanswered question in the black circles.

"What?" he asked again.

"You smell like alcohol."

"Oh, well. That."

"How much did you drink?"

"I had one drink. Last night." This was true if "night"
meant after eleven and before six.

"You smell like a bar."

He could still feel the numbing power of this morning's tequila and last night's beer, that floating sensation he'd missed so much while he was away. He wanted it again, wanted to lie down and let the alcohol carry him off, carry him back to Before.

"I thought they'd cured you of that. I thought you couldn't drink there."

He thought, She can't even say the word. His sweet little girl, his youngest, she always danced around an issue and never landed inside it. He put his arm around her and whispered "prison" in her ear.

"I know," she said. "I thought they fixed you." His little puritan princess, this one was. For one of those hippie types, she was the most uptight, the one who used to sniff his breath at night if he needed to drive, who checked his room for unexpected guests, for anything with the appearance of impropriety. Poor kid. He gave her so much to fret about.

"It's not illegal or anything. I'm not doing anything illegal." He put his right hand over his heart. "I will not do anything illegal."

She continued to stare at him, to squint her eyes and try to cull some information from him, some promise he couldn't make.

"What?"

"Just be sober on Sunday, okay? For Stevie's confirmation. And don't forget to show up."

"You, too? What's with you girls? Why wouldn't I be there?"

Eliza looked at her hands, and he felt nervous again, and sick, and too sober.

"Why couldn't God give me just one boy?"

"You've got sons-in-law. It's the next best thing."

"Oh, right. Your chubby little health-food Jew is just what I wanted."

Eliza pulled her lank blond hair into a ponytail, and she pasted a smile on her face. "I missed you, Belly."

"Oh, sure you did."

"I did."

Eliza stood up. She traced a line in the dust on the TV set. Belly spread himself out on the couch, lifted his right leg till his titanium hip screamed for him to stop. He wanted nothing more than to sleep, to sleep all day, to erase the four years of dawn wake-up calls, four years of strange sideways sleep-deprivation, of rising just when he felt it was time for bed.

"You want me to help you?" she asked. "I could take the day off."

"Help me with what?"

"Whatever you have to do."

"What do I have to do?"

"I don't know. Nora knows. You have to see your parole officer, you have to get a job, stuff like that."

"There's plenty of time for that."

"No, there isn't," she said.

He sat up on the couch, and she stood silhouetted in the window.

"If I need help, I'll tell you," he said, but that did not seem to satisfy her. "How's the art world? Still piddling with the paints?"

She smiled into her lap.

"What?" he asked her. "What?"

"Yes. Still piddling. With the paints. Sort of." She reached into her purse and took out a small notebook wrapped in tinted aluminum foil and handed it to him. The front cover was made of wobbly cardboard, and inside, blank pages of thick, uneven paper crinkled.

"I made it myself," she said.

"Thanks," he said, fingering the foil. "Is it candy or something?"

"It's an artist's book. It's my art."

"Can you make money at this?"

She blinked big and slow, like a baby doll. "I'm not the one who has to worry about making money," she said quietly.

"What? Can you say that a little louder, please?"

"Nothing," she said.

"What?"

"Nothing."

"What?" he yelled.

"Not everybody wants to make lots of money." She said, in a too-soothing voice, an imitation-maple-syrup voice, "Some of us would rather have less money and more integrity," softly, with too much sincerity, and he felt the weight of his empty pockets and empty wallet, and he felt last night's alcohol rise, he heard his own words come out with a wisp of slur, he watched her slump and make herself small like a feeble little animal, watched her seal her mouth in a tiny, fake smile.

"You're still just a little mouse. Look at you, skinny little mouse. You were supposed to be the strong one."

Eliza wobbled a little as she stood. She worked her lips into a wavering smile. She was still frail, and she looked afraid, but he hadn't noticed how tall she was, how she towered over him as he sank into the couch.

"Welcome home," she said, and she turned and went into the kitchen. He heard Eliza and Nora mumble in conspiracy, heard Nora laugh and Eliza make those murine, sad sounds of hers.

Belly rose, rubbed his eyes, stretched his arms, massaged the scars on his hips. He wound his way upstairs and to the bathroom. He turned on the water and tested with his hand until the temperature was just right. He slipped out of his boxers and tried to climb over the rim of the clawfoot tub, but his hips would not allow it, so he sat on the porcelain ledge and carefully swung one leg over and then the other, trying to ignore the fact that he was old. He lifted his arms and turned like a ballerina once under the spray, then turned the water off and stepped out and shook himself like a dog. He estimated the whole operation took under fifteen seconds.

Money or time, his grandfather always told him, a man can have money or time. He had no assets now, bank accounts depleted, pockets empty, and the days stretched out before him endlessly, punctuated here and there with a few minor appointments. He had three or four days in which to find a job, to find an answer to the inevitable question that would be posed to him Sunday at Stevie Ray's confirmation: What now?

He knew Loretta had his money, and he knew she was still somewhere in his town. He could feel it.

He walked up one more flight to the stifling attic, took out a clean pair of jeans and another white button-down shirt. One of the things you long for in prison is to wear your own clothes, and now he saw his wardrobe contained replicas of the same outfit, day after day in a kind of no-man's uniform.

His wife, Myrna, used to read the same book to the girls every night, a big red hardcover they'd taken out of the library and never returned. It was called something like *When I Grow Up,* and the one night a week he was there at bedtime, he always read it to them. It showed a Mexican fireman, a white lady-doctor, a black policeman, and a black lady-teacher. He knew it was supposed to show the girls that they could have any kind of job they wanted — black or white, man or woman, it didn't matter — but somehow the book had shut off his imagination: now, when he tried to summon up some vision of his future employment, the only choices before him were those four.

He made his way downstairs and to the kitchen, where Nora was waiting for him, and he told her, "I've decided to be a Mexican fireman."

She said, "Great. Let's go. Your appointment's in fifteen minutes."

"Where's Eliza?"

"Work," she said, lifting up the baby in her arms. "Work. Heard of it?"

"What about the boys?"

"Swimming at the Radcliffes. Let's go."

He watched the strip malls flicker like a TV screen along the highway as they drove to Ballston Spa. The town's Main Street was sleepy and slow, and he remembered that this was the original Saratoga Springs, but the water had dried up and they lost their resort privileges to the big brother next door. There wasn't one apartment available in all of Saratoga in August, but here "For Rent" signs peered from windows all over town. He could probably find a little studio for two hundred bucks a month, a carpeted hideaway where his daughters couldn't find him and he could work just a few hours a week to make the rent, spend the rest of his time drinking alone in leisure.

There was nothing spa-like about Ballston Spa: it was a northeastern ghost town. But it was beautiful, it was much more beautiful, really, than Saratoga, with its unassuming buildings no one bothered to renovate, all sitting patiently on Main Street not even waiting for change. All the cruddy storefronts had put in lace trimmings and changed their signs from "Junk" to "Antiques." Nobody believed it.

Nora dropped him off in front of the drab county office building, a big box of beige stucco.

"How about you get your license renewed sometime this week?" she asked.

"Oh, like you're too busy to drive an old man around."

"I am busy," said Nora, putting the car in reverse.

"Pick me up in half an hour," he called after her.

Inside it was just as beige and so air-conditioned he perspired even more, big jewels of sweat under his pits. A male receptionist — he looked mildly retarded with his jowly jaw, eyes too close together, and a pinstriped oxford shirt buttoned all the way to the top — sat at the front desk.

"Did you used to live at the Furness House?" Belly asked him.

The man looked up. "Can I help you?"

Belly saluted him. "I'm reporting to my parole officer within forty-eight hours."

"Name?"

"William O'Leary."

"Have a seat."

"I'd rather stand if it's all right with you." He patted his hips. "It's hard on the old joints getting up and down."

The man didn't look retarded anymore. He looked mean. "Sit," he said.

The only magazines in the waiting area were the self-help kind — lists of job agencies and healthy-living stuff. There was even a whole magazine for walking. If Belly opened up a place for people who'd just gotten out of jail, there would be *Playboys* all around. *Walking.* He shook his head at the strange ways of the working world.

"Mr. O'Leary?"

It was just his luck his parole officer had to be a good-looking redhead. Good-enough-looking, anyway.

"Belly," he said.

"Come on back, Belly." She looked at him over her shoulder. "You can call me Ms. Monroe."

He followed her down a long line of beige cubicles, watching her butt sway in her tight jeans. The face, the face was take it or leave it, but the ass was nonnegotiable.

"What's your first name, Ms. Monroe?" he asked.

"Ms. Monroe," she said. "Have a seat."

Her cubicle's prefab walls were covered in uplifting prints and slogans. A poster Nora had as a child hung above Ms. Monroe's desk: a gray kitten dangling from a tree with "Hang in there" written underneath. Only Ms. Monroe had crossed it out and tacked on a piece of paper that read *Quit your complaining.*

She looked over his file. "How's it going?"

He shrugged his shoulders.

"That good, huh?"

"Everything's fine."

"Adjusting okay?"

"It's only been a day."

She took a copy of his release plan from his file and listed one by one everything he had agreed to and he nodded at the whole list and when she was done he said, "You want me to pee in a cup and then I can go?"

We could walk across the street to Wendy's, he thought, and sit in a booth and drink Frosties till our mouths are nearly numb and then we'll warm each other's tongues. It'll be just like high school, but good.

But Ms. Monroe looked up from his file and said, "Actually, I'll decide whether you require a urinalysis. I'll decide how quickly you need to find employment and if that employment is suitable. I'll be visiting you at your residence and determining if that residence is satisfactory. So I suggest you take this seriously."

He wanted to kiss her.

"What's going on with the job hunt?"

"It hasn't even been twenty-four hours."

"That's plenty of time."

"It's hard because I don't have a driver's license."

"Well, get one," she said. "That problem's solved. What about the job here?" She tapped on the file.

"My daughter just arranged that for parole purposes. It's not a real job offer."

"That's not the kind of thing you want to tell a parole officer. That constitutes fraud."

Belly uncrossed his legs and leaned forward, resting his elbows on her desk. "Okay, it was a real live job offer, but it's not a job I want. I'm not working at the pallet company with my daughter's boyfriend, or whatever he is. I'm going to find something else."

"What?"

"I don't know." He took a pencil from her desk and twirled it in his fingers. "I can't do anything."

"What did you do before you worked in a bar?"

"I went to high school."

"What other job did you have?"

"Is this a trick question?" His longing to kiss her shortened and shrank. When did all the women get so hard?

"It's in your file, that's why I'm asking. You put it down here when you made your release plan."

He thought back to that one summer, his last summer of freedom before he met Myrna and knocked her up. He was a roofer, long hot days in the sun with strips of tar paper and a hammer, a belt with pockets for his number eights and sixteens weighing down his hips. It was the only job he had where he could see evidence of change. At the bar he saw patrons get drunk and drunker, he saw them fluff up or deplete bank accounts, but only when he worked construction did he see something grow and shift until it became a home instead of a shelter.

"I'm too old for that," he said. "I have fake hips."

"There are plenty of jobs like that without heavy lifting."

"You want me to drive a backhoe?"

"Why not?" Ms. Monroe closed his file. "Is there anything else you like to do? Anything you've always dreamed of?"

"I love to tango," he said. His feet automatically shifted a little at the sound of the word. He'd drunk and he'd screwed, but he hadn't danced yet.

"I'm serious," said Ms. Monroe.

"So am I."

"Listen, I'm giving you a week to find a job. I want you to have a certified offer of employment by next Monday. We'll meet again on Friday morning to see where you're at." She shut the file and looked at him. "Get it?"

"Why don't we continue this conversation over a drink?"

"Don't tell me you're drinking. Drinking is not allowed. You need a copy of your release plan?"

"No, no, I have a copy. I've got the thing memorized."

She put his file in a metal holder, then she tapped a pencil on the desk and looked at him out the corners of her eyes. "Listen, here's what I want to tell you: expect chaos."

"I do."

"No, really. Just expect it to be rough, and then you won't be surprised when it is."

"Okay," he said.

She handed him a form and told him to get it signed by anyone he talked to about work.

"Mr. O'Leary," she said. "I just want to remind you: You can't drink. You can't gamble. You cannot work in any establishment that serves alcohol or promotes gambling. But the rest of the world is open to you. It's a whole sea of opportunity, so get on it. Okay?"

"Okay."

"Okay?"

"Okay," he said, and she nodded for him to leave.

Nora was waiting for him out front, a box of Wendy's fries on her lap staining her jeans with grease.

"How'd it go?" she asked.

He reached over and grabbed a fry. "Swimmingly."

"What did the parole officer say?"

"I don't know. Nothing. Can you drive, or should we just sit in a parked car in Ballston Spa all day?"

Nora drove and the baby slept and Belly stared out the window. He felt like he'd been home for months.

She dropped him off on Broadway, at his request — he pretended he was going work hunting. He walked past St. Peter's, past the Catholic high school. He walked past the park that huddled at the elbow of the road, marking the end of old downtown and the beginning of the new. Across the street he saw the ruins of the torn-down strip mall where once there was a Woolworth's, where he sometimes lunched on a grilled bran muffin and black water with Cremora and read the *Saratogian* in a rare moment of anonymity as his dog, Seaver, waited outside for him to bring her his scraps. His Man-o-War bar, his dog, his park, his Woolworth's counter, all of it gone now or altered or fixed up beyond recognition, so all he could do was blink at the world with big blank blue eyes, with Eliza's open eyes, just blink and sigh and wonder.

Now, in the middle of the day, was when he felt the most tired. For more than thirty years he had slept through the noon hour, and now he had to venture out in the midday heat in search of a job, like a teenager. He could not think of any way to go about it, so he walked to the iron gate of Congress Park and peered inside to the casino and the springs and the remnants of monuments past that had mostly crumbled but whose iron teeth still rose from the grass. He tried to but could not enter. Too much, he thought, too much happened in that park. I don't need anything else to happen. For the rest of my life, I don't need a single other event to occur.

He walked up Broadway to the art supply store, his shirt soaked with sweat, his hips aching, and he peered in the big dirty windows. He could see Eliza in the book aisle, a feather duster fastened to her hips. He thought, What a sad life for such a talented girl. She seemed to sense him there; she looked up, and he stepped to the side of the doorjamb, hoping the metal bar would cloak him, but it was too late. She saw him, and she came forward.

"Belly, what are you doing here?" Eliza hung out the open door of the store. "You want to get lunch?"

"Yes," he said. "Lunch. Good."

"Be right out."

The sun, he felt, was killing him. The middle of the day in the middle of a heat wave, with nothing and no one to regulate the passing of the hours, just watching the world swim around him. Sunday, Sunday, Sunday, he repeated to himself. He would have it all figured out by Sunday. He wished Sunday would come now. He wished for a drink. He wished for a cold front to swoop down and save him. He wished he had his sunglasses. But that was four wishes, he realized, and one would have to go.

"Jatski's?" asked Eliza, and he nodded.

"I don't have much time, though," he told her. "I have to meet that girl at two."

"What girl?"

"The one who's staying in my room."

"Oh, Bonnie. Why didn't you say so? She's practically your daughter-in-law."

"What do you mean?"

A nervous, avian sort of look flashed across her face. "Nothing. She's great. I really like her."

"You like everyone."

They went next door to the diner, and he felt such a sense of relief upon entering that his hips almost gave out. It was exactly the same as it always had been, the plastic booths and the happy, empty paintings by Mama Jatski, and the fake plants. Eliza turned around, and Belly was still standing in the doorway.

"All right, Belly?"

"Never felt better," he said, and followed her to a booth in the back.

A few tourists — overdressed and scrutinizing the *Racing*

Form — lunched in the diner, but most of the patrons looked like locals, without the makeup and the jewelry and the anxious air of travelers. The same family was running the place, four or five siblings exactly alike, the boys and girls both, slinging coffee and hot plates of instant eggs. He looked, but he didn't see Loretta or the NYRA boys, anyone who used to frequent this old lunch spot of theirs.

"Good old Jatski's," he said as the waitress filled his coffee cup.

She said, "Ha," filled Eliza's cup with decaf, and dropped their menus on the table.

Eliza raised her mug. "To Jatski's," she said, and they toasted.

"Coffee-flavored water, just like I like it."

The menu was also the same, save for splotches of whiteout covering the old prices and new figures — just for August — etched in ballpoint pen. "Think I can get a little whiskey in this?" he asked her, smiling.

She didn't smile back. "I really wish you wouldn't start drinking again."

"I'm not *drinking*," he said. "I had a couple of sips last night, to celebrate. You should try it."

"I will never touch that stuff," she said. "Not a drop."

"Maybe that's your problem right there."

She didn't say anything, just made that little chirping *hm* sound. Did it signal an end to the topic, or was he supposed to keep saying *What, what is it honey, tell me what you mean, let's* talk *about it,* to try and drag the truth from her? Forget it. He'd rather sit there in the terrible silence. He looked at the girl, his daughter, and she didn't look familiar to him.

Eliza sipped her coffee, and Belly looked at every sandwich

and every omelet and every beverage. This was the first restaurant he'd been to in four years. He felt green and glowy under the fluorescent lights. Eliza hummed to herself, pretending to be impervious.

"Well?" he asked Eliza finally. "Don't you have anything to say?"

"I was waiting for you."

"What are you, the shrink?" Eliza had folded her menu and wrapped her hands around the white coffee mug. He said, "How's the art world?"

"Oh, well, I'm not really in it." She frowned. "Actually, I've kind of stopped painting."

"Thank God," he said. "You don't know how happy I am to hear that, kid. Jesus, those paintings with the blobs. Why don't you go back to drawing those cartoon animals? That's something you could make money at."

Eliza blinked, then closed her eyes for a moment. "That was in eighth grade," she said. Her knuckles were white around the mug. Then she began to nod, slowly, and she made big swooping movements with her head, her eyes still closed.

"Is this a seizure?"

She opened her eyes. "Belly," she said. "Can't you try just a little bit?"

"What are you talking about?"

"I think it must take so much work for you to be mean all the time. It must just exhaust you."

"I'm not mean. Are you crazy? What did I say that was mean? Tell me what I said that was mean." Eliza pressed her fingers out in a wave of protest, but he kept going. "That I asked if you were having a seizure? That's mean? That's a caring thing to ask. That's a thing you ask when you care about somebody, which you would know if you thought about anyone but yourself."

The waitress came back and tapped her pencil against her cheek, and Belly stared hard at his menu.

"What can I get you, Eliza?"

"I'll have the western egg sandwich on whole wheat. No meat. What about you, Belly? I'm buying."

"This is your father?" The waitress pulled her glasses down to get a better look at him. "Guess they let you out."

"Looks that way," Belly grumbled.

"Your hair got all gray."

"Thanks for noticing."

"Well, honey, don't complain. Look at my brothers. Not a gray hair on their heads, 'cause it all fell out."

"I come from a long line of not-bald men," he said, perking up. Now this, he thought, was a conversation. Why couldn't Eliza do this, just have a pleasant chat about nothing and go on about the day? The girl was so serious.

"What can I get you to eat?" The waitress flipped the sheet on her guest-check pad.

"Western egg sounds good. With meat, lots of meat."

Belly sipped from his lukewarm coffee and counted the paintings on the wall. Then he counted the booths, then the tables, the chairs, the stools at the counter, then he started on the napkin dispensers. Still, Eliza did not speak.

"So," he said. "They all know you here."

"I've been working downtown for eight years."

"That long, huh?"

"I was two blocks away from the bar for four years, and you never came down to see me."

"You try running your own business and see how much free time you have."

"Especially if you're running two businesses."

They had never discussed it. Not once. In all the time he took bets at the bar, Eliza never made mention of it, and when he was with her, he pretended to maintain his position as up-standing citizen, small businessman. He and Eliza never talked of the booking, of Loretta, of his third daughter, or of Eliza starving herself, and now he wondered what words had ever spilled out to fill the space between them. What could he possibly have to say? He didn't know what to tell her about it, how to explain.

Twelve booths, sixteen tables, fourteen stools at the counter, twenty-six napkin dispensers that he could see. She wasn't even trying to fill the silence. She was doing that hippie thing, that psycho shit: just staring, just sort of smiling.

"Right," he said. "What else is new?"

"Henry and I are in counseling."

"Jesus. Doesn't anyone have a happy marriage anymore?"

"I am perfectly happy being married to Henry," she said, her voice lifting a bit. "I simply think there are times in a marriage when perhaps one person can use a little privacy or a bit of extra space, and that it doesn't have to signal the end of everything."

"Are you telling this to him or to me?" Belly asked. He cleared his throat as Eliza continued her steady gaze upon him. "So, why don't we talk about what's happened to the retards who used to live on Union Ave.? There's a fine topic of conversation. Something a little lighter, please. Man fresh out of jail here."

"Surely you know something about being married and liv-ing apart."

"I know that I didn't marry some fat Jew guy who doesn't eat meat like the Bible tells you to. Some freak who doesn't like football and, you know, can't make babies."

"I really don't think his infertility is any concern of yours."

"Of course it is. The guy cannot make grandchildren. And you married him anyway."

She had her fake smile on again, but this time sadness seemed to seep out the sides. "Why would I want to bring children into a family like this?" she asked.

"I'm going to pretend you didn't say that."

"Why don't you like Henry? He's never been anything but kind to you. Think about how much Phil hates you. Is that better? Someone who punches you at a family picnic?"

"That's why I don't like Henry. At least Phil is honest. Kind men are not to be trusted, Eliza."

"Oy vey," she said as the waitress presented their sandwiches.

"Anything else?" she asked, placing Belly's plate before him. He tapped his fingers on the cool purple Formica.

"Nothing," said Eliza.

Belly leaned over the table and whispered, "Eliza, has he turned you into a Jew? You sound like a Jew."

A little groan escaped her.

"I'm not a Jew. I didn't convert. I'm Catholic till I die and maybe even beyond that, so please, Belly, please drop the anti-Semitism."

"Hey, I'm not against the Jews or anything. They're fine, just not to marry."

She shook her head. "Oh my god, you're just so pathetic."

"Don't say that to me."

She put her hand on his, but he swiped it away. She took a breath, then said quietly, "You're fucked up, Dad."

He'd almost never heard her swear. "Don't you talk to your father like that. Show a little respect. Jesus H. Christ, were you raised by wolves?"

Eliza lifted up the top piece of bread on her sandwich and laid it down again. "I was raised by you," she said, keeping her eyes on the table. "You raised me."

"Damn straight. And I didn't raise you to be no Jew-lover, either. And I didn't raise your sister to be no blaspheming man-hating dyke bitch."

Eliza stood and put a bill on the table. "Here's ten bucks. Get yourself some fries."

Twenty-nine paintings. Eleven different kinds of cereal in small cardboard boxes on display. Four waitrons. He took a bite of his sandwich. The eggs were no longer hot and the bread was a little soggy, but he dabbed hot sauce on top, and it was salty and it was good.

The truth is there was nothing wrong with Henry except he was an old-fashioned sissy and Belly would have liked someone a little more appropriate for his youngest daughter. One of their own kind. Someone he could pal around with. He had one gay kid, and another one was married to a man who hated him. The least Eliza could have done was shack up with someone Belly could talk to.

She'd married him so young, so fast, right after high school with no warning, no time to let the announcement sink in. A Jewish wedding with a girl Jewish priest in a big field in the park in a tie-dyed wedding dress, for Chrissakes. They'd stood under a giant tablecloth, she'd walked around him seven times, they stepped on some glasses, and that was it. She was gone. The worst part about it was he knew she was miserable with him, and that seemed to be what sealed them together: two resigned sorts of people smothered in their own sadness. He would like to see his baby daughter smile every once in a while, for her to have a man who could make that happen.

He wrapped her sandwich in a napkin, left the money on the table, and went next door. Eliza was helping a woman pick out some paints. She was bent over small glass jars of brightly colored powder, reading the labels and offering them one by one to the customer.

He slipped into the store, past the art books to the architecture section. He now owned a collection, four whole books on the architecture of Saratoga Springs that Nora had brought him while he was away. He could point out the difference between Greek Revival, Queen Anne, and Italianate. But he wondered what good that knowledge would do him. What could he do with that information other than walk down the street and point out the mansions of Union Avenue that were cut up into apartments in the depressed seventies, the ones that were all bought by rich New Yorkers and restored to their former grandeur while he was away. What sort of employment could he cull from that?

Eliza was bound to her own thankless job. The couple who owned the store — a fat duo, man and woman both going bald — watched every move their employees made with a security camera on the second floor, just sat up there all day and spied on their workers, wobbled down the stairs when they saw someone shelve a pallet wrong. Eliza worked here all through high school and college — they would only hire locals, she told Belly, never Skidmore students or summer people — and once, just once, Eliza had come home from a long August Sunday (they were expected to work six-day weeks in August), reached into her pocket, and revealed to Belly what was apparently a very expensive jar of cobalt pigment. He'd congratulated her on her theft.

"Did you like the books I sent you?" Eliza asked him now. "I never asked."

Belly hid the sandwich behind his back and leaned against the bookshelves.

"You mean the ones Nora got me?"

"They were from me."

"No, they weren't."

"Yes, they were."

Grease from the eggs began to seep onto his hands.

"That explains why you never sent a thank-you note," she said. "Belly, I'm sorry we got into an argument. You just got back and we don't have much time, so let's just, you know, start over."

He reached back and hid the sandwich in the stacks and put his other hand on her shoulder, elbow straight, and he said, "Apology accepted."

She looked at her shoes.

He walked to the door, but before he exited, he turned around and called to her, "Eat some meat, would you?"

Doe-eyed Eliza, the smallest baby of the bunch, the thinnest and shortest with the weakest bones. By the time she was born, Belly worked so much he would sometimes go days without seeing his children — he left for work just as they got home from school or day care or CCD, and he went to bed before they woke. It was not on purpose. It was not on purpose. But sometimes he thought if he stayed away long enough, he'd come home to find he had fathered a boy. When he saw them, his four pale daughters and his haggard wife, it was always a shock, always like he had woken up in someone else's life. He used to look at his youngest daughter with her watered-down smile and her pale spaghetti hair and wonder how she ever came from him.

After her sister died, Eliza was not hungry for a whole year. He'd bring home McDonald's, Oma's pizza, kung-pao chicken, but she'd eat nothing. She was not sick, he refused to believe that she was sick, but then she was eighty pounds and in the hospital, a feeding tube sucking at her arm, and when he arrived, his wife and two remaining daughters were already there, hovered over her, Eliza's pallid hair splayed out on the plastic-covered pillow, her soft blue eyes trained on the ceiling, and Belly couldn't go in. He left. She was there for a week. He sent her flowers and balloons and even a singing gorilla, but he never went inside.

There were things, perhaps, a father should not fathom. Sometimes he wondered if he was due for confession. Should he notice the way Eliza's hips were still too bony, pressing into her hippie hemp skirts like invitations? That her stomach poked out, almost like one of those African babies, it peeked out from the waistline of her skirt, that her legs were too long and skinny and she retained in her stance the air of a stork? Should he notice these things, and how a man might react to them? Should he wish that one child were thinner and another heavier and that both were prettier? Was that right?

He walked up Lafayette Street now, where the Orthodox Jews lived. It could be such a nice street, but they let it rot, turned it into a shantytown of dirty Jews on sloping porches, weird ringlet hair and top hats even in boiling heat, a whole clan of them camped out in the middle of the East Side.

He felt the weight of family life and all its messy complications, all the burdens that children brought, and how lost he would be without them, but he was lost now, and his daughters were strangers who could not console him. He had felt this way only one other time in his life, like he'd woken up and all the colors were off, everything smudged and soupy. It took a year, maybe two, to regain his composure after God pulled the rug out from under him, took his daughter away, but once the world looked crisp and clear to him again, he felt certain it would always be that way. Now he felt trapped in one of Eliza's paintings, in blobs of undefined, unnamable shades that swirled together to make a big beige universe.

The Basset Hound insisted on meeting him at the "new fancy coffee place on Broadway," as she called it. In the past hour, downtown had swelled with tourists, and Belly had to push his way through as he headed south toward Washington Street. He remembered now that it was Dark Tuesday, the track's one day off, and there was nothing for trackgoers to do but head downtown and shop.

He pressed the doors open to Café Newton. It was as if War Bar, his second home, had never lived in this space, had never existed. The walls were two-toned and matched the furniture, everything in the place some muddy autumnal shade that reminded him of Eliza's paintings. There were pictures of other coffee shops in the chain on the walls, every one of them exactly the same. Any evidence of the space's former life was gone now, and it gave him a sick and floating feeling, that gravity was no longer holding him down.

"It's two bucks for a regular coffee," he said as he sank into a purple velvet chair. "And they got pussy furniture here." The Basset Hound had her hair all piled up, thick black glasses on, all businesslike. "Plus, you know, this place used to be my bar."

"I know," she said.

"I lost my bar, and it's a fucking cappuccino palace. These are sad times for downtown Saratoga."

Bonnie laughed.

"What?"

"The way you say it, Saratoga. You say it like a local. *Seradoga*."

"I am a local. My family's been here for three generations. You carpetbagger types are the ones ruining it with your twelve-dollar coffees."

"But it's packed in here, Belly. I don't think people mind."

"These aren't people, though. They're tourists."

She took a sip and got a little milk foam on her face. He had the urge to lean over and lap it up.

"You know what's wrong with this place?" Belly asked. "You want an example of how fucked up the world has gotten since they sent me away? Hillary Clinton is our governor. That's what I'm talking about."

"Senator," Bonnie said.

"Whatever. Same thing. Hillary Clinton."

"I voted for her."

"I'm sure you did."

"What do you want to drink?" she asked, getting up. "I told you I'm buying."

"Whiskey," he said, but she just stood there. "The cheapest cup of coffee they sell. Light and sweet."

While she was at the counter, he glanced around, again dreading and yearning to be recognized. None of the faces focused on him. No one turned to take him in. Bonnie came back with a mug of bitter-smelling coffee, and as she sat down she asked him, "Why do they call you Belly?"

"Oh, you know. Christmas Bells, hell's bells, Hell's Angels, Big Fat Bellies. You know." It always disappointed people when he told them how he got his nickname, a departure from "Billy," just for slipping in and out of the house so often that the bells his mother hung on the door to monitor him were always ringing. She used to say that Belly's favorite sport was ringing people's bells, riling them up until they lost their tempers or until he did, and then he would bask in the glow of that victory — "The bell tolls for thee," his mother would say. Then, "Get back in here, Belly." Then his father would unhook the bells from the doorknob and whip them across Belly's shoulders, and then Belly stayed away altogether so the bells would finally stop ringing.

"You look so different from what I pictured," Bonnie said. "The way Ann talked about you I thought you'd be bigger. I thought you'd be as big as your name."

"In prison they called me Rosie. After Pete Rose? 'Cause he was in for gambling."

She took out a long, thin notebook and wrote down what he said. She told him, "The way she talked about you I thought you'd be, I don't know, less delicate. Less handsome or something. She never said you were handsome."

Belly thought about last night with Maybelline, about the little rings of fat on her stomach and hips that sipped open and closed as he entered her. He pulled her from his memory and put Bonnie back in, that smooth line of her long torso, endless legs that could envelop him.

"Should I call you Rosie, too?" she asked.

"It was the Chinese guy who called me that, Mr. Chin. I was in good with the Chinese because they're into the whole horse-racing thing, and they knew I was from Saratoga. Plus, I did it the Chinese way, without even knowing it. The Chinese have it all figured out."

"How do you mean?"

He wished he would stop talking. He wished she would put her mouth on his to shut him up. "Because the Chinese have their own organized-crime scene, believe me. But what they do is they agree on one guy to take the fall for the whole thing, and while he's in jail, they take care of his family until he gets out. Then you got nine hundred other guys in there, and they're all criminals. You can't trust anyone there except the Chinese."

Bonnie was nodding and writing and furrowing her brow.

"What?" he asked.

"So you took the fall?" she asked. "You took the fall, and the NYRA folks were supposed to take care of your family?"

He wanted to tell her. He wanted to broadcast how brave he'd been, and how quiet, and how he'd kept his mouth shut in service to his daughters, and how his mean Nebraskan mistress who'd brought him into the bookie business had stranded him there and absconded with his last reserves of laundered bills. He did it for his family, and they would never know. He wanted Bonnie to turn into Woodward and Bernstein and uncover the truth and tell his children, that they might finally forgive him.

But he just said, "Coffee makes me jittery. Let's go down to Caroline Street and get a drink."

"Do you really think we should? It's only two o'clock, isn't it?" she asked, but her question went up at the end, and he knew she'd come along.

* * *

Outside Ruffian's the blare of some strange mix of Irish and reggae music halted him. He cut the air in front of Bonnie with his outstretched arm. "Let me wear your sunglasses."

"Why?"

"Just because. Hand 'em over." She took them from the top of her head and put them on him herself. He noticed she had very short fingernails.

"What's a girl like you got these cop sunglasses for?"

"You don't want anyone to recognize you?" she asked.

"Yes and no," he said, leading her to the back. "Maybe after a drink or two."

They sat at a plastic table on the patio. The pretty little waitress from the night before came to the table. "What's the best drink for a man just out of prison?" he asked her.

"I'd say Jack Daniel's," she said, refusing to react. Maybe this kid knew who he was and didn't care. Maybe she wasn't from here, and hadn't heard of him. "What you had yesterday."

He nodded. "One for me and whatever the lady wants," he said, though he knew he couldn't pay for it.

"JD it is," said Bonnie.

It was hot, but the alcohol cooled something in him. He leaned back against the chair with the backs of his knees flat against the seat and his legs stretched out before him. He took out a cigarette and counted the remaining nine in the pack, his dwindling supply.

He looked at Bonnie and she was smiling at him. "You got kids?" he asked her.

She shook her head.

"I didn't think so. Not with a body like that."

"I have a dog," she said. "Tron."

"Like the video game?"

She nodded. "I used to have two dogs. The other was Pong. But he's gone now."

He couldn't help it. He laughed. "Pong is gone and Tron is not."

He thought she'd smack him but instead she held up her glass. "To Tron and Pong: one's gone, one's not." And they drank. The waitress brought the next round and they drank to other pets past, each round for a different pet, and Belly's mother had taken in many a stray cat in her day and so there were many rounds, and when enough hours had melted away they had a toast to his sweet old bitch Seaver.

The girls had named her. A fine mutt she was, half black Lab, half beagle. She would wander all over town by herself, visiting the various families who gave her treats, showing up at the bar around dinnertime for a burger. She was the only woman in his life who could take care of herself. He loved that dog. He missed her every day.

They sat outside at Ruffian's and watched the sun climb up the sky and start to descend like a child on a slide. He gave her back the sunglasses and she wore them in the late-afternoon orange glow. The sun and the whiskey baked them both into fine, fermented fixtures on the patio.

"Where's your dog now?" he asked Bonnie.

"She's home with Ann." The sound of his daughter's name felt like a change in the weather. "Jimi's allergic."

"I know that," Belly snapped.

"Besides, Eliza always brings her crazy dog over to Nora's."

"Didn't even know she had one," he said, but his speech was slurred, his brain was slowing.

"Eliza's the kind of person who gets a dog and doesn't train him just so she'll have something to hate. She has to be so nice to everyone all the time, she needs that kind of outlet."

The way she insulted his daughter just made him want her more. "You married?" He was heavy now with beer and whiskey and want.

"Not really." She fingered the gold band on her right hand.

"What does that mean, not really?"

"Not legally," she said.

He took a big gulp of JD. "So that means you're free for sex?"

He could swear her ears perked up like a dog listening for its owner's call. "Definitely not."

"Hey, sorry, I'm not trying to offend you."

She waved the topic away. "Can I ask you something? You haven't really talked about it, but I wanted to know, what was prison like?"

He motioned to the waitress for another round. "It was long," he said. "The older you get, you know, the faster time passes, but it was just a really long time in there."

"Was it scary?"

"No," he said. "A little. No. Not really. It's just, you know, drug dealers and a few fraud types. No murderers. It's not the worst. The thing about jail is it's incredibly boring. It's so boring. But they had a really good gym, and sometimes we saw movies, and I got a work release so I didn't have to do much. I played a lot of basketball before my hips gave out. It could have been worse. The hardest part was they tried to turn me into a morning person."

"How'd you get out early?"

"I was up for parole and they said yes."

"That's it?"

"Pretty much. I kept my head down and my mouth shut the whole time. It wasn't hard to do. It's not like TV in there. It's much slower than that."

Bonnie nodded and sipped and wrote some more and he wondered why she wanted to know these things and what she would do with what he said and if he ought to say something else, something endearing maybe, or something about how he'd reformed or what a good and solid citizen he planned to become, but he said, "What am I going to do now?" and she stopped writing. He lit a cigarette: he was down to five.

Bonnie said, "My mom told me she knew you. She used to know you. My mom said you were an excellent tango dancer."

"I was," he said. "Who's your mom?"

"Denise Annolina. We used to live on the West Side."

"That explains why I never saw you around. I would have remembered a body like yours."

"I went to Emma Willard," she said. "To boarding school."

"Oh, yeah." He grinned. "All girls."

The Basset Hound crossed and uncrossed her legs, her smile bloomed in benign tolerance, and somewhere in there, in the movement of her knees, he was hit with a memory. One of those late '80s parties, mounds of coke on coffee tables and mirror balls and Donna Summer and he walked in on this girl peeing — not this Denise woman, but some other dark-eyed Italian beauty from the other side of the tracks. She just looked at him with these huge brown eyes and stood up, her panties still around her knees and leaned back against the tank and he unzipped his jeans and screwed her right there above the toilet. She had big stretch marks on her stomach from pumping out the kids, and her loose flesh jiggled the whole time.

He exhaled a thin line of smoke. The past would never come back again. He'd have to watch it like a late-night movie, a rerun, a dramatization of a life.

"Anyway," he said now, "I can't remember anything before 1986. The last time the Mets won the World Series. The one good thing about 1986."

"You know, it wasn't all bad. Ann said you had a few good times."

"Oh, did she?"

"Yeah, she used to talk about this trip you all took to Florida, to spring training or something."

"Oh, that," he said, and he leaned back and drank.

"Yes, that," she said. "That's your one happy family memory. You should try to hold on to it."

He looked at Bonnie, at her taut body and her droopy face and he asked, "How do you decide who's right for you?"

She sipped from her drink and laughed. "You know what I do? I ask people what their favorite Elvis Costello song is and judge them based on that."

"I only know that one about writing the book."

"Everyday I write the book."

"Yeah, that one."

"That'll do." She drank again. "I live with Ann," she said. "Ann and I are married."

He looked at her again, the big boots, the belt buckle, the jeans worn low on the hips like a man, the short fingernails, the cop sunglasses. He could see all of this clearly while the rest of the world swirled around him. He looked at himself in the mirror of her sunglasses, his fine head of gray hair, the stubble over his cleft chin, and he could see her eyes behind the glasses and he knew she knew he was disgusted with her. He closed his eyes and thought, I will not say one more word to this person.

But she began to speak. She talked and talked, as if he'd asked her a question. Even though he kept his eyes closed, she kept talking, kept drinking, and the sun was fading in the sky like the drink was fading from his brain.

"There was this guy who used to stare at me in boarding school, at Emma Willard," she said. "One of the kitchen boys. And there were only fifteen kitchen boys and two thousand teenage girls so it was a big deal if one of the kitchen boys checked you out. The boy would stare at me, just lock eyes with mine over the salad bar and not look away. He had these really dark eyes, black eyes, and this long stringy hair, which in the '80s was so hot. And he played in a metal band, which was also hot."

Was she trying to convince him she wasn't all bad, that somewhere in her past she was a normal, healthy teenage girl?

He tried not to listen to her, tried not to picture her with Ann, and he couldn't see Ann, he no longer knew her face, and every time he tried to trace her cheekbones in his mind, tried to find the almond curve of her eyes or that one long hair on her right eyebrow, he could only see the heart-shaped face of his third daughter. He could not abide this so he tried again to call up Ann's face, but it was a decade in the blurring. He hadn't seen her since Eliza's wedding, and he had not talked to her for a couple of years before that. He'd sent her one letter and that was the extent of their interaction. Even when they did talk, he could never understand her.

"Then one day I was standing next to him, he was refilling the salad bar, so close I could feel this tiny softness from his arm hair — lots of arm hair, he was Italian — and he turned to me and this light went on inside me and he said, 'I've seen you.' He said it so darkly. And my whole mouth was just full of this blackness, this fear, and I couldn't look at him and I just stood there feeling his stare. And then I just shrugged and said, 'So?' "

Belly turned over in his chair so he was staring at the concrete floor of the patio. He thought of Ann with her defiant, square jaw and her thick glasses, Ann with boys calling at the house, at the bar, boys with cars and bikes and skateboards trying to track her down, and how he used to wonder why she didn't just pick one of them and proceed.

"The boy vanished, like on *Star Trek,* and I didn't ever see him at school anymore. I don't know if he hid when he saw me coming or what, but I could still feel his stare."

Ann was valedictorian of her class, the class of 1987, and she gave a speech, he remembered, a short, crazy speech about how the word *valedictorian* was made of *Victorian* and *edict* and how they were already beyond George Orwell's *1984* and there was no such thing as a valedictator. She gave this speech about how that word, *valedictorian,* means to say farewell, to fare well, that it means they should all go out and do good. She told them her sister had died in a car crash a year ago and that she would never get to go boldly where all those high school graduates were heading now. She told her classmates not to split their infinitives.

In the week after her graduation, Belly and Ann had the house to themselves. Eliza spent all her time at Henry's and Nora was suddenly, after disappearing for a year, back in town and engaged to Phil. Most days, Belly knew, Ann was out with her friends in the state park; she said her last month of high school was "All Stoned, All the Time," and Belly didn't care.

She'd go and suck the carbon dioxide gas from the dry crystal geyser spring in Spa Park and come back loopy and glazed and they'd sit home and watch the Mets, who returned to their role as black sheep of the National League the year after their big win; couldn't even snag the pennant.

One night they were on the couch with two Coronas and Johnny Carson and he had his arm around Ann, her head on his shoulder. He looked at her and said, "How'd I get three blond daughters? Nora's the only one who looks like me."

Ann had gazed at him, carefully, searching in his eyes and then staring at the floor. She took his hand from her shoulder and held it in her lap and she said, "Belly, I have something very important to tell you. I want you to listen very carefully and I want you to think about it before you say anything."

Belly prepared himself for pregnancy, or for her declaration that she was not going to college, he tried to imagine what announcement Ann the valedictorian could make that would rattle his world, but he could think of nothing that would muddle the clarity with which he saw her.

What she said was, "I don't like boys," and that was the last time he hit her.

He waved his open fist across her face and she hit the floor. He slapped her again and she cried and covered her face — stop, drop, and roll, just like Dick Van Dyke had taught her on the TV — she curled herself into a weak little ball and he yelled, "You were supposed to be the strong one." He'd left a triangular scar above Ann's right eye from his fake 1986 World Series ring and she had not spoken to him since.

Ann left. She moved in with the Kessels — Margie and Henry's parents — for the rest of the summer and when it was time for her to take the bus down to New York City for school, he told his other daughters it was August, he was swamped, there was no way he could meet them at Springway Diner to say good-bye to daughter number two.

Belly opened his eyes. She was still talking. The Basset Hound was still talking.

"And then it wasn't till about seven years later when I was at my fifth-year reunion that my old roommate Stephanie said he'd turned out to be gay and he'd moved to San Francisco to play in a gay metal band. Which was still hot, actually. But then I realized that the way we stared at each other and all that crazy hate and crazy heat I could feel between us was because he knew he was gay and he knew I was gay and it made us hate each other. It made us drawn to each other, and repelled. That's when I knew."

She turned to him. Belly pretended he could no longer hear her. He rose and walked out, leaving her with the bill, walked up the hill to his new home and laid himself down on the couch, the ring of the jukebox and Bonnie's voice still in his ears. He clamped his eyes shut and dozed to the rhythm of the Basset-Hound-with-the-hot-ass journalist girl's words, dreaming of fire and disco and blackness.

He woke to the rich smell of boiling meat. Stevie Ray and Jimi perched on the carpet below him, playing video games; the Mario Brothers theme, he remembered, had seeped into his dreams. King rolled in his walker, mesmerized by the TV.

"Why do you all have to have these crazy names?" he asked the boys. "What's wrong with William?"

"They've got a theme going," said Stevie Ray.

"He talks!" Belly said, but Stevie Ray clamped his mouth shut. "Well, it's a stupid theme."

"We like it."

Nora came and stood in the arch of the doorway that joined the kitchen to the TV room.

"It's kind of sad, isn't it, naming all your kids after dead guitarists when your husband is a dead guitarist?" Belly asked her.

"Excuse me?" She folded her arms.

"I mean, not dead, but failed. Didn't he want to be a guitar player or something?"

"He didn't fail. We decided to have kids instead. He took over his father's restaurant."

"Exactly. Same thing."

"Not at all the same thing."

"The exact same thing."

"He plays music all the time. He sings his sons to sleep."

Stevie Ray put down his joystick, while Jimi played more intently, fixing his eyes on the screen.

"When is he ever here at their bedtime?"

"Sundays."

Belly adjusted himself on the couch.

"Sound familiar to you, Belly? Only being home on Sunday nights? Does that make him a bad father?"

"Sure," said Belly. "I take it all back. He's a very happy man."

"Whoever said happiness was the point?"

He looked at his grandsons. Jimi pretended not to hear them. Stevie Ray stared. "That's not the point?" Belly asked.

Stevie Ray opened his mouth, but Nora stopped him.

"Would you please mind your own business, Stevie?" Nora asked him. "Look at your little brother, minding his own damned business."

The boy made a teepee with his hands and whispered a prayer to himself.

"I really wish you wouldn't do that," Nora said. "Do you have to pray every time I say the tiniest thing? You think Jesus cares if I slip once or twice?"

"Mommy, can I go outside and play?" asked Jimi.

"Of course, honey. You go ahead."

Stevie Ray followed Jimi outside, leaving them alone, Belly and Nora and the baby and the buzzing TV. The sound of a bouncing ball echoed off the side of the house.

"You don't think you might be a tad hard on the boy, do you?" asked Belly.

"Are you going to talk to me about playing favorites? I don't think so." She lifted the baby from his walker and plopped him into the high chair. "Stevie Ray," Nora called out the window. "Come back and set the table, and call Bonnie down. It's almost time for dinner."

He thought back to a time when his family was happy, the kind of happy that makes you feel dizzy and at the same time perfectly sober. It was a million years ago.

They'd been on two family vacations. The first one was Disney World. He took pregnant Myrna and Nora and Ann on a five-day vacation. It was miserable. Myrna fussed constantly over the two girls, didn't want them to go on any rides or in the water. She hovered over her children like a rain cloud, pretending she could protect them from the weather. He kept his mouth shut, or filled with St. Pauli Girl, most of the trip. She'd already called the police on him once by then, just for a single slap to the side of her head, and his father-in-law sat him down and gave him a long, long, boring lecture about how to manage his anger. So he did just what his father-in-law said:

every time he wanted to yell, he prayed. Dear God, he prayed, Please let my next child be a boy. Please, God, won't you give me just one boy?

God hadn't answered his prayers, or maybe he had and he'd just said no, but he sent Belly the next best thing: a girl who could do boy things, daughter number three. She could throw anything — baseball, Frisbee, boomerang. She could beat any boy her age at the one-hundred-meter dash and she could dance ballet, too. The perfect kid. God gave him the perfect kid and then He took her away.

Maybe happiness wasn't the point: he'd had so little of it. The one good vacation was to Port St. Lucie, Florida, home of the Mets spring training. Myrna went off to rehab and he left the bar in his father's hands and took the four girls on a plane, lapel pins and playing cards for everyone. They had all behaved themselves beautifully without their mother there to infect them. Everyone got along, and Nora helped out with Eliza, nine years her junior, who still needed extra attention. The girls swam and Belly watched, and they'd feasted on lobster and scampi and gone to Mets games, slept soundly all night piled into one breezy hotel room.

He walked into the dining room now and Bonnie was already laying out the plates, leaving Jimi to do the silverware and Stevie Ray to fold the napkins. They worked like an assembly line. He had the urge to run up and snatch the plates away from her, form a wall between her and the boys to prevent infection. But it was too late. The three of them were laughing, the baby in his high chair pounding his little fists.

Belly inspected the table. "Don't you boys know the fork goes on the right?"

Stevie Ray yawned. "No, it doesn't."

"I know that, I was just checking."

Nora entered with a steaming soup tureen. "Looks fancy, boys," Belly said.

"Good old-fashioned Irish beef stew," Nora announced. "I figured since you were actually going to show up for dinner tonight I'd make something you like. Stevie, get the potatoes."

As soon as they were seated, Nora started in on him. "So, you're going by JG's tomorrow?"

"Who's that?"

"The pallet factory. JG's. It's on your release plan."

"Can we not talk about this in front of the boys?" Bonnie got that reporter look in her eyes, like she needed a pen. "What are you looking at?"

"What's a release plan?" she asked.

"You fill out this paper saying what you're going to do when you get out of prison," said Nora.

"Interesting."

The boys stared at the food getting cold on their plates.

"Yes, and Belly signed a federal contract saying he was going to work for Gene. Now, if you'd gone out and found yourself something else . . . but you haven't. So you need to go there tomorrow."

Belly laughed. "You can't make me work somewhere I don't want to work."

"No," Nora said. "I can't. But Ms. Monroe can."

"You talked to my parole officer?" He lifted his napkin with the tines of his fork.

"Of course I talked to her. You don't think she called here to check out where you're staying? That's her job."

It was quiet, very quiet, with Bonnie and the boys all staring at their laps, and Nora staring at Belly, and Belly staring out the windows to the dilapidated front porch.

Nora cleared her throat. "We'll talk about it after dinner."

Belly said under his breath, "No, we won't."

"What was that?"

"Nothing."

"Good. Bonnie, would you say the blessing?"

"Excuse me? It's my second night back and Bonnie says the blessing?" He saw Jimi chew on a carrot. "Put that down, kid. You don't eat until you thank Jesus."

"Thank you, Lord," he said, and Belly pointed his index finger at him so fast that Jimi dropped the carrot.

"Bonnie is our guest," said Nora. "She can say the blessing."

"What about me?"

"You're not a guest," said Stevie Ray. "You live here."

"I don't live here," Belly said. "I'm just visiting."

"Let's all join hands," said the Basset Hound.

He linked his pinky with hers, and braced himself for a long, heartfelt, melodramatic thanks to the Lord.

Bonnie said, "Good bread, good meat, good Lord, let's eat."

Belly picked up his fork. "Couldn't have said it better myself."

"And there's one more thing," she said, pressing on Belly's forearm to lower his fork, "before we eat. I'd like to read a poem in honor of Stevie Ray's confirmation."

"Read it Sunday," Belly said, shoveling a lump of mashed potatoes in his mouth. They erased four years of instant potato spuds from his culinary memory.

"I won't be here."

"No?" he smiled. "Aw, that's too bad."

"Lay off, Belly," said Nora.

"Lay off, Grampa," echoed Jimi.

"You lay off, little man," he raised a pretend fist to Jimi, his tough little grandson. He could sort of see why Nora might prefer him to Stevie Ray's soft and willowy way.

Bonnie recited a poem, from memory, something about butterflies and caterpillars and suffocating cocoons.

"Thank you, Bonnie," said Nora.

"I didn't get one word of it. Not one word."

"I did," said Stevie Ray.

"Great, you like poetry now? Now you're definitely going to be a homo."

"Belly," warned Nora. "Enough."

"No, really, explain it to me."

"Don't talk with your mouth full, Grampa," said Jimi.

"It's about how hard it is to grow up," Stevie Ray explained. "How hard it is to turn into a butterfly."

"Very good," said Bonnie.

"Well, why not just say it then? Why not just say it like that?"

"She did. It said it just like that." Stevie Ray took a bite of beef stew. "You have to listen."

"Don't talk with your mouth full," said Jimi again. He put a dollop of mashed potatoes on the baby's tray.

"This is delicious," said Bonnie. "Thank you so much for cooking, Nora."

"You're very welcome."

Belly didn't say anything, just took tiny forkfuls of food and chewed quietly.

"Where's Eliza?" he asked finally. "I thought this was a family dinner."

"Aunt Eliza don't eat cows," said Jimi.

"Doesn't," said Nora.

Belly took a bite of beef and said, "Children, thank your mother."

"We don't have to," Jimi said. "It's her job."

"You going to take that?" asked Belly.

"What?" said Nora. "He's right."

"It's not your job. You don't have to feed them. You could put out a slice of pimento loaf and let them fight for it if you wanted to."

This was a game they played in prison. Someone would smuggle a treat from the kitchen, an extra slice of ham, a brownie, or, in the best of times, a ripe tomato. During recreation they'd put it in the center of a group of men, reverse dodgeball, and see who could get to it first.

He thought of telling them — engaging them in a prison yard game with his lemon meringue pie — but then he realized not one of them, not a single member of his immediate family had asked him what he had endured those forty-six months. Maybe they didn't want to know. Maybe they didn't care. Maybe they were embarrassed to have a felon for a father.

"She gets paid to raise us," said Stevie Ray.

"What do you mean?"

Nora served herself seconds. "I get an allowance, from Phil. Because I don't work. Because I can't work. He wanted to have a big family, so that's how it is. I get paid to raise the children."

He looked at Bonnie. "Aren't you going to say something? Aren't you one of those feminists or something?"

"It's great," she said. "It's brilliant. All mothers should get paid to raise their children. It's a job like any other."

Nora raised her fork and said, "Cheers."

"I never got paid to raise my children," Belly said. "I paid for them myself, every cent I made."

"You've got to be kidding. We all had jobs." Nora swallowed hard. "Eliza and Ann put themselves through college. What are you talking about?"

The chewing halted. They were all staring at him.

"What are you, a bunch of retards? Eat, for Chrissakes."

He rose from the table, went to the fridge, came back holding yesterday's lemon meringue pie, carefully and with ceremony, like it was on fire.

"What's that?" asked Stevie Ray.

"Dessert."

"It looks gross," he said.

"Well, thanks. Great manners, kid." He turned to Nora. "Great job on the kid."

"Do we have to eat it?" asked Jimi.

"Of course not, honey, but you should thank Grampa for getting it. That was a nice gesture on his part."

Thanks were mumbled.

"What's wrong with you boys? You don't like meringue?"

Stevie Ray pressed on the hard white top and said, "It looks dead."

"Can we have Popsicles?" asked Jimi.

"Go ahead. Clear your places first and then you're excused."

Belly looked at the Basset Hound. "You want a Popsicle too, or is that too phallic for you?"

She and Nora exchanged glances.

"I think I'll just skip dessert," she said, rising to clear the rest of the table. "There was enough sugar in all that alcohol we drank."

So Nora and Bonnie tended to the dishes, leaving the baby in his high chair, and Belly stared down at the sorry pie. He pushed it onto the baby's wooden tray. The kid mashed his fingers into it, gloves of yellow cream and white meringue coating his hands, crust on his fingernails.

"That's the way," Belly said as King grabbed handfuls of pie and tossed them onto the dining room floor.

It was light outside, and hot, and Belly did not know what to do with the still lake of hours laid before him. In the bathroom he smoothed his hair, tucked his button-down shirt into his jeans, straightened the pant legs over his cowboy boots.

He thought of something his father told him, long ago, when he asked for a loan to marry Myrna.

"Come back with a bottle of Jameson's," his father had said.

"Why?"

"Because booze is the answer to every question."

Nora was on the front porch, crouched down so her belly rested on her stretchy jeans, inspecting the floorboards. Spring Street was sleepy, and for a moment it felt like September, like all the tourists had returned his town to him.

"How's she look?" asked Belly.

"This will be the last thing to work on," she said. "Gene says the foundation's rotted. We've probably got to pull the whole thing down and rebuild, but that's a lot of paperwork, a lot of dealing with the design folks at the city to approve it."

"What a crock," Belly said. "The city can tell you what you can do to your house, that you own? That's bullshit."

Nora shrugged. "That's the way it is now."

They stared at the house across the street. Everything about it was new, but fake-old, with a fancy swinging glider on the re-stored porch, perfect lace curtains, intricately painted trim. He felt the slightest bit embarrassed to be standing in front of this

half-finished construction project parading as a house, like the
music had stopped and they were the only ones left standing.

"Who lives there now?"

"Yuppies," Nora said. "City people who come up on the
weekends." She straightened up, slowly, holding on to the
creaking rail. "So you're going to the pallet factory tomorrow,
right? Gene says you can work in the office, if you want. I
imagine you know a little bit about bookkeeping."

Belly looked at Nora. "It wasn't all me," he said.

"I know, I know it."

"There were lots of other people in on it, too."

"I know, Belly. You don't have to tell me."

He looked at Nora, swollen Nora with her secret fat boyfriend and her whiny children and her absent husband and he
said, "Okay."

"I'll take you over there tomorrow afternoon."

Belly pressed on the sagging wooden plank beneath his feet
and it gave a little, so splinters of dead wood poked through.
"All right," he said. "Okay."

Belly walked down Caroline Street, crowded and teeming
with drunken tourists.

He had lived in this town all his life, as had his father, and
he didn't recognize a soul. Somewhere in this milling mess of
people, he was certain, walked Loretta and the NYRA boys
and his old clients and his regulars. They must have found a
new home somewhere, maybe at the ridiculous fancy bar
Loretta preferred near the end.

He crossed Broadway, the dividing line between east and
west, and headed behind the bank, to the big blight of a super-

market they called the Ghetto Chopper — the slum version of Price Chopper. He bought two bottles of cheap Cabernet and a plastic pocket combination corkscrew/bottle opener and headed back south, through the perfectly restored little enclave of Franklin Square with its Italianate mansions that now housed a bridal shop and a funeral home.

He hooked back to Broadway and stood in front of the visitors' center, looking at the pretty little bungalow of a building, the numbers 1915 — the year it was built — sunk into a block of cement below it. He was a tourist in his own town, and the thought made him so thirsty. He kept walking till the sidewalk ended, all the way to that once-abandoned Tudor building by the state park that now housed the Museum of Dance. It was lit from below, looming like a mausoleum; the half-timber poked from the stucco like it was trying to break loose.

Tomorrow, he promised himself, he would not drink, he would not be cruel, he would follow the rules and obey. He would sober up and have his shit together by Sunday. He just needed one more night of swimming in alcohol, of losing himself in it, and then he would come back. He sat on the dried-up lawn while cars streamed along Route 9, he opened both bottles with his new corkscrew and he drank one while he waited for the other to breathe. He felt sorry for the grass, so brittle and beige and begging for rain. Even after the sun set the air was still thick, and he laid his head back on the lawn and waited for the world to cool.

He saw the women of his life swaying before him, his daughters, mistress, wife, parole officer all dancing on the SPAC stage, led by some prima ballerina in a toga, a girl with a beautiful, doll-like face. He was on the dais, prostrate, the women as whirling dervishes around him, concocting some spell, choreographing a tour of his wrongs and misdeeds, his grand mistakes. They were lifting him up without touching him, the lady in the toga — it was Grace Kelly in *Rear Window* — leaning over him, tickling him with her blue eyes and blond hair and her perfect features till he could stand the tickling no longer and he reached out to grab her by the hair and her hair came tumbling out.

It was the grass. The grass tickled his face. His face was in the grass, sharp little blades digging into his cheeks. He'd drunk both bottles, slipped straight into oblivion and did not realize it till he was on his way home. He raised himself on his wobbly hips and his knees were stained green and the world seemed new in that moment, and also it seemed like a big mean place, like a woman with a full cart of groceries who would not step aside to let him buy his one little thing.

The walk home was long and hot and then he felt a few drops of rain. He thought, The rain is coming, but it was only a small rain, a sprinkle that taunted him, and when it left, the temperature rose like a laugh that gets bigger before it stops abruptly and makes you wonder what was funny in the first place.

3

IN THE morning Bonnie nudged Belly awake. "You're on the couch again," she said.

"I can't make it up to the attic." He rubbed his eyes and sat up. He'd slept in his clothes, and the zipper of his jeans had carved a neat vee in the flat skin of his stomach.

"Coffee?" She handed him a rainbow mug with big brown letters that read *World's Greatest Mom*.

"Aw, you're sweet," he said. "For a man-hater."

She laughed. "I was warned about your tongue."

"Oh yeah? You been talking to my old girlfriends?" Something about this girl opened him, or closed him, he couldn't tell which, something that compelled him to push on her or pull her toward him.

"Well, no, that's not what I mean, but more power to you. I heard you already found yourself a nice young one."

"Maybelline."

Bonnie handed him a scrap of paper with a phone number on it. "She called four times last night."

He crumpled the paper and tossed it toward the trashcan. He missed. "She's just a distraction."

"From what?" Bonnie asked.

"Anybody else call?"

"I don't know. Maybe. You can ask Nora when she comes back. She said to tell you that you're going to the pallet factory around 12:30 so you better haul your ass up and look for another job if you want one."

"What a sweet girl."

Belly got up and stretched, set his coffee mug on the TV, went to the bathroom and brushed his teeth. He'd skipped toothbrushing for two nights, and now he felt the enamel coated in a filmy mush. He came back and Bonnie was still sitting on the couch, those long legs, those tight jeans — even her knees were sexy — and he picked up the mug and sat down next to her. He was too tired this morning to summon his disapproval. He hated her for making him want her.

"Are you excited for Stevie's confirmation?" she asked.

"I don't know if that's the word. I just hope I don't catch fire the moment I set foot in St. Peter's."

"Been out sinning?" she asked.

"For years."

"Well, you went in there all these years you were divorced and nothing happened, right?"

Belly rested the mug on his pants. "Who said I was divorced?"

"Ann did."

"I'm Catholic," he said.

She said, "So am I."

"Well, I never divorced her, and as far as I know she never divorced me."

She cocked her head to the side. "But you wear no ring."

"Never did. Men didn't wear rings back when I got married, back in the Stone Age."

Belly's hips were stiff and his head ached and his mouth was dry and his gums were sore and parts of last night were chipped and faded or not there at all, and he did not want to talk about his wife.

"Listen," said Bonnie. "I don't want to offend you or anything, but I have the feeling that if you keep drinking and don't go out and look for a job you're going to piss some people off."

"Oh, people," he said. "You mean my family?"

"Yes. Your family. Sounds like your parole officer, too."

"What can they do? Send me to prison? I've been there, and I can tell you, it's starting to seem like a pleasant alternative to this nuthouse." His empty words did not impress her; he didn't even believe himself.

"I highly doubt that."

He shrugged. "I still have a few days to get a job before I violate my parole, and the least the family can do is, you know, give me a little time to relax." He looked for his cigarettes but could not find them. They seemed to have fallen from his pocket, swallowed up by last night's grass. He searched through the kitchen cabinets until he found Nora's mostly untouched Marlboros, snuck one from the pack, and returned to the couch. "My family's not the ones I have to worry about pissing off, anyway, " he said.

Bonnie lingered there a moment, her mouth opening and closing like a dying bass. What did she want to know, what did she want to tell him? He could see her fingers tapping at the couch cushions, wanting to walk toward his hands, what? Maybe she wanted to comfort him, and he wanted the comfort, too much: it made him feel sick.

"I'm going downtown now, anyway. I've got something lined up."

"Sure you do," she said.

"I do."

"I've got to go," Bonnie pulled her hair back in a ponytail, taunting him with that long neck.

He said, "You're leaving? What a shame," and he smiled at her so she stood and shook her head. He smoothed out his shirt and rebuttoned his jeans and snapped his folded hand open and shut in a fake wave good-bye to his daughter's wife. He put the unlit cigarette to his lips and pretended to smoke it, just like Nora did.

When she left he felt the ghosts of Nora and Phil and the children following him around the house. He turned on the radio, a song: *That ass, the dick* or *What a Wonderful World* or too-smooth country music, and he turned it off. He sat in the brown recliner and the TV talked to him about elands and football and the heat wave and the big Whitney race and a girl who'd tumbled into a stretch of the Hudson overflowing with PCBs. He listened to the television chatter and to the telephone's silence and when the same thought bubbled up inside him he said aloud, "Stop thinking about that." He said, "No," he said, "I don't care," he talked himself inside out but the thought would not go away. "I've got to get a job." The word, *job,* felt like a prescription to spend the rest of his life in a dentist's chair.

By now, they should have called him. They should have sent Loretta over with his money and acclaim, maybe a mysterious letter from the bank that Nora's mortgage had been paid. But their silence felt like a warning now, like an omen: he was on his own.

He thought of one thing, one small possibility that lingered in his peripheral vision, a long shot. He tucked his shirt in and ran his fingers through his hair and he walked downtown, this time taking Circular to Lake and dipping down the steep hill, past the firehouse and the police station, avoiding the old War Bar altogether.

The empty corridors of City Hall echoed, the marble floors so shiny they looked wet. It was over-air-conditioned in the lobby. It was fucking freezing, and somehow that made pools of nervous perspiration swim inside his shirt. He was a teenager again, again an insecure, unsettled adolescent, as if the first round hadn't been bad enough.

The building hadn't changed much since he'd first walked in there, almost thirty years before, to file a DBA. The way it had worked, the way it had always worked in Saratoga, was you got the Republican chairman's imprimatur on any piece of paperwork and you got what you wanted: a building permit, a summer job at the track, your parking tickets waived. Belly just figured he would walk down to City Hall and someone there — McSweeny or Bill Fisk or any of the NYRA boys lingering in the halls — would find him a sinecure, or shake his hand, leaving a rolled-up wad of twenties stuck to the palm. Somebody there would repay him for his silence.

He eyed the empty halls and no one burst from the doors to greet him. He waited a minute, two minutes, and then he looked at the directory — small white letters on a felt board, so old-fashioned — but he knew none of the names written there. No McSweeny, no Fisk, nothing familiar on that whole right-hand panel of the board except Margie Kessel, town planner, Eliza's sister-in-law. So he would not see his people yet. They were still hiding. They were waiting for the right time to contact him, that was it. They were waiting for the dust to settle, to make sure the new DA — whoever that was — hadn't fitted him with a wire or tapped his daughter's phone line before they came to give him back his money and his woman and his life.

He moved his hips up the one wide flight of stairs to an office with drop ceilings where a secretary sat behind a too-tall desk. She had nice eyes but her hair was too big.

"Margie Kessel here?"

"Your name?" she asked, keeping her eyes trained on a messy pile of papers.

"Belly O'Leary." She looked up then, took him in. He knew she was putting a face to the name in the headlines. He ran his hands through his hair before he folded his arms across his chest.

"I'll tell her you're here. Have a seat."

He lowered himself into a hard plastic chair, picked up a lone copy of *National Geographic* dated 1983. Spit and Spat, the statues in Congress Park, were on the cover, young children playing in the pool between them.

"This is a strange surprise," said Margie from down the dark hallway. She motioned for him to come toward her. "Step into my office."

He nodded, raised himself from the seat, and followed her like a pet. Her office was a small room with very high ceilings and one huge window sealed shut. It was covered in papers, blueprints, odd little maps with tiny colored plots. "What a mess," he said. "What's with the temperature?"

"Hot outside, hot inside," she said. "AC's broken in here. Sit down." Her armpits had half-moons of sweat stains beneath them.

He pulled a chair up to the desk and sank into it. The air-conditioning hummed overhead, dripping Freon into an old rusty bucket.

"You seem to have some trouble getting around," she said.

"New hips."

"When'd you get those?"

"Prison," he said.

"Great. That's just what I want my tax dollars to pay for. New hips for old criminals."

"Do you have to always start a fight?" he asked.

"Do you?"

He looked at his lap. "Bill Fisk here anymore?"

"Not for ages. Can't you tell? It even smells better in here."

"Give me a break."

"This is a much better place to work without the old Republican guard in place. I know they were your friends, but it was very hard to get anything done."

He nodded. Okay, he thought, they're really gone. All of his old friends had vacated the premises, the plan. He was alone with no friends at City Hall now, no one downtown to save him.

"Do you mind telling me what the hell you're doing here?" she asked.

He took a deep breath. "Listen." He pressed his hands against the air in a gesture of stopping. "I thought you might help me get a job."

"You're kidding."

"No, I mean, you were talking about the Small Business Association and everything, and maybe there's some job for me. I had a bar for thirty years, maybe I can kill the corporate takeover, make sure the Golden Grill doesn't close up shop."

"Have you been down Phila Street, Belly? The Golden Grill is gone. It's a café."

"Another one?"

"Listen, you're just in time for the reign of the big-box shop. Wal-Mart's the biggest corporation in America and one just opened up by the old mall."

"I didn't know there was a new mall."

"My advice to you, Belly, is to go out there and get yourself a job at the Wal-Mart, in the liquor section or something, if they have one. They're hiring a couple hundred people."

"That's rich."

"Listen, the economy was really good until about two weeks ago, so a million of these giant stores moved in over the last couple of years, thanks to a nice tax break courtesy of the governor. We got Target, Lowe's, Home Depot, whatever you like. Those are the jobs, unless you want to work at Ball or GE or Quad Graphics and those are heavy union and all the guys your age are already collecting their pensions." Margie blew her nose. "You brought the rain with you when you came."

Belly covered his mouth with his hands. He said, "Fuck."

"Why don't you go work for Gene? He's got that thing he does with the wooden things."

"Pallets."

"That's right. The pallet company. Nora will know all the details." Margie winked at him.

"What's that mean?"

Margie looked at her hands, stretched her fingers, and twisted her wedding ring.

"Haven't you seen him? He's at Nora's house every day." She coughed. "Maybe he's just steering clear for your return."

"How do you know?"

"Everybody knows."

"Everybody knows what?"

"About Nora and Gene."

"What are you talking about?" he asked, though he knew, and he didn't want to know.

"Listen, it's not my place to talk about it. It's Nora's affair."

"What the hell do you mean by affair?"

"Don't give yourself a heart attack, Belly. You probably won't get the government to pay the medical bills now."

He sank back in his seat. "I'm so thirsty," he said.

"Belly, thanks for stopping by. I have to work now."

He tugged at the collar of his shirt. "It's so hot in here."

"It's an old building," she said, and she placed a hand on his shoulder as he rose.

They stood there for a moment. He knew she was waiting for him to leave, and he looked at his shoes, he looked at the fluorescent greenish light flickering in the ceiling, he looked at the stained, gray, corporate carpet on the floor, and still he did not move.

"Is there something else?" she asked.

He kept his eyes trained on the condensation forming on the windowpanes as he asked her, "Can you sign this form?"

"What is it?"

"I have to show my parole officer I was looking for a job."

"Oh, Jesus," she said, but she wrote her initials in the appropriate place on the form.

"Listen, Belly. Good luck. I mean it."

He said, "Thanks," and walked down the hot, dark hallway, out the building into the blazing sun, and he did not know which direction to walk. He felt like a man with no zip code as he headed home to his daughter's house.

He tried to erase from his memory any image of what had just happened, tried to pluck it right out. Instead he recalled, it must have been in 1980-something, how Eliza had started disappearing for days at a time. Not that Belly noticed. But Myrna told him one morning when he came back from the bar that Eliza was spending nights at a house two blocks south, at the home of her friend Margie. They were vegetarians, Myrna said, with both fascination and contempt. They were hippies. Belly didn't know why she was telling him: was he supposed to intervene somehow? Was he supposed to go over there and drag her home? Let them feed her, he thought, and house her, too. Less money for us.

One Sunday morning in their old house on Phila Street the doorbell rang. Usually this was a bad sign: even the Jehovah's Witnesses knew to come to the back door and knock hard. Myrna was passed out on the couch — nine o'clock on a Saturday morning was not the O'Leary family's best time — and Belly opened the door in his pajamas to find a woman in a dashiki and a man in a T-shirt that read *Thank you for pot smoking*.

Belly said, "What?" and the woman held out a loaf of homemade bread.

"We're Henry's parents," they said.

"Who?"

"Henry. Your daughter's sweetheart?"

"Which daughter?" Belly asked. He crossed his arms and wondered if his third daughter had gone and got herself a boy without telling him.

The woman was still holding the bread.

The man said, "Your daughter Eliza," cocking his head to the right.

"It's banana bread," the woman said.

Myrna mumbled "What the hell's going on?" from the couch, and then she raised herself and wafted over to the door like a ghost and managed to smooth down her hair and paste a smile on her face. What was it about women that made them instantly able to turn from drooling drunk to gracious hostess?

Myrna invited them in, and they ate banana bread, and later Myrna fixed apple martinis in the old silver shaker that had belonged to his father and they sat and talked like real couples with real families. The Kessels had driven through Saratoga on their way back from Canada, they said, where they'd hidden from Vietnam, part of the caravan of carpetbaggers who took a detour and were so charmed by the town they never left. There were hordes of them then, twenty-five, thirty years before, kids Belly's own age but living on a different planet entirely, young parents who let their children run around in nothing but diapers, outside where everyone could see them. Kids who opened up hippie restaurants that served tasteless mush and wouldn't respect the food chain.

That whole day faded away: the two couples, the banana bread, the drinks, a game of Twister (Belly just observed while Myrna tangled herself up with the neighbors), the swapping of family histories, some polite comparison of the children's grades. Belly watched in awe as his wife rotated her whole personality to accommodate these visitors from another world.

The doorbell rang again, and this time when Myrna stumbled to the door, a chubby girl with a cyclone of brown hair stood there with her arms crossed above her wide stomach. She said, "Tell my parents it's lunchtime," and turned around, stepped off the porch, and fell like a truck on the pavement, spraining her ankle.

He'd watched the Kessels spring into action, rescue their daughter Margie from the sidewalk and help her home, one parent on each side boosting her up, and a horrible sting of guilt circulated through him, so much guilt and so little alcohol left in the house, and when night came and the booze wore off completely he found himself in a rage, on a rampage, swinging his arms around like a machete until every woman but one in his house received a welt.

The Kessels and the other hippie types were gone, or hardened now into solid citizens, just their children left to cling to scraps of worn convictions like faded tie-dyed T-shirts. Margie was in charge of the town, somehow, and Eliza had married Margie's boring brother who couldn't make her happy. This was not how he meant it to be, when he was first married and first running the bar, when, for a few months at least, he envisioned a life with a pretty wife and a couple of kids in the town that he loved.

Everything that happened happened long ago, twenty pounds ago, two girlfriends ago, a hundred thousand gray hairs ago, and not one thing about that life had stuck. No more wife, no more mistress, no more bar, no more books. Since his third daughter left him, he hadn't been able to hold on to one thing, not one semiprecious thing could he retain.

* * *

How'd the job search go?" Nora leaned against the doorjamb with the baby on her hip. The boys were playing Grand Theft Auto and Belly had reserved the right to play the winner, but what he really wanted was to nap.

"You think these boys will ever let me sleep?"

"You can't sleep in the middle of the day, Belly, you have to get a job."

He shifted himself on the couch. "Did I get any calls?"

"Are you expecting any?"

"I don't know." Jimi's guy died on the TV screen, drowning in bad-luck theme song.

"Well? The job?"

"Not good," he said to Nora. "Nothing."

"Well, it's pallets for you, then." He shook his head. She sat down next to him on the couch and put the baby between them. King flapped his arms like a bird. "I know it's only the third day, but you can't sit around here playing video games. You've got to do something."

He nodded.

"Well, let's go."

"Where?"

"To Gene's. He said for you to come in this afternoon."

"Fuck," Belly said.

"I'll pick you up in a few hours."

Belly planted his feet in the plush, stained carpet.

"It's only for a few hours," she said. "What else are you going to do?"

He thought of the Piels in the fridge and the Jameson's and tequila in the cabinet, and those sounded like wonderful friends to spend an afternoon with, but he said, "Let's go."

*   *   *

The pallet company was out by Quad Graphics, in the industrial part of town that had not yet been claimed and subdivided by developers. Just a little low building with big, mean, yellow machines out front moving stacks of wooden planks from one pile to another, and a hand-painted sign that read "JG Pallets."

"Who's the J?" Belly asked.

"The boss," said Nora.

"I thought Gene was the boss."

"He is. Sort of."

She put the car in park, left the motor running, but Belly just sat there. He sat there sober.

"Off you go," said Nora.

"Give me a minute."

"Don't be late on your first day."

"It's not my first day."

"It is. I told Gene you'd come in at one p.m. and it's already five after."

"I'm an old man," he said. "Give a little respect, would you?"

"Right."

Belly lit a cigarette he'd stolen from Nora, cupping the filter in his hand as if he could keep her from seeing.

"Get out of the car," Nora said. "Come on."

"Let me finish this."

"No," she said, and she got out, walked around to his side, and opened the door. A group of men milling in front turned to look at them.

"Nora, don't make a scene."

"Out," she said.

"Fine." He stabbed the cigarette out and saved the unburned part in his pocket. His right hip screamed at him as he climbed out, an ache right above the metal joint. But he didn't say anything. He tried to let his stoicism kick in.

He didn't say good-bye to Nora, just walked toward the front door, looked at the men, and said, "Women, what're you gonna do?" Then he wondered if they would think she was his girl, his pregnant girlfriend instead of his daughter. Even a big girl like Nora would give him some points, being so much younger than him.

Men sat at picnic tables, hard hats and safety goggles lying next to their open lunchboxes, and Belly thought he should say something else to them, some old male salute, some regular way of interacting that he must have known before he was surrounded by men, day and night of men, not one of whom you could trust, before he stopped shaking hands or slapping a fellow on the back, all locker-room interaction forbidden in prison because it led to things unspeakable. He said nothing. He walked past them and said nothing.

Inside, big metallic machines gnashed and gnawed away, sawdust everywhere, churning out these plates of wood, and for what? Pallets. Just slabs of tree so people who actually had something to ship, some real product, could do their jobs. In all his dreams as a boy, he never could have imagined that this is how his life would be, fifty-nine years old and starting a new job smashing pallets together.

He found Gene in the back office, a dank little room with greenish fluorescents buzzing above. Gene. Fat Gene. Back when Nora was in high school, Belly and his old pal Phillip Sr. used to call the kid Fat Hands when he came by the house or the bar to collect her. He hadn't really gotten fatter, just more swollen, slower, big bags under his eyes and big pores and a big sad smile. He was the kind of guy you immediately felt sorry for, like you wanted to buy him an ice cream cone or a beer.

"Belly, good to see you." Gene looked at the big old school clock above the desk. "You're a little late."

He should say sorry. He should say, Won't happen again. He should say, Thanks for the job. But he'd been his own boss for thirty years. He said, "So this is it, huh? I thought it was a bigger operation."

"It's what it is," Gene said. "It's a job. Here's some paper-work to fill out."

"What is it?"

"An application and stuff. Background."

"What kind of background?"

"Everybody here has to fill out an application. It's not a test." Gene handed him four sheets of paper and a pencil. "You can sit outside with the guys if you want."

Belly had nothing in his stomach but the residue of last night's cheap wine. He made his way to the blinding bright-ness outside where the men all sat with packed lunches from their wives. Their wedding bands gleamed in the sun.

He sat down at a table and filled out his name and age and Social Security number, scanned a little notice about health risks and asbestos and sawdust. Then, for some reason, he could not make his hand grasp the pencil anymore. The connection between his brain and hands faded in the sun and he couldn't write anything, not one word could he elicit from his fingertips.

"Where's your lunch?" asked a man with a walrus mus-tache. All these men were interchangeable, men with big beer guts and bad haircuts and ranch houses and pictures of their kids in their wallets. Men leading the good life, the boring life, the empty life, the life with no adventure and no tall tales. Fucking men. He'd had four years of nothing but men, men's naked bodies in the shower, men's naked bodies doing things to each other Belly never, ever wanted to recall. He'd vowed to himself he would never be around men again, only women, women forever, and here he was, surrounded.

"Must have misplaced my lunchbox," Belly said.

"He's got nothing to eat," said mustache man, and then the men each took something from their lunchboxes, half a sandwich, a bag of potato chips, three Oreo cookies, trail mix, Fig Newtons, Doritos, a pile growing bigger and bigger.

"That's plenty, guys," Belly said. "Enough." He looked at the pile. He said, "Thanks."

Mustache man was looking at Belly and Belly said, "What?"

"We're taking a poll," he said. "Not to be rude or anything, but are you the guy? The racetrack guy?"

"That's me."

"Belly O'Leary."

"Live and in person."

What was the problem? This was great. This was work. Lunch with the guys. Oreos. He could tell his stories, about Loretta, about the parties in the back room on Travers night. A built-in audience. This would be fine.

"Did you do it?" asked a short guy with a receding hairline.

"What?"

"Did you take all that money from the government?"

"What are you talking about?"

Someone said, "Weren't you the embezzler?" The guy had cookie crumbs in the corners of his mouth.

"I didn't embezzle shit," said Belly.

"From the government? That wasn't you?"

"There was no embezzling. It was bookmaking."

"Yeah, but it was all Mafia, right?" asked the short one. "Wasn't there a whole Mafia thing, some scam, and you took all that money from the city?"

"That was our tax money," said cookie-crumb guy. "That was money for my kids' school."

Belly felt the wind shift, the mood change. He knew how easily a few men having lunch together could turn into a lynching mob. He'd seen it many times in the last four years, though he had escaped unscathed. No one in Schuylkill had anything against him.

"Listen, I'll tell you what it was," Belly said, his hands high in the air. "It's really very simple. Instead of betting at the track, they bet in my bar, tax-free, and then a few people got more money than they would have, you see what I'm saying?"

The men were all listening to him, five, six men, alert to his every word.

"All it was was more money for the people and less money for the track."

The men were not convinced.

"Less money for the city," said cookie crumb.

"It's all right," said mustache man. "We'd all do it, too, if we could figure out how."

That seemed to calm them.

"How much money you make?" one asked.

Belly shrugged.

"Come on, tell us. What are we gonna do, turn you in?"

"A lot," said Belly. "I made a lot and I blew it all on a woman."

One guy raised his soda and said, "Here's to that," and then they all raised their drinks, or their sandwiches if they didn't have a drink, and they toasted to "blowing it all on women."

"What do you guys think of Gene?" he asked the group.

They exchanged glances.

"What?"

"Aren't you a friend of his?"

"He's a friend of my daughter's."

"Right. The daughter."

"What's the problem?"

"Nothing. Nothing. Gene's fine. He's what they call one of those micromanagers."

"What do you mean?"

The short guy said, "He comes over and, like, looks at every pallet to see if the screws aren't sticking out. This other plant up in Glens Falls got all these OSHA citations and now he's obsessed with making sure we don't do anything wrong."

"It's kind of a pain in the ass, if you want to know the truth," said mustache. "We keep trying to think of how we can get someone else to be foreman. Get Gene one of those fake promotion things so he can worry about the bills or something and leave us alone."

Belly thought, I could be foreman. Bump Gene out of here, out of Nora's life, boss these boys around. I could get a little money in my pocket, my own money, maybe even today, and I could call Loretta, tonight I will call Loretta, she must not know I'm out, that's why she hasn't called. He was sweating now, and dreaming, and not really listening to the lunch chatter of his new companions, some guys to watch the game with, a barbeque, a new apartment, maybe with a deck, a porch, a man must have a porch to watch the dancers waddle by in their little outfits in the summer. Loretta will fix drinks, he thought. I'll tend the grill. It would all work out fine.

And then, again, he could not summon up her phone number. He couldn't remember. All seven digits were erased from his memory, and he panicked, and then he was back, in front of the pallet factory with his blank application.

"The only time he's in a good mood is when your daughter's around," said cookie crumb, and then they all started to laugh.

"What?"

"Nothing, nothing, just, you know, she's always around, they're always in the office having these powwows with the doors closed."

Belly stood up. "What are you saying?"

"Nothing man, calm down."

"No, fuck you, you got something to say about my daughter then get up."

He didn't know how it happened. He didn't even know why he cared. So Nora was pregnant and humping her fat high school boyfriend, so she was cheating in plain view of this captive audience. What business was it of his? But the same way he couldn't keep his fingers filling out the application, he couldn't keep them from flying into the faces of these men, these men who had donated their lunches to him — now they were the enemy, that's what his hands thought, they fought without his okay, they reached for the mustache and the cookie crumbs and the receding hairlines, and then there was Gene, big bubble of referee, pulling him out, seating him in the corner, the principal's office, detention, or worse, expulsion, and like that his work day was done.

*   *   *

Don't say anything." Nora had one hand on the wheel and the other on her unlit cigarette.

"Hand that over," he said, feeling the other cigarette crushed in his pocket, leaking tobacco in his jeans.

"Nothing!" She was yelling at him. His own daughter, yelling at him.

"I can't do heavy lifting."

"Jesus, Dad. Jesus." She shook her head. He took a cigarette from her pack on the dashboard and smoked it in silence as they drove down Route 29. They passed a liquor store, and the neon lights called to him, curves of bright red beckoning.

"It was work," he said again. "Something you wouldn't know about."

"I know about work," she said.

"What job have you ever done?"

"I had my own business once."

"For about five minutes," he said. "It folded."

"So did yours," she said. "And I was a beer back, illegally, in your very own bar, if you recall," she said, and then he didn't want to talk about it anymore. Why was Nora so stubborn, always trying to fight with him? Why couldn't she be a good daughter, like Eliza, or like his third daughter, gentle with her father, and supportive, and sort of far away instead of up in his face all the time? He remembered what it was like when Nora worked at the bar, how she would obsessively clean the taps and reorder the top-shelf scotches alphabetically, and how she'd hand him the phone, her whole face encased in scowl, when a client would call. How she would straighten up his stacks of boxes with the receipts, and cover them with benign labels like "Taxes — 1987" or "Paystubs" or "Napkins," doing her best to hide his flagrant misdeeds. With his other kids, he could pretend to be an upstanding citizen, but with Nora, with Nora, he could only be himself, all the loose threads of his flaws hanging out.

Of course she knew everything, knew the contents of every slip of paper in her dead sister's toe-shoe boxes. She must have known that someday they would catch him, and she got out long before she could be implicated. A smart girl. So how had she ended up with this '50s sort of life, this housewife nightmare, when there was so much she could do?

Inside the house, he watched her remove the skin of an entire apple in one long ribbon of peel, this tiny perfect moment of home economics, and this was the life she chose. Her boys sat in the next room glued to the TV, waiting for their predinner snack, baby birds, waiting for their mother to serve them.

Belly looked at the list of repairs on the fridge and then he stood on a chair and opened the cabinets above the sink. They stuck, so you had to tug with all your might to open them. He inspected the hinges that were rusty and crooked and maybe just needed some WD-40, a little grease to get them going.

Nora looked up at him.

"You have any 3-in-1 oil?" he asked.

"What are you doing up there?"

"I'm going down the list," he said. "Cleaning up house."

"You don't have to. Gene will do it."

"That's all right. I can handle it."

"Don't bother, Belly. Come on, come down. We're going to Eliza's for dinner."

"Listen, I had planned to help out around the house. I

would have fixed the porch railing, but Gene did that. Maybe I could've cleaned out the gutters, but Gene did it. You know what I'm saying?"

"Not really."

He could see that Stevie Ray was only half playing the video game. He lowered himself from the chair and hid deeper in the kitchen, nodded for Nora to follow. The baby waddled by in his walker.

"What?" she asked.

"Listen," he kept his voice low. "What I'm saying is, you need to leave something for the men to do. The other men, the ones who live here." He came and put a hand on her shoulder.

"What are you talking about?"

"I'm talking about Gene. You and Gene."

Without taking her eyes off Belly, Nora called over her shoulder, "Boys, go and clean up your rooms. Now."

They protested lightly and she repeated, "Now," and they scampered away.

Nora took Belly's hand off her shoulder and led him to the kitchen table. "Sit down," she said. He obeyed, and she put the baby in his high chair, poured herself a cup of decaf, and sat down across from him. "I'm only going to say this once. I never want to hear you speak about me and Gene. Not ever. You are not to speak one word against that man, or talk about his place here in this house. He is our family friend, and that's all. You don't know anything about any of it."

"I know what I know," he said. "I got the fill-in from Margie, not to mention the whole pallet factory."

"Don't," she said.

Jimi called from upstairs, "Mom, Stevie broke my Game Boy."

"He broke it himself. He stepped on it." Their screams echoed through the house.

"Stevie, apologize to your brother," she called up through the vent. "I'll be right up."

"Go ahead," said Belly. "We'll talk more about this later."

"We will never talk about this again." Jimi was crying now, heavy sobs filtering through the house. "It's okay, sweetie, I'm coming."

"You should have had girls," he said. "That's your problem right there. Boys will give you nothing but trouble."

"Watch the baby," she said, and headed upstairs.

He did. He watched the baby. He lifted King and took him back into the TV room, he sat on the couch and flipped on Animal Planet and put the baby on the floor, surrounded by a rainbow ring of plastic toys. The baby had a full head of brown hair, and Phil's brown eyes, the same chubby cheeks Nora had as a baby. At least the baby looked like Phil, as far as he could remember. The man was never home for Belly to lay eyes on. The kid must be Phil's. Gene had some kind of light-colored eyes, and once his third daughter had explained it to him, how brown eyes have the most power and blue eyes have the least and if the two parents had light eyes their children would have light eyes and if one parent had light eyes and the other had dark eyes it could go either way, and how if both parents had dark eyes then you could never tell. But two light-eyed parents could not have a dark-eyed baby, so this baby could not be Gene's. The baby had brown eyes.

His third daughter was so good at science, so good at school. She never had to try, and instead of asking him for help with her homework, she would explain it to him. Geometry, history, Shakespeare — she'd stop by the bar every afternoon, unwrap her silly pink sweater and sit atop it on the barstool, just so she could see her father for a few minutes before she went to dance class, and she'd go over what she learned that day. His third daughter would teach him.

He'd stopped learning since she was gone. It was as if from that moment he could retain no more information in his head. There was no more logic. If only she were still here he felt certain he would not have lost his way, he would not have taken those bets, gone to prison, lost his bar, alienated Ann, let Eliza marry that hippie Jew, pretended he didn't know that Nora got knocked up her senior year of high school and went to Mexico and did God knows what with the baby. If only his daughter had lived, none of this would have happened. She would have explained everything to him.

"Where's the baby? Where's King?" Nora appeared in the doorway.

"How should I know?"

Nora searched frantically under the couch, behind the TV, in the kitchen cupboards. "You were watching him, dammit." She was screaming and he heard chairs squeal and cabinets slam.

The baby crawled in from the dining room, crawled right over to Belly, hoisted himself up with his hands on Belly's knees, stared straight into Belly's eyes, and made a cooing sound.

"Help me look!" Nora yelled from the kitchen. She ran into the TV room and saw her father and her son together on the couch. "You bastard," she said.

"What? He's right here. He's fine."

"You bastard." She hoisted the baby to her hip.

"What? I was watching him. He was here all the time."

Her lips trembled and she closed her eyes and exhaled. She

counted out loud to ten. In a low and steady voice she said, "You may not watch my child again," and went upstairs. He heard her voice waft down to him. "It's okay, King," she said. Sometimes the lack of soundproofing in this old house was a blessing.

"*Train whistle blowing,*" she sang. "*Makes a sleepy noise. Underneath the blankets go all the girls and boys. Rocking rolling riding, out along the bay. All bound for morningtown, many miles away.*"

Belly laid himself down on the couch and he fell asleep.

Get up!" Nora yelled.

Belly sprang up on the couch so fast he wrenched his hip. "What the hell?"

"Get up off that couch right now, Belly, you cannot just sleep away the days."

"It's the evening," he said.

"It's time to go. Eliza's waiting for us."

"Jesus," he said. "Give me a minute, will you? I'm an old man."

"Since when?"

In the bathroom he checked himself in the mirror. He had aged more since his release than the whole time he was away, a parabola of flesh drooping under each eye.

They piled into the truck, Belly and the baby and Jimi in the back, Stevie Ray in the front passenger seat. They climbed in and Nora started the truck and they drove to the end of Spring Street, left on Court, another left on George, halfway down the block, and Nora said, "We're here."

"Why did we drive one block?" Belly asked Nora as she unstrapped the baby and walked up the bumpy brick sidewalk in front of the house. "It's environmentally unsound." Jimi and

Stevie Ray ran into the yard and Belly heard a dog bark, not a real bark but a weak sort of yip instead.

Nora pushed open the front door and Belly said, "They don't lock their house?"

"Belly, please behave yourself. Just once, won't you please be good?"

Eliza came to the front of the house in a dirty apron. "Gimme gimme gimme," she said, taking the baby from Nora. "Hi, Belly," she called over her shoulder.

"Right," he said. His youngest daughter's house seemed pickled — preserved in the same sad state of disrepair as when he'd last seen it five years ago. After Henry's parents retired to Florida, he and Eliza moved in and vowed to fix it up, resurrect it, and match it to the bloom of renovated houses that surrounded it, keep up with the dusty roses and antique yellows of neighboring Victorians. Then they could sell it and make a profit. It was a little brick Italianate townhouse with a sloping side porch and no grass in the yard. The house hid behind Eddie Maple's old colonial mansion on Union Avenue, the wide street of towering estates that ran from the park to the racetrack and then broke into a narrow highway out to the lake. The mansion's yard housed great pine trees that shed their needles on Eliza's tiny plot of land, making grass impossible. The yard was still nothing but dirt, spotted with piles of dog droppings.

Inside he saw the same warped pine floorboards and peeling wallpaper, the puce-colored couch backed against the wall. The whole living room was drowning in books, books on shelves and on the floors, great piles of the things leaning anywhere they could.

"Where'd you get all these books?" he asked, picking up an oversize hardcover with dark photographs of jazz musicians. "Do you get a discount on all these?"

Stevie Ray called from the kitchen, "She gets the five-finger discount," and he heard Eliza scold him.

One bookcase was made up entirely from the self-help section, he noticed. *Codependent No More. The Dance of Anger.* Even a couple of classics he recognized: *The Seven Habits of Highly Effective People. How to Win Friends and Influence People.* Every book on the top shelf had the word "Divorce" in the title.

"Who's divorced?" he called.

From the kitchen he thought he heard someone say, "You are." But that couldn't be.

"Did the Kessels split up?" he asked Nora. She didn't respond. He leafed through *How to Survive Your Parents' Divorce.* "I bet that old hippie got himself a Ferrari and a tight young piece of ass."

"Oh shut up, Belly," said Nora, pushing gently on his lower back to steer him toward the kitchen. He stopped, and reached back to press her hand harder on his sacrum, to see if she'd massage the maelstrom right out of him. "Move," she said.

The kitchen had undergone such extensive renovation it belonged in another house. Warm terra cotta tile — the kind they'd had years ago in their hotel room in Florida — and a doublewide fridge that took up half the east wall.

Eliza sat at the table with King. Belly ran his hand along it, a huge slab of oak. "It's called a farmer's table," she said.

"You need one of these," he said to Nora.

"If someone fixes mine, I won't need to buy one."

A small dog wound his way into the kitchen.

"What's this thing?" he asked.

"This is Audrey," Eliza said, her face nestled into King's neck. "My dog."

"What kind is it?"

"A mutt."

"I'll say." Belly pulled a stool up to the stainless steel island in the middle of the kitchen. "This dog is an insult to the memory of Seaver." He looked at its runny black eyes. "What's wrong with it?"

"She's going blind. She's diabetic."

The boys chased Audrey around the kitchen table, reaching for her skeletal tail. The dog ran to Belly and hid behind him, her tail flopping between his legs.

Nora said, "Jimi, don't you touch that dog."

"She kind of reminds me of your husband," Belly said. "Where is the guy, anyway? I thought he had summers off, gets to sit around all day and read books for money, or something."

"It's just us," Eliza said, without elaborating. She handed the baby back to Nora and stood up. Her spindly little legs jutted out from a batiked miniskirt, her shoulder blades like wings poking under her shirt.

The table was set already and Eliza took a saucepan and a wooden spoon and dropped a pile of beige mush on each plate. The boys took their places at the table, frowning at their dishes. Belly saw them look up at their mother and saw her nod her head, a whole dictionary of movement that only parent and child could read.

On a small plate in the center of the table was Eliza's egg sandwich from two days ago, cut into triangles and rearranged to look like a sailboat.

"Come to the table, Belly."

The dog followed him as he sat down, and he asked, "What are you serving us here, Eliza?"

"Millet," she said. "Very high in riboflavin."

"Well, thank God. I can just feel the riboflavin deficiency I developed in jail."

Stevie Ray actually cracked a smile, but Jimi began to cry softly. "I don't want to, Mommy, I don't want to eat this," he whispered.

"It's okay, sweetie," said Eliza, holding a wiener on a fork. "I made NotDogs." He stopped crying and Eliza put it on his plate and Nora cut it up into bite-sized pieces.

Everyone ate in silence until Belly said, "What's going on here? Where's Henry?"

"Well," Eliza said. "Belly, I wanted you to come over today so I could tell you something."

Nora and the children looked at their plates.

This had happened to him before. An intervention. Way back in the dark ages of the O'Leary family he had woken up one summer midday to find all his children and his wife and mother and even his no-good drunk of a brother there to tell him he had to go to rehab. But now he wasn't drinking, and no coke, not at this moment, and he hadn't hit anyone in years, and he felt the bile rise in his throat as his family cornered him like they were trapping a feral cat. "Whatever it is, no," he said.

"Well, you don't actually have a say in it, Belly."

"You know, you girls have got to stop interfering in your old man's life."

"Belly, just listen to me," said Eliza.

"What do you mean interfering? I'm the one taking care of you," said Nora.

"What do you mean, taking care of me? I'm not your child."

"Prove it," Nora said.

"Oh, fine, go ahead, lay it on me. What did I do wrong?"

Eliza took a sip of organic juice. "Nothing, Belly. This isn't about you. Believe it or not, this is about me."

"Oh." He looked at Nora and she shook her head at him.

"Yes. I wanted to tell you that I'm going to Alabama."

"When? Why?" Belly carved an *x* in the thick mush of millet. "Alabama's not even a real state."

"I'm leaving tomorrow and I'm going to study with a woman at the University of Alabama."

"Study what?"

"You know that book I made you? I'm going to do more things like that. They have a master's program in Tuscaloosa."

"Tuscaloosa, what the hell are you talking about? Tuscaloosa," he howled. He looked at his family and they were laughing. At him. They were laughing at him. "Tuscaloosa to make crafts." He felt the unspeakable piercing of sobriety. "Tuscaloosa."

"Book arts," she said.

"What would you want to go and do such a thing for? You're thirty years old, Eliza. You should be staying home and having some children." Belly looked around the table at his family. Jimi munched away on a fake hot dog and Nora sipped her water and Stevie Ray looked right at him, a little smirk lining his lips. The baby rested in Eliza's arms and stared up at her.

"Wipe that smile off your face, young man."

"Whatever," said Stevie Ray. "Ask her who's paying for it."

"You know what, Stevie? We don't need your input here," said Nora.

Eliza stroked the baby's hair. "Ann is paying for it all."

"Jesus," Belly said. "She's paying you to leave your husband. Why do you think that is? She's trying to convert you."

"Oh, please," Nora said. "That's the best one yet."

"You can't go," Belly said. "Stevie Ray's getting confirmed on Sunday and I just got here."

"I don't care," said Stevie Ray. "I think it's cool."

"You shut up," Belly told him.

"Don't tell Stevie to shut up. Apologize to him." Nora wagged her pointer finger at Belly.

"You tell him to shut up all the time," Belly yelled. "He should be a good boy and keep his mouth shut."

"You shut up, Grampa."

Belly pushed his chair back and hovered over his grandson with his hand raised like a big white flag.

"Don't you dare put a hand to my son," said Nora, standing too. "Belly, you sit in your seat and be quiet and listen to your daughter." She put a hand on his shoulder and pressed down. "Sit," she said.

"Daddy, sit down. Sit down. It's okay. Everything's okay. I talked to Stevie Ray about it before and he doesn't mind, and Nora doesn't mind."

"So you all talked about this behind my back." He speared a piece of hot dog and shoved it in his mouth. The hot dog tasted like rubber and he spat it out. "You go on and on about me being there and you're not even going to show yourself."

Eliza adjusted the baby on her lap. "Belly, I feel bad that I'm leaving so soon after you're back. But I just have to go. I'm sorry. I have to."

"What about Henry?"

Eliza just shook her head. "He'll be okay for a while on his own."

He said, "That's great. There's this man who's stood by you and supported you and you're leaving him?"

Eliza blinked at him.

"And you're living off your dyke sister?"

She rubbed the baby's soft forearm.

"Just great. Wonderful. Just like your mother. Just abandoning everyone right in the middle."

"Grampa, you're an asshole," said Stevie Ray, and Nora did not shush him.

They heard a truck roar down Union Avenue behind them and that was the only sound. The rumble of the truck made brown pine needles float by the window, down to the dirt where no grass would grow. Then King began to cry. Belly watched the baby's face contort and the tears coat his cheeks and he had no urge to comfort him.

Eliza rose and let the screen door slam behind her, walked down the back porch steps to the dirt yard. She stood under a white trellis covered in vines that never flowered, cooing softly to the baby. He quieted in her arms. Belly thought about the architectural glossary in the back of one of the books they'd brought him, and about the definition of the arch: two weaknesses that, leaning one against the other, form a strength.

Belly went to her, sidled up next to her under the trellis, and leaned against her a little, and she rested her head on his shoulder and the baby looked at him with his big brown eyes and father and daughter looked at the brown lawn.

"Daddy," Eliza said, and the word weakened him. "Ann is coming instead. To the confirmation. Ann is coming to see you."

She looked so hopeful, Eliza with her doe-in-the-headlights eyes turned up to him, the pale straw of her hair staticky against his shirt, and he said, "Eliza, this is a terrible thing you're doing. This is absolutely unforgivable."

She backed away from him, up the steps and into the kitchen. He heard his daughters murmuring, chairs scraping against the tile floors, plates clinking in the sink. Then laughter. Nora pushed open the screen door and said, "Time to go, Belly. We're out of here."

He walked through the yard to avoid going back into that falling-apart house, looking into the face of his falling-apart daughter. He didn't want to watch her make the same mistake over and over again.

Belly sat at Nora's kitchen table drinking a beer, and he said to her, "I can't believe this doesn't bother you."

"It doesn't."

"Not even a little?"

"Not one bit."

Belly took a swig and offered the can to Nora. She shook her head. "You know, Belly, this is something Eliza's been talking about for years now, this whole book-making thing. Let's just let her go, she wants to go."

"Why can't she wait a week?"

"Because it starts when it starts and it starts now. There's orientation on Friday or something. It doesn't make any more sense to me than it does to you, the artist stuff. I'm not saying I get it, but I get that it means more to her than her husband does."

"Well, isn't that nice? Somebody must have done something wrong, if she thinks making these book things is more important than her family."

"I wonder who that could be?" She wiped the condensation off the table where Belly's beer had rested. "There's no use getting upset about it. She's been planning this for months now."

A crackling, cooing sound wafted from the baby monitor and Nora put a finger up to keep Belly silent. She cocked her head to listen, but the baby's voice faded away.

"Good," she said. "I need a few minutes off from motherhood."

"What you're telling me is she knew about this before," he said. "She's always been planning to leave."

"I didn't say that."

"She knew when I was getting out and she made arrangements to leave."

"I didn't say that, either."

He stared at his daughter. He stared at the gurgling fat collecting under her arms. He stared at the stretchy blue fabric affixing her maternity jeans to her booming stomach.

"What do you want me to say?" she asked him. "Tell me, and I'll say it, and then we don't have to talk about it anymore."

"You don't see some sort of problem with Eliza leaving her husband, with her sister financing the whole thing?"

"Ann. Your daughter's name is Ann."

"Yes, Ann. I know her name is Ann. Ann is corrupting Eliza."

"Okay, that's it. No more. End of discussion. You're delusional."

"Oh, I'm delusional, that's rich. You're the one living in your little dream house with your boyfriend and no job."

"That makes no sense."

"Sure, sure, he's just a friend."

"Belly, keep your voice down, the whole house is sleeping."

It was too late. The baby's cries seeped out of the monitor and Nora scooted her chair back and headed upstairs.

"The jig is up," he called after her. "Everybody knows."

He walked through the TV room and the dining room and stood at the bottom of the stairs and called, "You're supposed to be the strong one. You're supposed to be the one keeping everyone together." He heard her whisper to the baby, heard her tell him, "There, there, my little King, hush now, it's okay, you're okay, little boy."

He wanted to call Loretta, Loretta whose phone number had fled from his mind, Loretta who was silent and absent and somewhere in this town. But he couldn't. So he left the house and walked to Springway Diner, looked in the window to see Maybelline cashing out, finishing her shift.

"Let's go to your place," he said when she saw him. She was so glittery, big shiny teeth stretching out into a smile. It seemed she was the only person in the whole town glad to see him.

"Don't you want to take me home? Don't you want me to meet your family?"

No, he thought, but he said, "It's late. They're sleeping."

She rubbed the fuzz on his arm with her index finger. "Please," she said. "You want them to meet your new girl, don't you?"

He did not remind her that they'd only been out once.

The younger the girl was, he thought, the faster she moved. He'd forgotten so much about women, about how clingy they could be, how fast and how far they leaned over. No one had tried to hold on to him for so long.

She brought him a brand-new pack of Newports and a

watery cup of coffee, and he felt reborn. He lit his cigarette with his cherished de-childproofed lighter, and they sat in a booth, smoking and drinking. Belly slurped a big sip. "Shit. Burned my tongue," he said. "I'll have to put some whiskey on that."

"How long you planning on staying with her?"

"With Nora? Jesus, I don't know. Till whenever I feel like it."

"She doesn't mind?"

"Why should she mind?"

Maybelline rubbed his hand with her pointer finger. He tightened his grip around the coffee mug. "You're interrupting her life," she said.

"What do you mean? I'm her father."

"Okay, okay, sorry, don't yell." She scooched in closer to him in the booth and said, "Kiss me."

"My tongue is burned."

"Where do you want to go? I'm off. Let's go somewhere."

He finished his coffee. "Let's go." He pushed himself up from the back of the booth.

"Where?"

"Come on. Get in the car."

He directed her down Broadway, toward town, told her to take a right onto Spring.

"Where are we going? To a bar?"

"Nope."

He motioned for her to turn into Nora's driveway.

"Where are we?"

"Home," he said.

His truck was in the driveway, and the house was dark. He parked May's tiny Hyundai on the cracked and drying line of tarmac. When he unlocked the back door and led her through the kitchen, a heavy silence nested in the house.

"It's so nice," said Maybelline. She ran her hand along the cupboards.

"It's getting there."

"Everything's so new."

"They're fixing it up. Nora wants to get the plaque. She's the only person on the block without it."

"What's that?"

"The plaque thing. That thing you see on the houses around here that says what year it was built."

"What do you have to do to get it?"

"Dole out ninety bucks and fix it up the way some assholes tell you to." He pulled her close to him. "Kiss me," he said.

"I thought your tongue was burned."

"Fuck me," he said, turning her around and pressing her against the kitchen counter, her back to his front.

"Not here, Belly. Where's your room?"

"In the damn attic."

"Take me there."

They climbed the red-carpeted stairs to the second floor, sweating in the muggy night, his hips aching the whole way. He took her through the creaking door and up the rickety back stairs to the attic.

"It's hot," she said. "And dirty."

He took her to the little single bed.

He heard a car pull in. It must be Phil, coming home. He heard the door open, and the murmur of wife meeting husband, and then Stevie Ray's voice calling to his father.

"Take all your clothes off," Belly said. The house filled with the sounds of a late-night family, and he tried not to think of anything but the feel of this woman beneath him. "Make some noise," he said. "Say my name."

She was loud like last time, her voice bouncing off the rafters, and when they finished he did not want to touch her. She pulled him toward her on the narrow bed, she tucked her orange head into his armpit, and he stared at the slices of streetlight seeping though the cracks.

Afterward, they sneaked down the stairs and out the front door.

"Can't I meet them?"

"Not right now," he said. "It's so late."

"You don't think they heard us, do you?"

He opened the passenger door to her car and helped her in. "Don't push me, Belly."

He took her keys and sank into the driver's seat, turned her car on, but Phil's pickup took up too much space behind them. "Shit. I can't get out."

Nora was standing on the back porch, arms crossed above her wide stomach.

He stuck his head out the window. "Nora, move your car."

She walked down the stairs and over to his window, leaned in, eyed Maybelline.

"It's Phil's truck."

"Move it," he said.

Maybelline started to extend her hand across Belly and toward Nora, but he stopped it with a karate chop.

"Ow," she said, and blew on it like her nails were wet.

Nora and Belly stared at each other. "Move it," he said again.

Nora stood up so her pregnant belly filled the driver's side window, then she leaned down again. "Don't come home tonight," she said.

"Oh, Nora, don't be like that." He reached his hand out the window, up toward her, but she slapped it away.

"I don't want to see your face again today. Come back tomorrow and try to act like a human being."

"Move your car."

Nora backed the truck out. Belly put the car in reverse, backed out with a squeal. It was the first time he'd driven in four years. "Your car sucks," he said to Maybelline. "It's got no pickup."

Maybelline cried softly.

"Jesus. It's no big deal. She's always like that." He turned left on Circular Street. "Okay, listen. Stop crying or I'm not going to your house." He pulled over, in front of the garish flower display at the entrance to Congress Park. "Chinese fire drill," he said. Maybelline didn't move. He leaned over, opened her purse and found a tissue, handed it to her, and got out. She stayed in the passenger seat, still crying. He walked around to the passenger window, leaned in. "Bye," he said.

He stepped into the park. Goddamned Congress Park, where everything happened to him. He got one foot in the park and could go no further. He was so thirsty the whole inside of his throat hurt. He turned back around to Maybelline's little car, where she sat like a sick child in the passenger seat, chewing on her palm-tree-painted nails. He drove her home.

On the way, she kept asking about Labor Day. Picnics and barbecues and did he want to meet her sisters.

"Are they hot?" he asked and she punched him in the shoulder, too hard for not even a week of sex. Especially cause she was into the gentle sex, all this "slow down, slow down" and talking and stuff, all the stuff that gets in the way of actual sex. "I'm gonna be with Nora and my grandkids. Sorry."

She pouted. "Well, I don't have to hang out with my family. I see them all the time."

"No, you should be with your family and I'll be with mine."
Her eyes shrank to dark little slits. "I'm sick of my family. I
can't stand being with my sisters and their stupid, boring husbands one more minute. I want to hang out with your family."
She put her hand on his, the long nails on his bitten-down
stubs. Then she squeezed his pinky. "I haven't even met them
yet." She kept squeezing his pinky nail, hard, then harder,
till he had to snatch his hand away. "Except for that incident
with Nora."

"Maybelline, listen." He didn't mean to use the break-up
voice. He saw her twitch, hands tighten around her purse, her
back in the air like a freaked-out cat. Then he saw it come off
her like heat monkeys: the psycho vibe.

He knew women like this. He knew their possibilities and
their limitations and he knew what a woman like Maybelline
was good for. She was the kind of girl he took to family events,
to parties, to places where he could show her off but might
not have to talk to her. A filler for the times Loretta snubbed
him, a way to get other women to pay attention to him. He
would not love this girl, and the realization depressed the shit
out of him.

At her house, she brought him whiskey and he put her on
the lacy bed. Turned her on her stomach. She was ready for
him with that stretchy black skirt and no underwear and he
pulled her hair up, exposing the back of her neck, the one part
of her that was not orange with fake tan, and he put one hand
on her ass and tried to take her from behind like that, closing
his eyes and pretending the face pressing into the frilly pillow
was Bonnie's, that his hands were scooping the perfect globes
of her high, white ass.

But it wouldn't work. He tried, but nothing happened.

She turned over in the bed and drew him toward her, and he let himself go down, his face wedged between her prematurely saggy breasts and he felt her heart beating against him, the lonely girl he would never love. "Take me home," he said.

She shook her head.

"Yes," he said. She lifted his chin and placed those bleary, orange-smudged lips on his, she parted his lips with her tongue but his mouth would not cooperate.

He said, "Yes," again and he pushed on her this time, just a light shove but she was too soft, she was made of water, and she slid away from him and he was drunk and he was tired and he was not in love.

Maybelline slipped her skirt back on and he followed her out to the car. As she drove him back toward town, toward the bright fluorescent Stewart's sign beckoning from Route 50, the place where Maybelline used to work, he fantasized that she maneuvered the car toward the high-octane gas pump that glowed from the road and then erupted into a mushroom of fire when she drove clean into it, turning the whole place crazy orange, with little cups of blue that ate at the bricks and sipped the dripping metal.

Belly crept into the house like a naughty teenager. He tiptoed up the stairs and as he reached the top he saw the light go out in Nora's room. The door was still open a crack and he pushed it open a few inches more and the moonlight and streetlights came streaming in the window and he could see how her eyes were wrenched shut.

"Nora," he whispered. "Nora, honey, I have something I want to tell you." But she did not open her eyes and he only said, "Good night."

BONNIE THE Basset Hound came through the TV room carrying a big frame backpack, a bandanna on her head. Her clomping steps woke him and she stood there in a tight tank top and he tried not to look. He tasted stale beer on his breath, his head pounding like someone wanted setting free in there.

"Climbing Everest?" he asked her.

"Heading home today. Back to Ann."

"Sorry to hear that." He smiled.

"Is there anything you'd like me to tell Ann? Any message?"

"I've got nothing to say to that homewrecker."

"Okay then."

"Nothing."

"I heard you."

"Not one word."

Bonnie put her pack down. "Why don't you come with us to the bus station? Nora's dropping me off."

"Why would I want to do that?"

"What else are you going to do?"

"There's a point."

Nora called from the kitchen, "Take a shower first, Dad," and he thought he heard forgiveness in her voice. So he climbed up the steps and peeled off his clothes — again he'd slept in his clothes — and he took his fifteen-second shower, a bodywide ablution, and climbed to the attic and changed.

Bonnie waited for him at the back door, and then offered her hand to help him down the side porch steps. "I'm not a gimp," he said. "I just had my hips replaced."

"I thought you could use a little help," Bonnie said. "You seem worn out today."

They leaned against the car, waiting for Nora and the boys, and Bonnie told him, "I talked to Ann this morning. She said to tell you hello."

"Sure she did."

Bonnie cleared her throat. "She feels bad about everything that's happened."

"What's happened? Nothing happened. Nothing that should matter to her."

"She feels responsible."

"For what?"

"About what happened to her sister."

Belly shook his head. "I don't want to talk about it."

"She told me that your daughter said something to her, a

week before she died, something about how she wanted you all to be closer, that she might not always be around to keep you together."

Belly clenched his teeth and forced air out his mouth. He said, "Listen, you better stop talking about this. I mean it. Now."

"Ann feels like that was some kind of portent. She should have kept a sharper eye on her little sister after she said that. She feels like maybe it was her fault."

Belly banged his fist on the top of the truck.

"Shut the fuck up," he said.

"Maybe you could tell her it wasn't her fault," said Bonnie, so maddeningly calm.

Nora and the boys were watching them.

"What?" he said. "What is everybody looking at? Let's go before this one misses her bus and we have to keep her another day."

He climbed into the truck with the big boys in the wayback and the ladies up front; he sat back and snapped his mouth shut and watched the town roll by and erased that last conversation from his memory bank. They passed Margie walking to work, and Nora beeped at her. Margie waved.

"How you doing, Hebe?" Belly called out the window.

"Belly, Jesus," Nora said.

"She doesn't care. Jews are known for their sense of humor."

Jimi giggled. Stevie Ray was sullen as usual. The baby fell instantly asleep.

They turned left on Broadway, past the demolition of the strip mall across from his old bar.

"That building is going to be beautiful," Bonnie said.

Nora nodded. "I can't wait. There's going to be a Gap there."

"Oh, for Chrissakes. Just what we need, another one of those chain stores. If that was here when you had your store you would have gone under, you know that?"

"It did go under."

"Even so," Belly rolled down his window, lit a cigarette with his special red lighter, and kept his elbow propped on the half-open glass.

"They have good sales," said Nora.

They pulled into the Springway Diner parking lot. Bonnie hopped out and removed her pack from the wayback. Nora and Stevie Ray and Jimi all climbed out; they formed a human Stonehenge around her.

"Thank you so much," Bonnie said to Nora. "You were wonderful."

"Anytime, come back anytime you want."

Bonnie and Stevie Ray hugged and he said, "Bye, Aunt Bonnie."

"Bye, honey."

Jimi was holding on to her leg. "Let go, sweetie," said Nora. "Aunt Bonnie has to get on the bus now."

Bonnie tapped lightly on Belly's half-open window. He rolled it down all the way and she put her hand on his shoulder and said, "Later, Belly. Thanks for the chat."

He said, "Okay."

"You can have my room now," she said.

"I'll be getting my own room soon enough," he said.

"Oh yeah?"

"I've got plans," he said, and he could hear the emptiness of his claim. What landlord would take him now, with a felony on his record, with no income to speak of, with his misdeeds published and trailing along behind him? He'd have to move to some shack in Ballston Spa, some trailer park full of convicts like himself.

He pulled himself out of the back seat, walked up the handicapped ramp and into the diner. Coffee, he thought, I need coffee, but as he stood at the counter, keeping his profile turned from the dining room in case Maybelline was working, he found no change and no bills in his pockets, and he returned to the car.

Nora and Bonnie talked a bit, hugged, talked more, and hugged again, weaving him out of some pattern. He sat in the passenger seat with the AC on and the door half open, and finally Nora got back in. Bonnie waved to them all and ducked inside to buy her ticket.

When Nora turned on the car and rolled up the windows, Belly started in on the kids. "Aunt Bonnie?" he said. "Aunt Bonnie? She's your aunt now, after staying with you for a week?"

"She's married to Aunt Ann," said Jimi.

"That's impossible. It's illegal, for one thing."

"Belly," said Nora, backing out, "they've been together for over ten years. If you and Ann had been talking all that time you would have known her."

He covered his ears. "Don't talk about that stuff in front of the boys," he said.

"The boys know all about it."

"It's a sin, for God's sake. It's against the laws of the church. It's against the laws of nature, for that matter."

"We don't care," said Stevie Ray. "I know tons of gay people."

"What gay people? Where?"

"All over," he said. "I'm going into ninth grade, Grampa."

Belly rolled down his window and lit a cigarette. The lighter was getting low on juice, and he had to run his thumb along it three and then four times to get it to spark. "At least the dyke bitch is gone."

"Don't say that word in front of the children."

They waited at the edge of the parking lot to turn left on South Broadway. A small black Hyundai shaking with Mariah Carey music pulled around them. It was Maybelline, singing loudly and off-key, a long cigarette poking from between her fingers.

"Belly, there's your whore," said Nora.

"'Bitch' is wrong but that word's okay?"

"'Dyke,' don't say 'dyke.'" Nora stopped the car in front of the ex–Dairy Queen. "You want to get out? You want to get out and talk to your whore?"

"Keep going, and don't call her that."

"Maybelline's a whore and Bonnie's a bitch," said Jimi.

"Enough," said Nora.

"Whatever. I'm just glad she won't be here to ruin the confirmation."

"She might be back," said Stevie Ray. They turned right on Spring Street and coasted down the hill, past the park, hovering at the traffic light for just a minute. "Aunt Ann is supposed to come on Sunday." He sat back in the seat. "She might."

"Oh, that would be a sight. That would be something for the children to see. Their aunt and wifey making out on the couch."

"Enough," Nora said again.

They pulled in the driveway and Jimi asked, "Ma, can we go swimming now?"

"I don't know, you guys. I've got a lot to do and Stevie Ray has confirmation homework for CCD."

"I'll take them," said Belly.

"Yeah, Grampa'll take us."

"I don't know." They pushed the screen door open and she looked at Belly. "I don't know."

"What? I'll take them. I can take them."

"Okay, but you both have to wear water wings."

Stevie Ray put his hands on his hips. "Mom, do I need to remind you that I'm nearly fourteen years old?"

"Okay, fine, you don't have to but Jimi does."

"I don't care," said Jimi. "I'll wear them."

Belly sat at the table while he waited for the boys to change, and Nora puttered around the kitchen. "You have to be careful with them," she said. "I'm giving you one more chance, just so I can have a moment to myself."

"I can watch the kids," he said. "I can help with that."

"Thanks. I've got it under control."

"But if sometime you want a babysitter or something you can just have me."

"I'll think about it."

Belly fiddled with the salt and pepper shakers. "I'm just saying, if you're going to pay someone to watch them, it may as well be me."

Nora looked at him. "How much money do you have left?"

He stopped playing with the salt and pepper. "None," he said.

"Jesus."

"I know. It's just temporary. Some money's bound to come through."

"From where?"

"They're bound to call."

"Shit," Nora threw down a dishtowel. "Don't you get it? They're all gone. They've cleaned the place up."

"They owe me," he said.

She stood next to him with her hand on his shoulder, bent down to look directly into his eyes. "You act like you're some kind of hero for going to prison. But it's your fault. You never should have gotten mixed up with them in the first place. You've shamed the whole family and now you act like everyone's indebted to you, like people are going to just call you up and offer you money, offer you a job, as if you don't have to work like the rest of the world."

"You're wrong," he said. "Just wait. You'll find out you're wrong." The boys stood in the arch that joined the kitchen to the TV room and they watched Belly. "Let's go," he told them. "I thought you little wimps wanted to swim." They moved through the humidity trapped in the kitchen, escaped to the outside.

"Watch them," Nora called after them. "You have to really watch them."

Stevie Ray walked five paces ahead of him, and Jimi stayed close to his side, mimicking Belly's wide steps, avoiding the cracks in the concrete. They turned right on Court Street and then right again on Phila, and Belly could almost hear the sharp clack of his old dog Seaver's paws as a soundtrack. This was their old route: him and the pup on their midday walk to retrieve the late paper, the stillness of weekday afternoons when the whole world was at work and Belly was just waking, when Saratoga belonged to him.

He pretended she was there, his sweet little mutt, he pretended these grandchildren were his girls, he pretended all four of his daughters and his dog surrounded him like bodyguards as they approached Mrs. Radcliffe's on the south side of the

street. Belly stood with his back to the house where once he'd
lived with his whole family unscathed.

"That's the house where Mom grew up," said Jimi, tugging
on Belly's sleeve to turn him around.

"I know it," said Belly. "I was there, too."

Stevie Ray unlatched the Radcliffes' rickety wooden gate
and led Belly and Jimi inside. In the small yard a big above-
ground pool squatted, surrounded by a cheap pine deck. A
middle-aged woman in a Day-Glo lounge chair lay with her
tired stomach hanging out of her bikini, a towel over her face.
This couldn't be, how could this be Mrs. Sylvia Radcliffe, the
same woman who rescued him from the street the morning after Nora's wedding? Two teenage girls floated on tubes in the
pool, holding magazines.

"Hi, Mrs. Radcliffe," the boys called.

She took the towel off her face and he wished she hadn't.

"Mr. O'Leary," she said, beckoning him forward with a
manicured hand. "It's been years."

The girls put their magazines down and glared at him.

"You'll remember they call me Belly," he said, making his
way slowly up the steps to the deck, running his hands along
his hips.

"I know that," said Mrs. Radcliffe. "Girls, say hello to Mr.
O'Leary."

They mumbled from the water.

The boys splashed into the pool, making the girls squeal.
Jimi did not wear his water wings, and Belly didn't make him.

"Feel free to go in," she said. "Our pool is your pool."

"I don't swim."

"No?"

"No."

"Never?" She leaned over so the stretch marks on her breasts curved like waves.

"Never."

She lay back again. "Me neither. I hate the water."

"Me, too."

"I'd take a dry shower if I could."

He laughed. "Me, too."

"Isn't that funny?" she said. She glanced at the kids in the water. "You want a drinky?"

He remembered this woman, his across-the-street neighbor, as shy and private, as law-abiding and churchgoing and meek. It was as if she'd blossomed in middle age, opened some secret compartment inside her that made her seem shiny and new, like an irresistible toy.

"What you got?"

She pulled out a small plastic tub from below her chair. "Wine cooler?"

"You're kidding."

"Yeah," she said. "I'm stuck in the eighties. I can't help it. I miss them."

"Me too."

"The drugs."

"Yeah."

"The parties."

"I know."

"The money."

"All of it," he said. "Me, too. Except the wine coolers. I don't miss those." He took another look at Mrs. Radcliffe. Gray roots poked from her dyed brassy hair. She had it pulled back in a neon green cloth, and a little trail of makeup ran down her left cheek like tears. "I never used to see you at the parties," he said.

"When I lived across the street. I don't think I ever saw you out and about even one time. I didn't know you partied."

"I was busy being Catholic," she said. "A good Catholic housewife with a kindly husband. I miss it mostly because I never really got to do it."

"I'll take a wine cooler," he said. "The least disgusting flavor."

She popped open a lemon-lime and handed it to him. "Gross," he said, chugging it down in one gulp. "Give me another."

"Don't tell Nora," said Mrs. Radcliffe. "She thinks I don't drink. Especially when the kids are swimming."

He wrapped his lips around the bottle and said, "My lips are sealed," his words echoing into the glass.

"How are things at the farmhouse?" she asked.

"What do you mean?"

"That's what we call it, Nora's house. The last white-trash house in the neighborhood."

Belly gulped his drink. "Looks all right to me."

Mrs. Radcliffe said, "Sure," and shielded her eyes with her hands, staring out at the pool. "These children were born in the eighties," she said. "My girls were born in 1986. That's something, isn't it? I guess that's when the eighties were over for me."

"Me, too," he said, but he did not remind her why.

One good thing, there was one good thing that happened in 1986. The Mets and the Red Sox in that seven-game set, that famous Bill Buckner play in game six, eight glorious days when nothing existed but baseball, the first time since July, since his third daughter died, when he'd woken up hopeful, when he'd found a reason to rise.

Mrs. Radcliffe was staring at him. She looked right at him with a wine-cooler glow in her cheeks and she said, "What do you think of life on the outside?"

He said, "I don't know."

Stevie Ray was hanging on one of the girl's floats, and the girl lay on her stomach with her head on her arms and they were talking close like that, and Belly felt the foot of space between his lounge chair and Mrs. Radcliffe's like a precipice. He was too sober to fall in.

"Did you hear there are gay people in the eighth grade?" he asked her, taking another wine cooler from her.

"Who told you that?"

"Stevie Ray."

Mrs. Radcliffe sipped a big swig of wine cooler, she smoothed the wavy lines of flesh over her stomach. "Must be one of the Kennedy boys," she said. "They always wear pink — I think it's part of their religion or something, but everybody calls them gay."

"Remember when it was bad to be gay? When people had to hide it? Whatever happened to that? When I was little I didn't even know a single gay person, not anyone who would admit it. People just flaunt it these days. Where is the shame?"

Mrs. Radcliffe swiveled onto her hips. Flesh pooled on the lawn chair, red stripes from the plastic slats decorated her thighs. "You must have met some gay people in jail, I would imagine." She didn't smile.

"Never." He rested the wine cooler on his jeans. It made a dark circle and he ran his fingers around the circle.

"I've seen *Oz*."

"Are you trying to tell me Dorothy was gay?"

"I mean the HBO show. Haven't you seen it?"

"No premium channels in prison," said Belly. "I'm out of the loop."

"How about *Midnight Express* then?"

"That was Turkish prison," he said. "And I don't remember any buggering."

"In the movie or in the jail?" she asked.

He took a big sip of sugary carbonation, this stuff would never make him drunk enough, and he said, "I've seen some things," and he would not say more. She was leaning over, her painted lips were parted and she wanted the details, and he downed the rest of the spiked soda and he would not say more.

The two girls floated in the center of the pool, and the boys made a whirlpool around them, running alongside the plastic walls until a current bubbled and the girls began to twirl.

Mrs. Radcliffe said, "My husband used to use your services."

"I remember," he said. "Whatever happened to him, anyway? He just disappeared one day. He came in, I used to see him once a week, and then he was just gone." He vaguely recalled the heavyset man, balding, always a little dab of saliva caught in the corners of his mouth.

"What happens to any of them?" she asked, and served herself another bottle. "He found himself somebody younger." She raised one eyebrow at him and he thought maybe she was coming on to him, maybe he could take off her bikini top and let those stretch marks hang down over him, maybe she would whisper to him while he worked at her, maybe she would take him inside that big warm house and hide him.

He thought about Mr. Radcliffe then, about Bruce. Bruce was a talker. He'd stop in on his way home from work for a pint of Guinness and relate the family woes. He'd had some kind of tumor erupt on the side of his face, nothing serious, but it looked bad, some giant ball of pus at his temple. And Mrs. Radcliffe's appendix burst, they thought it was period cramps or something, and they'd all held a vigil over her hospital bed; Bruce had been left to care for these girls, they were twins, that's right. Bruce had always been thankful that their problems were solvable — "The best kind of problems to have," that was his motto. No one had died, no cancer, no long-suffering illnesses, no losses.

Belly wondered what it felt like to stick it out with someone like that, to seal yourself to another human being by surmounting adversity together. He'd never had the chance. Myrna left him before they could survive their tragedies. But then, the Radcliffes hadn't made it either.

"That's what you did, isn't it?" she asked. "You left Myrna for that Loretta woman?"

Belly shifted himself on the chair. His flesh clung to the plastic slats. He tried to reposition the chair so the sun would not glare at him so directly, but the sun, it followed him wherever he went, it forced the booze from his pores so no matter how much he drank now, here in the pounding heat of the late afternoon, his brain refused to succumb.

"She left me," he said. "Myrna left me."

"Is that right?" she asked, her voice tinged with disbelief.

"She left me a week after the funeral," he said. "I got home from work and she'd just packed up all her things and put them on the front porch, all these liquor boxes she'd pilfered from the bar."

"I remember," said Mrs. Radcliffe. "I remember I went over there to borrow some coffee liqueur and Nora said she'd moved out. I just assumed you told her to."

Belly shook his head. Maybe the wine cooler was working. "I couldn't believe she just left me with the girls like that. First Nora took off and then, she, then my daughter." He swallowed. "And then I come home and Myrna's just gone. No warning. She said she just could not stay sober and stay with me. What did she expect me to do, stop working at a bar? Stop keeping alcohol in the house, just because she couldn't keep a lid on it? But I mean, her own children. What kind of woman would do that?"

"I remember so clearly that it was coffee liqueur I wanted."

"It was all her idea. I remember the biggest box she had, it was all booze. She'd written "booze" on it in a big fat black marker. She took all the booze in the house with her and she dumped it in this big Dumpster by the highway. She took *my* booze." He was getting worked up, his voice rising so the kids stopped in midwhirlpool and stared, water whooshing all around them.

One dance, they'd tangoed together, a little joke of a twisty drunken dance at the senior prom, after six months of dating, tangoed just the way his Grampa taught him, she got pregnant that night, and they'd never unraveled, not until the day she'd told him she was moving to her own bungalow in that dead little town to the west.

"Is your daughter going to be there?" asked Mrs. Radcliffe.

"Which one?"

"The one who lives in New York, Ann. The news one. She never comes around." She adjusted her breasts in her bikini bra. "The gay one," she said, winking at him. "The kind they all know about in eighth grade."

Myrna's leaving should have ruined him, should have shamed

him into submission. Or he should have begged her to stay, or to return, or to stop drinking and stand up to the task of raising her three remaining children, should have dug up the marriage license and tapped on it with a pencil and recited, "till death do us part," but he just dropped her off and purged her from his memory. He should have kept the house on Phila Street for the last years that Ann and Eliza went to high school, should have kept their bedrooms preserved with the posters of Shawn Cassidy and LPs of the Cars and the Who and A-ha stacked to the ceiling. He should have given his wife some opening in case she wanted to come home.

"I don't know," he said. "Maybe."

The wine coolers stranded him with a miserable headache. Mrs. Radcliffe's stretch marks looked like fingers, beckoning him. She smiled her sugary wine-cooler smile at him. "Well, Myrna will be there at least. She's still a churchgoer."

He should have left the door open for her. But he couldn't stand to see his third daughter's belongings, and even when he shut the door to her tiny room at the top of the stairs, he could see everything inside it, the towering boxes of toe shoes and her textbooks and collection of black dolls and all of her earrings posted on a red ribbon in a ripple above her dresser. And her goddamned pink sweater with the alligator. He couldn't stand to see his wife, they looked so much alike, and he couldn't stand to be inside that house, and he hated his three remaining daughters and he hated himself for hating them and none of it was good, nothing worked, nothing pleased him except his mistress Loretta, who erased all his agony with her smoky perfume and that cloud of rusty red hair.

"Well, all that miserable business happened a long time

ago," Mrs. Radcliffe said. "I just wanted to thank you for being so discreet," she said. "For not giving up any of your clientele. That was very brave of you."

Her words, they soothed him. They shut him up. He didn't tell her that none of the clientele was ever in danger, that only gambling promoters could get in trouble, not gamblers. He didn't tell her that Loretta and the NYRA boys had threatened his family, that far worse would have happened than prison had he given up names. He just let Mrs. Radcliffe's words wash over him like some kind of breeze, some little wisp of relief he'd been waiting for. She patted his hand. "Another wine cooler?"

"No," he said. "Got to keep my eye on the boys. I promised."

Mrs. Radcliffe chatted on about her daughters, talked about how they'd all be there on Sunday for Stevie Ray's confirmation party and what she and the girls were going to wear — the three of them had matching outfits for church.

"Boys, let's go," he called. "Time to go."

Faint whines escaped from the boys as they climbed out of the pool and gathered up their things to leave. Belly noticed how Stevie Ray lingered on the edge of the pool, his bare foot catching the edge of one of the twins' rafts. Two conflicting thoughts rushed at him simultaneously, compounding the headache: he was both proud and jealous of the boy. He followed behind Stevie Ray, watching his walk, shoulders hunched forward in a huddle. He didn't play sports, this grandson of his, he didn't hang out with other boys, he caved in on himself when he stood, and Belly realized his oldest grandson was exactly the kind of boy he'd picked on back in junior high.

Belly remembered the morning after his third daughter's funeral, when all the decibels were too high and too tinny, and even the soft thud of the *Saratogian* hitting the front steps jolted him awake. He had padded down the carpeted stairs, the *swish swish* of his Grinch slippers on shag, out to the porch. Mrs. Radcliffe had stood on her front lawn, watering her begonias, pregnant with the twins. She set the hose down so it sprayed a big dark slash on wet macadam. She came to the middle of the road, no double yellow lines, just newly smoothed tar in time for the racetrack. He slumped into the road to meet her. She lifted her arms, soft pads of fat jiggled below her biceps — how he missed women's bodies before aerobics and Madonna and Jazzercize — he smelled flowery deodorant and sweat and coffee breath — and he meant to rest his head in the perfect round nook between her shoulder and chin, but she took one hand on either side of his Brillo-pad cheeks, she pulled his face to hers and kissed him full on the mouth, slid her tongue in to meet his and licked the filmy enamel of his top teeth. He shook his head now, trying not to remember.

In the kitchen, Stevie Ray popped open a can of Coke, and Belly stared at the black face of the computer. He said, "How do you work this thing?"

"What do you want to do?"

"Stevie, come over here and turn this thing on."

"It's right here, Grampa." He pushed a little round button and a green stripe lighted within it.

"Show me how to e-mail."

"You don't know how?"

"This whole Internet thing exploded while I was gone. I know what it is, I just don't know how to work it."

"Well, you have to have an account first. You have to have an address."

"I'll use yours."

"No way."

"I'll use your mother's. She has one, doesn't she?"

"We have a family one," he said.

Belly tugged on Stevie Ray's soggy sleeve. "Aw, come on. Give Grampa a break."

Stevie Ray squished into the chair with Belly, his fingers dancing over the keyboard. He felt the warmth of the boy's body, smelled the sharp scent of chlorine and sunscreen, and the boy concentrated fiercely on the computer screen. Belly reached up and tousled his hair, but the boy squirmed out from his hand, and then his hand hung there in the air a minute, like Wile E. Coyote before he noticed there was no more ground beneath him.

"You know how to type?" Belly asked. "They teach you typing already? When I was your age only the girls took typing, and the boys took shop." Stevie Ray ignored him.

The computer made a terrible whining sound and the screen turned blue and then white. Stevie Ray typed something in and another screen opened and he said, "You can do it now."

"How do you make it go to someone?"

"What's the e-mail address?"

"How should I know?"

"Who are you writing to?"

"Your aunt."

"Which one?"

"Ann, dammit. I'm writing to Ann. Make it go to Ann."

Stevie Ray typed her address at the top.

"Is that the real CBS?"

"Yeah. She took us to the studio where Dan Rather does the news and everything."

"Well." He could think of no response. "He's probably a mean boss."

"She makes a lot of money."

"Probably not that much."

"You can type now, Grampa."

Stevie Ray got up off the chair.

"Where you going?"

"I don't want to see."

Stevie Ray headed toward the living room and Belly called, "What do I do when I'm done?"

"Hit *send*."

Belly typed. He picked out the words with two fingers as they came into his head. He did not read over what he'd written, he just typed and typed and hit *send*.

"Stevie," he called. "Turn this thing off."

"Belly," Nora stood in the doorway. "What did you just do?" She pressed some buttons on the computer and the screen went dark.

"I e-mailed."

"Who?"

"Your sister."

"Which one?"

"Listen, I just want to let her know that I know that homosexuals are sinners."

Nora opened the fridge and took out a Piels, opened the can, and handed it to him. "Okay, go ahead and believe that."

"Thanks, I will."

"Kids," Nora called. "Change out of your suits and get ready for dinner. We're going out." She turned to Belly. "Thursday is family night. We have pizza at the restaurant with Phil, up at the bar." She hesitated and he wondered if she wanted him to come.

"Very wholesome," he said. "Good wholesome family fun."

He vaguely remembered something like that in his own household, some weekly dinner, one night he would take off and spend with the girls, a ritual he looked forward to every week. A real gourmet feast. He tried to recall where this happened, and when, but then it came to him: it was only a TV show his third daughter used to watch. It never happened to them. What they really ate, what Myrna fixed them, was spaghetti, pizza, grilled cheese, hamburgers. It was basically the kids' meal at Friendly's. Really, prison food was better than Myrna's crummy culinary creations. He thought of telling Nora that, but then maybe she would want to know more, more about prison. Or worse, maybe she would want to know nothing. He wanted to go with them to dinner but he didn't know how to ask.

She came to him, she reached her hand out for his and he took it. She pressed her palm against his palm and when she removed it he was left with a fifty-dollar bill stuck to his lifeline.

Belly sat on the couch in the empty house and flipped through every channel on the TV three times and drank beer and smoked cigarettes on the porch. He put the fifty in his wallet and let it brew there. Then he climbed the stairs to Nora's room, he opened the drawers of her dresser one by one: underwear, socks, diaphragm, rubber things he did not want to identify, and he did not know what he was looking for until he found a Ziploc bag with two joints stashed behind her short-sleeved shirts. Underneath the bag hid a pile of crisp twenty-dollar bills and he looked at them for a moment. He put out his index finger and pressed on the pile — trying to remember what it felt like to hold a wad like that, to remember how you could feel the weight of a grand or two or ten. He didn't want to, he didn't mean to, but he picked up a twenty, he lifted six twenties from the pile and stuffed them in the pocket of his jeans.

He sat on her chenille bedspread and smoked one joint and looked at the pictures affixed to her mirror, pictures of her children and her mother and her husband and Gene, Eliza with Henry and Ann with Bonnie and then an old school photograph with his third daughter smiling in the center.

Ann was still gone and Eliza was going and the third daughter had been gone such a long time. Myrna had left him and Loretta had forsaken him and he wondered which, if any, of these women would come back. Who would stay with him?

Downstairs, back in the TV room, the heat was unbearable. Belly lay in the fringed La-Z-Boy recliner waiting for night to set in, for Nora and the children to return so someone could distract him from himself. He lay in the chair with a Piels in one hand and the remote in the other and he thought, This cannot be my life. It's Thursday night and this can't be my life.

Outside the sun was setting; an orange haze seeped into the house and out the window he could see a sliver of moon rising. He raised himself up and stood on the back porch and watched the sun fall behind the trees, felt the heat intensify when it should diffuse, and he could not name the feeling settling in his solar plexus but he knew it was unbearable and he knew no amount of alcohol could cure it.

Then an apparition rose from the sidewalk: a black figure circled in light, a walking silver lining. It could be Loretta, or Phillip Sr., or his third daughter. It could be someone called back from the beyond to retrieve him, and he steadied himself, he readied himself, for the next world.

It was only Eliza. Eliza walked down the driveway, silhouetted against the fiery sky. She walked up to him and took his hand and said, "Belly, I thought maybe you could use some company."

He shook his head. "I'm fine," he said.

"You want to do some errands with me? I need a few things before I leave tomorrow."

"No," he said.

She said, "Please? Daddy, please?" and he turned and looked at his youngest child, her pale stringy hair and her pale eyes, everything about her light against the darkening sky and he felt something strange, some foreign object clogging his throat. I'm giving birth to an egg out my mouth, he thought, and then he coughed and made a sound and he thought, What is happening to me, what is this? and Eliza put her skinny little arms around him and said, "It's okay, it's okay, Daddy," and he still didn't know, he could not see out his left eye and he let his head hang down on her bony shoulder and he shook and her shoulder was wet. It was all over in a minute. Then the sky was dark.

Eliza said, "Come on, Belly, I'll take you with me."

He put his beer can on the back porch steps and let her lead him around the corner to her house, to her old Subaru station wagon, and he strapped himself in the seat. She drove down Union, past the bed and breakfast where the retards used to live and past the mansions and past the racetrack and the arts colony and he said finally, "Where are we going?"

"Wal-Mart," she said, shifting into fifth gear.

"Oh, Jesus, what the hell?"

"What?" she said. "What's the problem?"

"You're the last person who should be going to a place like that."

"Why do you say that?"

"Aren't you and Margie the antichain gang or something? You hippie types hate that shit." He wondered if she'd spoken with Margie, if this was the official Wal-Mart intervention program, national get-your-father-a-crappy-job day. But he looked at Eliza and everything about her seemed far away, disinvested. His youngest daughter was already gone.

Eliza turned onto the old road to the mall, past the former dump on one side and the new skating rink on the other and she said, "I know it's wrong, but I love it."

"That's just what your mother used to say," Belly told her. "About drinking."

"Well, that," Eliza replied. Then, "Let's not talk about Mom."

"No, you know what? Let's do. Let's talk about your mother. You guys are constantly giving me shit and no one seems to mind that your mother up and left you, you were still in high school and she left you. Now why do I get such a bad rap and your mother is a saint? You don't remember picking her up off the floor in the morning? You don't remember how she was passed out on the couch when you came home from school?"

"I do. I remember all of it. I remember going with her to rehab. Checking her in. I remember bringing her things at Four Winds, her perfume and stuff. I remember riding my bike over there after school during visiting hours. I remember how I would never let Henry come in the house. We remember all of it."

"Then why? You're not mad?"

"It's too hard to talk about," she said.

He put his hand on Eliza's hand as she downshifted to

second and they pulled into the ocean of Wal-Mart's parking lot, lit up like a football game. A big gray box with green light streaming from it and a giant red, white, and blue "Grand Opening" banner stretched across the top.

"This is what everyone's talking about?" he asked.

"It's new," said Eliza. She wandered off in search of he didn't know what. It was so big, so bright, he felt paralyzed.

He walked along the endless rows of cheap electronics, past the "Join Our Team" flyers that decorated every aisle, past the new employees, young and old, in blue smocks, and he recalled a promise his nineteen-year-old self had made: to never wear a uniform for work. A banjo player, an older fellow with a gray beard who looked vaguely familiar, strolled through the aisle strumming a Dixieland song — the tune Belly remembered but the words fell away — a big "Ask me: I'm here to help" button on his lapel interfering with the strings.

The light from absurdly high ceilings cast a green glow over everything. Belly got the feeling Wal-Mart was a giant terrarium in God's garage, each aisle a treadmill, a maze, too many items, too many people, nothing familiar, nothing small, nothing real in the whole box.

And then he saw Loretta.

She was wearing the same old kind of outfit: gold lamé hot pants and high heels and a ferocious fuchsia tank top, low cut. It was so low cut. His Nebraskan prairie girl all dolled up for the little northeastern city. Behind her rolled her son in his futuristic wheelchair, blowing in a plastic tube to propel it forward. Belly pressed himself against the shelter of a My Little Pony display and tried not to look at the boy, and the boy, he realized, Darren, must be thirty-two or thirty-three by now, a grown man. He could not believe this was the same stoned kid he sent to pick up his daughter at dance class in his 1972 Mustang, the kid who crashed into the back of the Shoe Barn, the car all covered in moccasins and his daughter with her head snapped back like a Pez dispenser, landing the car and his daughter in the duck pond in Congress Park. If he looked at the boy the ghost of his dead daughter's face rose like heat monkeys on tarmac.

He remembered the time they ran into a neighbor of Loretta's on the street, a young woman with a six-week-old, and after they left her Loretta said, "That was one ugly baby," and he loved her for her heartlessness. He wanted to see her, he wanted her to see him, but not like this, not with tears dried on his unshaven face and sweat stains on his shirt and the whites of his eyes dyed red from beer and pot and unsound sleep.

He wended his way through the endless store, tiptoeing into the aisles like a cat burglar, trying not to let Loretta catch him. He found Eliza perched before the deodorant display, reading labels.

She stood up when she saw him. "Did you see her?" she asked.

"Yes."

"Did she see you?"

"No."

"Are you okay?"

"I think so."

"I don't know what you ever saw in that woman."

He looked at the contents of Eliza's yellow plastic basket: she'd managed to find the only products in there with the words "all natural" written across the packages. He thought of her fat Jewish husband at home, slathering organic hair gel on the site of his male-pattern baldness, he thought of their sickly dog, and he said, "You can never tell what goes on between two people."

Eliza looked up at him. She put her hand on his shoulder and said, "That's so true."

She asked him, "Do you need anything? Deodorant or anything? Shaving cream?"

"I'm using Phil's," Belly said. "He doesn't know it."

"Oh, Belly," she said.

Eliza pivoted around in the toiletry section, filling her basket with Barbasol and Old Spice and Gillette — anything remotely manly, Belly noticed — a whole bathroom cabinet's worth of macho supplies, and then she led him to the checkout.

They waited in the long line at the register. He read *Reader's Digest* while she cashed out and they headed toward the door, but Belly stopped. He told Eliza to wait and he turned around and walked to the customer service desk, his cowboy boots slippery on the shiny white faux-marble linoleum. He walked up to a young black girl in a blue vest and said, "Let me have an application." She ripped one off a pad and handed it to him. He folded it in half and then he looked up and asked her, "Is it okay if it's folded?" and the girl shrugged her shoulders and said, "I guess," and he folded it again and put it in his back pocket. If he dropped off a filled-out application later, he could get some nineteen-year-old manager's initials on his form, buy himself a little time to find a real job.

Outside he saw Eliza, a postanorexic aging hippie leaned up against a piece-of-shit Subaru. A tiny twinge pricked at his chest: she'd be gone so soon.

She said, "Okay?" and he nodded.

They sat in the car, in the heat, and Eliza handed him a small plastic bag. "I got you a present."

Inside, an aluminum flask with faux alligator skin wrapped along the sides hugged the bottom of the bag. He looked up and she smiled at him. He couldn't remember how to smile back, the gift made him so suspicious. He unbuttoned the top of his shirt and fanned the fabric against his chest. "Can you turn up the AC?" he asked.

"I don't have any," she said.

"Jesus, why not?"

"Can't afford to get it fixed."

"Get your sister to pay, maybe."

"She's already giving me money for school, as you know."

He rolled his window all the way down. "I meant Nora."

"She doesn't have any extra," said Eliza. "They're paying out all this money to Gene to fix the house."

"They pay him for that?"

"Of course, you think he just fixes stuff for free?"

Belly looked at his hands. "Yes," he said. "I did."

Eliza shook her head. "They're getting ready to put on an addition, for the new baby. King will need his own room and they only have the three bedrooms, and with you there, that means they need more. They've got to fix it up according to the design guidelines, you know, whatever those historic preservation people say."

"Maybe we know somebody at City Hall who can get them around all that rigamarole. I can make a call."

"Oh, Daddy, don't even say things like that. You know you don't have friends there anymore."

He stared out the window.

"Anyway," Eliza said. "I'm not going to need a car in Alabama. It's just a little town. I can walk to everything. It's kind of like Saratoga used to be." Belly rolled his window back up. "I was thinking of leaving the car with Ann and Bonnie, so they could get out of the city."

"Great," he said. "Then they can come up here all the time. Go ahead and make my life miserable."

"Well, I don't know that Ann would come up here, anyway."

"I thought you said she was coming for the confirmation, instead of you. Wasn't that the bargain?"

"Well, yes, I thought maybe she would, but I talked to her tonight and I think she's not going to." She turned up the vent. "I think it was the e-mail you sent her."

"I asked her to come. That's all I said. I said we should try and keep the family together and she should come here." He loosened his seatbelt. "I told her I missed her," he said quietly. His heart rate increased, he had trouble breathing, and he told himself if he cried again he would smash his own face in. He pretended he was his father, silencing him with the old equation: one punch for every tear, you little weakling.

"It freaked her out, I guess. First of all, she didn't even know you knew how to use e-mail. She's never even gotten a letter from you in her life."

"That is not true. I sent her a letter once, when she went to college. I even apologized."

"That was when you went to AA for a month and you apologized to every person you'd ever met. You didn't mean it."

"Well, I meant it this time. I just asked her to come visit, but forget it. I don't care if I never see her again, if that's what she's like."

"She might come or she might not. She's deciding."

"Jesus!" Belly banged his fist on the dashboard. "You're all so ungrateful. Every one of you." Every time he blinked he saw Darren and his daughter, the wreck, the shoes, the car as it fumbled into Congress Park and landed with the front end in the water, burned strips of metal convulsed into strange silver sculptures on the ground. He propped his eyelids open with his pointer fingers. "Your mother leaves you and you forgive her, and all I do is send this nice e-mail thing and you all turn against me."

"Nobody's against you. We're all for you. We all, you know, we forgive you as much as we can. Mom was drunk, but she —" Eliza stopped. "She was never mean."

"I wasn't mean."

"She never hit us," Eliza said softly.

And what could he say? She got him. It seemed like that was another man, an episode of *Cops,* someone else's life or body or mind. It wasn't he who hit these girls, his lovely daughters, it was a phantom, an invasion, body snatchers. What could he say?

"Mom didn't leave us, you know," Eliza continued. "We knew she was leaving. She told all of us, and asked if we wanted to come."

"What? She tried to turn you against me?"

"No, not at all. She just said she needed to get out and that she was going to Stillwater and we could come, but we wanted to finish high school in the same place." She took a deep breath. "And, frankly, by that time Mom was getting sober and we were more worried about you. We wanted to keep an eye on you. We wanted to make sure you were all right."

"Oh, right, you did it for me."

"I told you we shouldn't talk about it."

"You're making that up. To make yourself feel better. But I don't blame you. If my mother walked out on me I'd make up all kinds of lies about it, too. Good job. Very creative. You're so creative, Eliza."

She looked for a minute like she was going to cry, and Belly sat back smug, a vague sense of accomplishment rapidly fading to regret.

Then Eliza said, "Did they give you shaving cream in prison? Could you have razors?"

He looked at the window.

"I was just wondering. About things like that."

"Under supervision," he said. "You used razors under supervision."

"Oh, Daddy," she said. "I'm so sorry."

"Whatever," he said.

"Did you use those meditation tapes I sent you?"

"My Walkman broke," he lied.

"You poor thing. How did you listen to music?"

"Oh, there was the heavy percussion of guys banging their tin cups on the bars."

"No, really."

"Really."

"It wasn't like that, Belly. It was federal prison."

"How do you know what it was like? Did you ever come down to see me?"

"I sent you things."

"Right."

They passed the dump again, and he noticed no putrid smell rising from the grassy knolls of garbage, and he wondered at all the changes and technology and how they could keep a landfill from stinking and how they could get the whole town to come out to a Wal-Mart on a Thursday night and what had happened here?

"You know, I just couldn't make it all the way to Pennsylvania with Audrey and everything."

"Who's Audrey?"

"My dog, Belly. You met her yesterday."

"Right. The dog."

"She needs insulin shots twice a day, and Henry has his very strict diet."

"The only vegan on the Atkins diet. That's all much more important than visiting your father in prison."

"Yes," she said. "But Nora always told me about it. And Ann. She told Ann, too."

"Who cares about Ann? Apparently she doesn't like it when her old man's nice to her." He rubbed a smudge on the car window.

"Ann was glad to hear about you, though. Bonnie gave her the full report."

"What does that mean?"

"All that stuff Bonnie was asking you."

"What about it?"

Eliza glanced at him for a minute before looking back at the road. They drove by the other big Catholic church in town, St. Xavier's, and the little city park called the East Side Rec — the "poor man's park" to townies — and it was dark now but still the air was suffocating. All the marijuana had evaporated and no more beer circled in his veins.

"That was all stuff Ann wanted to know. She was getting the scoop for Ann."

Belly said, "Oh," and he wanted to know more but then again he didn't, and he leaned his head against the plate glass and watched the town roll on by.

"I'm leaving tomorrow, Belly."

"I know."

She squeezed his hand but he made his fingers limp.

"You can come down and visit me if you want. You and Nora and the boys. We can have a family vacation."

"Right."

"It'll be just like Florida," she said, and when she smiled he saw for the first time tiny crow's feet stretching from the corners of her eyes.

Belly said, "Sure it will," and he patted her shoulder.

"How did you meet Loretta, anyway?" Eliza asked him. "I never figured out that part of the mystery."

Belly sighed. "After your mother left, I just spent more and more time at the bar and Loretta starting coming in there — she was dating the bouncer, you remember him, that kind of fat Malazzi kid? She used to like big guys before me. Goombahs. And I just noticed her after all those years of not really looking at her."

"That is such. . . ." She hesitated, then said quietly, "Bullshit."

"What's bullshit about it?"

"You were seeing Loretta years before Mom left."

"I was not."

"Yes, you were."

"I absolutely was not."

"Oh my God." Eliza pulled over.

"What are you doing?"

"I'm having a heart attack." She put her hand on her chest. "Belly, you are going to drive us all mad."

"Drive the car."

"Just give me a minute."

"Drive, dammit."

"Are you honestly telling me that you didn't start seeing Loretta until after Mom left? I mean, honestly you're telling me that, but what I want to know is if that's what you actually believe, because if you believe yourself you are in some serious trouble. I mean, go ahead and lie to me, but don't delude yourself like that. That is just scary."

"Will you drive the car, please? Will you please drive the car?" He pounded his fist on the dashboard again, and this time a small whitish indentation formed in the aging gray plastic.

"I'm driving, I'm driving." She pulled back on the road. "Don't worry. You'll be out of here in five minutes."

"I have a minor fear of small, enclosed spaces. You can imagine."

Eliza turned onto East Avenue, the line between the old and new parts of town, and kept looking at her father out of the corner of her eye. "Well?" she asked him. "What about it?"

It was Loretta he craved, Loretta he loved, Loretta who reaped the profits from his life-on-the-side, Loretta whose rabbit-fur coat and designer clothes he financed with the betting, Loretta who hid out in the apartment above the bar while he still lived with his family on Phila Street, who waited for him every afternoon with open arms and a flat stomach and breasts that called him awake, Loretta who delivered the weekly winnings and skimmed her share off the top. Even after tragedy carved a deep scar in their connection, he wanted her.

"I did not start seeing Loretta until after your mother left."

"Then why was Darren picking my sister up after dance class that day? Weren't you with Loretta that afternoon?"

Belly opened the door and a rush of hot air blew in.

"Christ, Dad, shut that, shut the door. What the hell are you doing?"

"Stop the car. Stop the car. I'm getting out."

"Stop it, Belly," Eliza screamed. "Close the door. You're going to kill yourself."

"Pull the fuck over," he said. She stopped the car on the corner of Spring and East Avenue and Belly stepped out into the blistering night. He slammed the door and headed down his daughter's street and he hummed that Dixieland tune hovering in the back of his fading memory, just grabbed the notes from the ether to keep from thinking about anything. He did not want one single thought to circulate through his brain. He wanted a drink and that was the only thing in the whole world that he desired.

He sneaked in the front door of Nora's house and walked through the living room and TV room to the kitchen. Nora had replenished his Piels supply. Voices wafted in from the side porch and he peered through the screen door to see Nora and Eliza surrounded by a halo: Nora was smoking a cigarette, a lit one. Their voices rose and fell like a mountain range. He shouldn't listen, he knew he shouldn't listen, but he stood with his shoulders pressed against the doorjamb and he sipped his beer and eavesdropped.

"He didn't even have deodorant," he heard Eliza say.

"He can get that stuff himself. He can walk to the Rite Aid," said Nora.

"It's not there anymore. They tore it down."

"Whatever," Nora said. "Menges and Curtis is still there. He's a grown man."

"Nora, I don't think you're taking this seriously."

"Listen, you can criticize me when you take him in. Let's see what happens when he gets old and decrepit and needs his diapers changed. Let's see who takes care of him then."

Belly took another beer from the fridge and downed it in one desperate slug and opened another, slowly, so they wouldn't hear the pop.

"I would, Nora. I would take him in but you insisted."

"You're leaving, Eliza. You're leaving and you always knew you would, so don't pretend to be the saint."

"What's that supposed to mean?"

"What a coincidence that you've decided to go back to school just after Belly gets back. I wonder how that happened?"

"This has nothing to do with Belly. This is about me, about my marriage going downhill and about my art. If you don't want me to go, I won't go. Say the word and I'll stay here and help you with Belly. With the kids."

"No. Don't. I'm sorry. I don't mean anything. I'm tired. It's a stressful time and I'm saying things I don't mean. I'm happy to take care of him. I have the room, I already have the chaos. What's one more child?"

They both laughed.

"Well, it's true," Eliza said. "You have the bigger house. And after you're done with the renovations you can sell this place for a mint and get a nice big place in Geyser Crest with a real yard and a bigger driveway and you can park all your SUVs there."

"What are you talking about? I wouldn't sell this place."

Belly took out beer number four.

"Oh, I just figured you'd rather live in the 'burbs," said Eliza. "You always seemed to aspire to that traditional sort of life."

"You know what? We're trying to fix this place up, all right? I realize I am now surrounded on all sides by rich people who are making Spring Street look like Main Street at Disneyland, but I can't quite keep up. It's hard when your husband works a million hours and you have three little kids. But of course you wouldn't know about that."

"That's what happens, I guess, when you have that '50s life. The housewife thing and all."

"Fuck you, Eliza."

"Don't talk to me that way, Nora. I'm your sister."

"Don't give me that high-and-mighty crap. You're not any better than me."

"Than I," corrected Eliza.

"Fuck you. Really." Nora flicked her cigarette onto the driveway. "And eat a cheeseburger or something. You're too thin."

"I don't eat meat."

"If you're moving to the South, you better learn. They lynch vegetarians down there."

He heard Eliza protesting, trying to smooth things over. Poor Eliza could never hold her own against Nora. He thought he heard her cry.

Belly rescued the two remaining beers still strangled in plastic and took to the couch. He turned on the TV to a *Jeffersons* marathon and turned it up loud, loud enough to hear outside on the side porch. He cradled the two beers against him as he finished the other and when Nora came in she stood in the archway with her arms folded above her pregnant midriff and they did not look at each other. She stepped through the room and headed up the stairs and they did not exchange a single word.

When the house was quiet he climbed to the second floor

and walked down the hallway to what had been Bonnie's room. Only now did it occur to him that this little bedroom at the back of the house must belong to Jimi, that the boys were doubling up to make room for Bonnie, and now for him. On the walls were pictures Jimi had drawn, second-grade scribblings with pictures of the perfect family, a mom and dad and three boys all holding hands, and a whole astronomical motif of stars and suns and planets and galaxies swirling around him. He could feel Bonnie's presence lingering in the room, the nutty scent of her perfume. He looked at the bed where she had been sleeping and he could not lie there. He returned downstairs, to the couch, to the television, the one spot in the whole house where he felt safe.

Belly finished his beers and sang along with *Moving on up, to the East Side,* and when he heard Eliza leave he tried again to call up the numbers in Loretta's phone number. They returned, all seven digits, and he felt so giddy he leapt from the couch, forgetting his old man hips. He ran to the phone, he forgot to be nervous, he didn't care anymore, but when he dialed an angry triad of bells announced to him that the number had been changed. No forwarding information was available.

His heart pounded in an unnatural way, the way it did at the end of a long night of cocaine, but he would not be deterred. He knew where she was, where she always was, the glitzy bar she preferred in their last years together, when so much money was coming in and she no longer needed to bother with War Bar, or the riff-raff of Ruffian's. He walked downtown, to Casey's, in an old bungalow on Throop Street, strewn with tiny white Christmas lights and fancy folks with rainbow shades of martinis — pussy drinks — and he went inside.

Loretta. Loretta sat at the bar, her diamond cross swinging

around her neck, three shot glasses lined up before her. And that, too, scared him and made him feel safe. He remembered he was supposed to summon some fury at her, there was some business, maybe, they were supposed to transact, but all information scattered when he saw that woman, his woman, alone at the bar.

He sat down next to Loretta and she didn't see him. She was leaning toward a younger man on her left, a handsome young man, a man far too young for her, but he was leaning toward her, too, a goddamned human teepee, and he caught a word or two of their whispering. "My house," and "later," and "when," and "good," and "I hope so," and even though he was over her, man, was he over her, the bitch, he wouldn't take her back if she begged . . . something terrible happened. His heart descended into his stomach and sat there, malignant, he felt the infection all through his veins. He missed her. He missed her beautiful body wrapped around his, the seamlessness of their fit. Before Loretta, he used to get a blow job twice a year — on his birthday and New Year's Eve. Only Ann was born one New Year's Eve, foiling his plans from the moment she got here because, yes, he was going to make Myrna do it, nine months' pregnant and all. Myrna wouldn't even have regular missionary sex on the Christian holidays, not even the ones that were more about candy than God, not even Easter. He used to say, "What do you think — Jesus is going to see us doing it from all the way up there in the sky? Christ is risen, but not my dick." Sometimes, Myrna used to hit him back.

He took a breath and leaned next to her, and he said what he said to her the very first time they met: "You're one of the few Catholics I've seen who looks like she can really enjoy pleasure."

She looked up. She turned away from the young man, not so handsome, Belly saw now, and drunk, and no match for her. Loretta was looking at him, glassy eyed and painted, her lips a little too full, the skin on her face a little too tight. She had had work done. On her face. Loretta's perfect face was taut and flat and covered in a beige glow that hid her freckles, so taut a smile barely broke through. She wasn't surprised to see him. She nodded at him and raised her glass and said, "Needlepoint it on a pillow for me." He loved that line, that first thing she ever said to him. That line alone made him look at her again, made him monitor her glass and keep it filled that whole first night, keep her anchored to the bar so he could keep looking at her.

Now she poured the shot down her throat and the skin there was looser and lighter and looked so old. She pushed one of her shot glasses over to him.

"You can take the girl out of Nebraska," he said, and she laughed. He could still make her laugh. The only woman he could ever make laugh. He remembered now, how she had that hold on him. She was like a superhero, a drunken superhero with a gambling habit and plastic surgery.

Belly downed the shot.

He thought about the first night they met, at the bar, this beautiful redhead letting the bouncer buy her beer, newly divorced and in a new town and so indifferent to him that he had to have her. He'd told her a joke — what had he said? — and she'd laughed, and when she laughed she opened her whole mouth, he saw all the way back to her uvula, and seeing that little teardrop of flesh at the back of her throat made him feel so close to her, that prairie-fed girl he'd only just met.

"Jesus Christ, I think I'm in love," he said to her reflection now, and she tilted her head down and smiled.

"Join the club," she said, and lifted her drink up to toast without turning to look at him.

He remembered the way she looked that night, more than twenty years ago, with dark red hair and freckles splashed across her face — he loved freckles on grown-up skin and he liked her skinny body. He'd said to her that night, "You're the kind of thin only ladies with no children can be," and he was so wrong. She took a picture of her fourteen-year-old son from her wallet, a gangly boy with a greasy mullet and a splotch of acne stuck to his jaw. He remembered thinking that the boy was just too trashy for his girls, his beautiful girls. He knew he should never put the boy in the same room as his girls. But then he did. He did it for Loretta. Two years later, he gave Darren the keys and sent him to fetch his daughter and while he sat in the faux-cow-covered La-Z-Boy with Loretta's mouth and legs and arms all around him, Darren was swerving through town, twirling his daughter through the sleek, humidified streets. He was coming and she was going and it was all Loretta's fault.

He looked at Loretta now and her hair was bleached to the moon, and makeup hid the freckles and he had never seen a chin job up close. It did not look right. It looked plastic. It looked like somebody took the beautiful woman he used to love and rolled her in Saran Wrap.

"What are you up to?" Loretta asked him, and she could not have seemed more bored.

"I'm out," he said.

"That I see. But what are you up to? What's the plan?"

He shook his head.

"New bar?"

"No. I can't."

"Ah." She nodded. "Still under house arrest?"

"It's not house arrest," he said. "It's probation."

"Whatever."

"It's for a year."

"The old man's going to have to get himself a job."

He nodded. "Got any contacts?" It was surreal, this conversation, this interaction he'd waited four years for, and now they were shooting the shit like old buddies.

She eyed him from the side. "None. I'm out of the loop. I'm a good girl now." She lifted her left hand and showed him the giant diamond sparkling below her knuckle, below the bubblegum pink of her nails.

This was all too much. Too much information. Too much news. He wanted to drink it away. If he drank, the truth would fade into the background, into the low hum of bar chatter and the pounding bass of classic rock that surrounded them. It would leave with the tourists at the end of the month and he could have everything back the way it was.

Loretta nodded at the bartender and he placed more glasses and more booze before them, and she pushed another shot toward him and said, "Don't get a DUI."

He drank and said, "I won't," and he and Loretta sat facing the mirror behind the bar, not looking at each other, not looking at each other's reflections, and inside he was on fire with nerves. Four years, four years he'd been waiting to see her, to hear her voice again, to place his mouth on the salty skin above her collarbone and drink in her smell, and now she sat next to him, the coldest thing in this heat wave, not even talking to him. Not offering help, not offering her hand or her heart or her body or his money or her connections or her time or even her attention. He could not remember why he loved her, if he ever loved her at all. For the first time in his whole life, he wished Loretta would ease herself away. He wished he could close his eyes, just for a moment, sip a quick breath of darkness and open to find his wife on the barstool next to him, the life they maybe could have had without the four children suffocating them, and then the three children tearing them apart.

When he'd met her that night, his midwestern refugee, she'd told him the story of how she came to live in Saratoga, how her daddy took her to the races when she was little and all her life, all her youth in Omaha she had dreamed of this beautiful town — she came from the Saratoga neighborhood of Omaha, went to the Saratoga school; it was destiny.

He emptied his glass again, fast, and his new best friend, the bartender, took good care of him. He would not be thirsty tonight.

He wanted Loretta to talk to him. He wanted to hear the same story she told him all that time ago, hear her smooth voice cure the creases inside him, hear how she begged her husband to move them out of Omaha, anywhere but there, and he'd bought her a house in Council Bluffs, Iowa, and moved her ten miles across state lines.

To Belly, who had only twice traveled out of the tristate area and never got anywhere close to the Mississippi, it had sounded so exotic. Council Bluffs. She'd said to him, "Council Bluffs is to Omaha as Ballston Spa is to Saratoga," and he'd said, "Oh," and then she'd told him how she tried so hard to get her husband to follow her but he'd just let her go.

Now Loretta put on fresh lipstick and blotted her mouth on the cocktail napkin. He loved it when a woman did that. He picked up the napkin with the stamp of her lips on it. The night they first met, when the conversation finished, he took her to his office behind the back room of the bar, put one foot up on the tufted leather admiral chair, and slid her down his knee, the back of her head resting on the bull's eye of the dartboard, and he'd had to reach and pick out three darts so their flights didn't catch in that red hair. He looked at her now and he couldn't remember how the two of them had got there, what he had said to make her melt.

"What kind of name is Council Bluffs?" he asked her now. "What does that mean? God, that's a strange word. Bluff. Bluff. Say it. Bluff. It's a horrible word."

"You're drunk," she said, and he nodded. "Mormons. They wanted it to sound official to keep all the brown people out."

"Jesus," he said. "Saratoga is the only town that makes sense."

Maybe he and Loretta would be friends. Maybe he would meet her most nights at the bar and they could talk about geography, and he wouldn't have to do anything to her, to anyone. He wouldn't have to lay a girl down and perform the impossible task of making love to her, or making her love him. He just wanted to drink and talk and listen and stare, and maybe he wanted Loretta to put her hand on the small of his back, her fingers cold from the ice clinking in her glass, and let the temperature lower in that one small square of his body.

Their glasses were empty, painfully empty. Without liquor before him, he would have nothing to say to Loretta. "What are you drinking?" he asked.

"I was drinking Glenlivet," she said and her good taste in booze made him achy. "It was a top-shelf night, but I moved down to Bushmills. Then JD. Now I'm on Early Times." She lifted a glass to him. "I love Early Times."

The bartender refilled their shot glasses again, and Belly sipped from his this time. He remembered when certain regulars would show, their hard times plain upon their faces, and something coming off them, something radioactive, that alerted him to their drinking needs. He called those times Night of the Big Whiskeys, or sometimes fifty-whiskey nights. He'd refill their glasses until they couldn't recognize themselves, call Spa City taxi, and send them on their way. He used to feel sorry for them, and now here he was in his own fifty-whiskey night. It was too loud and too hot in here, and now he looked at Loretta, swimming in her drunkenness, and he put his hand on the counter and inched it down toward hers, but she curled her fingers around the glass and she lifted it to her perfect, painted, plastic mouth.

"Don't," she said.

"Why?" He felt small, he felt he was shrinking and Loretta was so big, so much big blond hair and so colorful, such a beautiful bird he couldn't catch.

"Don't touch me," she said.

He flattened his fingers on the sticky bar and asked again, "Why?"

"Because it's over." She drank some more. "It's so over. It's been over for such a long time and I don't want to talk about it."

She took two cigarettes from her purse, her long, light cigarettes and she lit them both in her mouth and handed him one, and he tried to touch her fingertips but even those she took away from him.

He said, "You have my money and my heart."

Loretta laughed, a mean, choking laugh. "They're both long gone," she said. "You'll never get them back."

He gripped the lip of the bar with his hands. "Where's my money?" he asked. "What did you do with it?"

"It's not cheap with a quadriplegic son, let me tell you."

"You got insurance money for that," he said. "What did you do with it? You owe it to me. You owe me."

She laughed again. "Nobody owes you anything," she said. "You did what you had to and so did I. Expect nothing and you won't be disappointed." She blew a long line of her smoke at her own reflection in the mirror. "Because that's what you're going to get. Nothing. Expectations are just resentments waiting to happen."

Belly started to shake. He pressed his wrists against the bar and watched his palms wobble. He clamped his fingers down on the polished wood to keep them from hitting her. "It's bad luck to be a bitch," he said.

She waved her diamond ring at him. "I don't need luck anymore, Belly, I've got money."

"My money and my heart," he said again, digging his nails into the wood until his fingertips turned white.

"Oh, poor fella. Had to sacrifice a few years of his pitiful little life in exchange for what — how many thousands did you take in? How much of that money did you blow on coke? On cars? You want me to feel sorry for you?"

He laid his head down on his hands and he refused to cry. He said, "Yes. I want you to feel sorry for me."

She drank. "Sue me," she said. "I dare you."

Belly watched as his own shaky hand reached for Loretta's windpipe, as it clasped the chicken skin of her neck and pressed. She watched him, and he watched her; it was like they were dancing. His hands were eating at her jaw, his fingers were sipping from her larynx and then when she smiled, she floated away.

"I dare you," she whispered. There was no fear in her eyes and he loosened his fingers and let them rest on her collarbones. She reached up and pulled his knuckles to her hairline, rubbed them against the hidden scar from her facelift. "Just let it be over. Let it be done."

He thought of all the times he hit his wife; he hit Ann, and Nora, and Eliza, and he never hit Loretta, and he never hit his third daughter, but that did not absolve his hands, and right now, with those guilty fingers, he was capable of murder.

She said, "I got the needlepoint line from Mel Brooks. You know that routine, about how you take the *M* from 'Midwest' and add it to 'moron' and you get 'Mormon'?"

Belly took his shot glass and slammed it on the bar. It shattered. He yelled, "I thought you made that line up. You said you made it up."

She shrugged her shoulders. "I'm used to disappointing people."

And then there was trouble, chaos, the bouncer lifting Belly from his seat; suddenly Belly was so small, and he stumbled toward home, wherever that was. A long beige Cadillac raced down the street, two teenage boys leaning out the window. "Go home, Grampa!" they screamed. And he should. He was a grampa and he should go home, alone, with no mistress and no money, all the stars in the sky laughing at him and all he wanted was to sleep.

5

H E OPENED his eyes and it was still dark. He knew right away that he was not in his pod, not in his cell, where the lights never completely dimmed. But his pupils were too dilated and the walls were too far away and he had to piece together again what was real, right there in the dark. He was home; he was back in Spa City, but he was not home. He was back in Saratoga, but it was not the same town; he had no home. He was staying with Nora. It was Nora's home. And Eliza did not live there anymore. And Ann, he could not remember her, maybe she had never lived there at all. Maybe she was never real. And daughter number three, she was here, she was sitting next to him on the couch with a cup of hot tea and a chunk of potato bread to mop up the alcohol making the rounds inside him, she was studying, she had fallen asleep on the couch with her glasses tilted over her closed eyes, and he took off the glasses and set them down carefully on the end table. He covered her in the red, blue, and purple afghan knitted by his great-grandmother, spun and dyed herself from her very own sheep, he stood there and watched her safely sleep.

He blinked, and then he saw the drop ceiling and the matted blue carpet and the worn plaid of the couch beneath him and he was alone in the still, hot, middle of the night, last night's clothes sticking to him. Right in the center of his chest a stinging began, first a soft sort of singing and then something louder and full of feedback, fingernails on a chalkboard but inside. Please, he thought, please put me in the bed. Please put me to sleep. Rub my back, scratch my back, make my back small and smooth and hot and clammy, make me the back of a child, the small back where two adult hands can cover it. Make me small. Make it go away. But it wouldn't go away. The stinging reached out until it covered his whole chest like a blanket, he was one long cloth of ache, he was mummified in it. He could not get away. He could not sleep.

He had a beer can cradled in the crook of his elbow and one stashed between his legs. He shook them. Both empty.

He lay with his eyes open and focused on nothing, focused on the dark, and every thought that passed through his mind, every acceptable image skipped out into the dark and left him with the same implacable ideas. He tried to think of baseball, he tried to think of Mookie Wilson's tenth-inning ground ball through Bill Buckner's legs in the '86 World Series. He tried to picture Ray Knight's seventh-inning solo homer. He tried to think of that one good moment in 1986, that one little flash when he thought maybe he could feel all right again. Maybe he could feel. But the rest of that year circled before him: standing in the doorway of the morgue, watching his wife touch the toetag on his daughter's bluish body, seeing how the kid's pinky finger splayed out to the side of her hand in an impossible right angle, the way her bed was made from that day forward, never again a wrinkle in the sheets, the soft leather of her worn-out catcher's mitt with her name in crooked black block letters.

He just wanted to rest in peace. He just wanted to sleep. Why wouldn't sleep come and save him? Why wouldn't morning come to let him out? He needed light to breathe. He needed to stop breathing.

He wrenched himself from the abyss of sunken couch cushions and walked through the dining room and living room and out the front door to the abandoned porch. In just his faded black watch boxer shorts he stepped down to the sidewalk, bare feet over tiny tufts of grass that poked out from the cracks. He walked to the center of Spring Street and looked east, trying to find a hint of horizon hiding behind fir trees and big Victorian houses. His town was sleeping, every single body horizontal in the whole place, every life but his held in the peaceful secret sideways place of dreams. He waited there until one side of the sky lightened to the color of pale fire; he waited, hoping one last lone drunk driver would fly up the fault line of Spring Street and not see him in the softness of that almost-morning light, hoping his inebriated savior would whip down the asphalt and lift Belly from the road, make him rise like flame from the hot concrete, let gravity release him so he could just float away.

Far in the distance horses began to bray. The racetrack was waking up. A truck rambled down Nelson Avenue, an open-backed pickup filled with the little brown men who rode into town every year with the weanlings and yearlings and two-year-olds. The backstretch workers — grooms, stablehands, and hotwalkers. He thought of those men, paid next to nothing, men with families stashed in unnamed southern countries, men who slept pressed into tiny tack rooms on the outskirts of the track. How did they do it? How did they sleep through the night in their mud and concrete prisons? He'd heard once that when a backstretch worker got sick — less than minimum wage and no health insurance — he'd go see the vet.

The sun rose and the sky filled with dusty blue, and for a moment the stinging inside him subsided. He turned and stepped inside the sanctity of Nora's sleeping house, he laid himself back down on the couch in his dirty boxers, and when he closed his eyes now he saw baseball and thoroughbreds, and his daughter's dead face was filtered away.

The boys made their way downstairs and played Grand Theft Auto while he watched them from the couch, and Nora wiped the kitchen counters, and he heard the paper Wal-Mart application crinkle in his back pocket. Nora handed him the phone, holding it away from her like it was something infectious. He thought, This is the call I've been waiting for, but when he said hello it was only Eliza's small voice on the other line.

"I'm sorry about leaving you, Belly," she said.

He said, "Whatever."

"You know, Ann still might come. Maybe if you call her or something and tell her you want her to."

"Let me just ask you this: what kind of person are you to leave that little blind dog? That diabetic dog?"

She did not respond.

"You're just going to leave your dog like that?" He heard sniffling on the other end. "Don't cry, don't cry," he said. "Do not cry."

"I'm sorry," she said again. "If it wasn't for me, we'd all still be together."

A dangerous feeling growled in his stomach. "I don't know what you mean."

"That day," she said.

"Don't."

"I was supposed to meet her at dance class. Henry was going to drive us both home, don't you remember? But I wanted to go to this exhibit in Albany so I called you and you had Darren pick her up. Don't you remember?"

"Shut up, Eliza. Just shut the fuck up." And that was the last thing he said to her.

His grandsons turned off the TV and left him with that strange static aftertaste buzzing through the air: the presence of absence.

In prison, his podmate received a letter from a son he never knew he had. The man passed the letter down from cell to cell, pod to pod, hungry hands reaching out for the crumpled hand-written paper. The man said he knew it was his son: their I's slanted the same way. Belly read it three times before he passed it on. The son did not want anything from the man except possibly to know what he looked like and a bit of his medical history, and to meet him someday if the father consented. The son wrote that he had a good job, a girlfriend, and a son of his own, and was not seeking money. The son wanted only to talk. Nothing more.

The letter caused a rupture in Belly — a great big hunger right above his diaphragm. He kept trying to think about Ann, his second daughter, who would never come to see him, never talked to him again after that day he hit her on the couch. He wanted the letter to make him want her. He wanted to want her back. But he could only see his wife's eyes in his third daughter's pale, freckled face, her thick blond hair, her pink sweater: his baby who died at sixteen.

His podmate had told him, "If you don't got kids, you don't got nothing to live for. You don't got nothing to fight for."

And now he sat here with the phone face down on his knees, entwining the curlicues of phone cord around his fingers, and he knew he should call Eliza back, he should call her back to him and beg her not to leave. But he leaned against the couch and closed his eyes and saw his third daughter's face, still with him after all this time, edging out the faces of the other girls.

The phone went dead, the strange seesaw tone erupting from the wire, telling him to hang up.

Nora slapped the knees of his jeans with a dishtowel and said, "Belly, you have got to get yourself up and ready to meet with your parole officer."

He said, "That's not for hours."

"You've got to get yourself there today. I've got too much to do before Sunday."

"How do you expect me to get to Ballston Spa?" He stood and hung up the phone.

"Take the bus," she said.

"What bus?"

"The CDTA."

He didn't even know what it stood for. But he conceded.

He went upstairs to change, too tired to face the shower, and he slipped on his last clean pair of jeans. They were his favorite, worn to perfection at the knees, the most slimming Levis he owned. They were all the same size, but some hung awkwardly, some were too tight, but these, these fine jeans hugged his bones perfectly and made him feel young. He took a clean white shirt, same as the others, and buttoned it high, to cover the tiny sprigs of gray chest hair that sometimes poked through.

He came downstairs carrying his dirty jeans and white shirts and socks and boxers and said, "What do I do with these?"

"Leave them by the basement door and I'll wash them," Nora said. "They'll be here when you get back."

Outside, Saratoga greeted him with thick waves of heat. His beautiful town, birthplace of the potato chip, the world's most attractive horseracing track, home of the twenty-two springs of crystal-clear water that ran straight up from the fertile ground, water people came from hundreds of miles to drink though it tasted like old shoes. He meant to walk to the bus stop, but he followed his feet down Union Avenue, past the glorious mansions, and he ticked off their architectural styles one by one — Dutch colonial, second empire Victorian, Greek revival, Queen Anne, Richardsonian Romanesque. He'd gone through a whole town tour's worth of houses and he came to the beautiful Saratoga flat track.

The racetrack burst at its seams with Friday peddlers. He remembered Ann selling lemonade and brownies out front, getting fifty-dollar tips from Trifecta winners, getting nothing but scowls from the losers, putting the money away and not taking it out until she needed to buy something for the senior prom: she wore a man's tuxedo.

Man O'War, Upset, Secretariat, Jim Danon, Onion, Four Star Dave, all the great horses had run here, and he'd seen some of their great races. His own family history wound around the track — it opened the same year his grandparents escaped famine-infested Ireland and hopped the wave of immigrants coming upstate to work in the foundries and factories, to build this very racetrack with their rough Irish hands, to build these mansions and the carriage houses behind them, the buildings downtown, the ones that burned and those that still stood. His family had settled on the West Side — they called it Little Dublin then, and then they called it Little Italy and then Little Harlem and then the family moved east.

At the main gate, a gaggle of teenagers hovered in security outfits. The uniforms draped like chintz curtains from their bones, they looked dressed for Halloween. And when he sidled up to the cashier the kid actually wanted to charge him an entrance fee. "My brother's a Pinkerton," Belly said.

The kid wrote a look of skepticism into his eyebrows.

"A Pinkerton," he repeated. "My brother worked security here for forty years. I never paid to get in here once."

"You mean a Wackenhut," said the boy, as a security guard approached.

"What seems to be the trouble here?"

Everything, everything, he wanted to say. I am troubled by everything in this goddamned town, like somebody cleaned up and put everything back in the wrong place.

Belly looked at the logos adorning the security guard's lapel: Wackenhut. He said, "No problem at all," paid his first-ever entrance fee to the track, broke the spell of the fifty-dollar bill hiding in his wallet. How had it happened that spending two lousy dollars could hurt him so? They returned to him two twenties and a five and three ones, and the weight of paper made him safer.

He prepared himself to be disgusted at the changes, steadied himself to lament the loss of the old-time characters, refugees from William Kennedy novels, to see instead the wholesome families and rich New Yorkers who suddenly thought racing fashionable instead of repugnant. But they were there, all of them, the old-timers and families alike, the poor and the rich. It used to be like World War I in here, he thought, used to be only the children and the old men. But now the racetrack served as the meeting grounds for all different folks, the oval of dirt like a kiva — an architectural term he'd learned from the books Eliza gave him, a Native American word for meeting place. They'd fixed it up. Entire "family areas" graced what used to be empty plots littered with cigar butts and plastic beer cups, video gaming machines lined up like lemmings under white domes.

Old men with mangy faces and bandannas sold their homemade tip sheets. "Get the edge," called one man. "Yesterday we had five exactas and the Daily Double. Only two dollars." Belly reached into his pocket to the dwindling supply of bills and took the sheet. Two dollars poorer.

The names, numbers, the odds, the owners, the jockeys, the trainers: it all seemed like a foreign language to him after so many years away. The tip sheet recommended two yearlings, The Muse and Gentle Strength, numbers two and five, for the fourth race. Belly made his way to the paddock where the jockeys paraded their horses and he matched them to the numbers on his page. He watched a silver Akhal-Teke clomping around on the dehydrated grass, number twelve, named Legz, and above the betting windows flashed his odds, an unassuming six to one. Ignoring the tip sheet, Belly put a whole five dollars on Legz, to place, and another five on Thirty Percent Gray, number eight, to show, and he made his way to the front of the clubhouse. Low odds, that's what he wanted. He wanted a sure thing.

A bugle wafted over the airwaves, *Call to the Post*. Patrons flocked to the monitors, stared up at it with their pink *Racing Forms* tucked under their arms, clutching tiny paper tickets. "It's post time," he heard, "And . . . they're off," and when the starting gates flung open and the horses came barreling down the dirt track, Belly's breath shortened and he felt faint. Around him he heard the familiar cries, "Hit the whip, hit it," calling out numbers and names. Number twelve, he prayed, first or second, come in number eight, first or second or third. He needed the money. He needed something good to happen.

What a strange thing, he thought now. Is this even a sport? It's not like you had team loyalty, not like the Mets. He'd never bet on the Mets, not once, not even last year during the Subway Series. It was never money he'd wanted from his home team, just the glory. But money was all anyone wanted here, that's all they had rooted in the win.

He watched the last lap of the race, his horses so far at the end of the line — out of the money, they called it, when a horse didn't even show — and he felt tired and thirsty and half-dead. The race finished, he watched the body-English of all those gamblers, exulting or despairing. Gentle Strength and The Muse came in first and second, respectively, his unused tip sheet dead on. He tossed his paper ticket in the trash and an old man said to him, "Don't worry. Most people lose."

"It was a sure thing," he said to the man.

"That's why they call this place the graveyard of champions."

He wandered over to the Big Red Spring, where a Dixieland band wearing red suspenders played between races. He vaguely recalled these old fellows, and he heard someone say to the band, "I come here every year just to see you guys play," and the banjo player nodded at Belly as his hands raced across the instrument. The banjo player, the one who'd wandered around Wal-Mart the night before, played that same song, and now Belly heard the words: "The World Is Waiting for the Sunrise." He looked over at Belly, nodded, called, "Welcome home," to him, then said, "Don't think you're supposed to be here," all of this over the glorious old-fashioned music.

Belly ran his hand under the springwater, over the mottled mess of calcium deposits that covered the spigot, tasted a bit of Saratoga's most famous offering, a sulfury sip of the stuff. He swallowed the putrid water and listened to the music, his feet involuntarily tapping, as he recalled his grandfather's stories of when Congress Street was a red-light district, when Meyer Lansky was jailed in Ballston Spa, his grampa's old saying, "Politics and poker make the average guy a heavy smoker." He thought about his old pals at City Hall and the NYRA boys and Loretta and their conspicuous silence since his return. All had evaporated, all associations melted, leaving him alone with the memory of how it used to be weighing on him like cardiac arrest.

He thought of that first bet: such a haze he was in that month, with Myrna gone and Loretta permanently drunk and her son in the ICU and his third daughter in the ground. Loretta's sweaty fifty calling from the countertop, and how from there, from that timeless slow moment, other bets came in. He'd won Loretta's fifty from her, and the other lazy drunks who couldn't walk the mere eight blocks to the track decided to wager their money against Belly's. The money poured in and out like the tide, and he had trouble keeping track, high or low. He'd bought a fifty-cent miniature spiral-bound notebook from Woolworth's and wrote down dates and first names and race numbers and the horses and the odds as they flashed on the TV screen and held just seconds before the starting gates opened. When the notebook filled, he bought another, and kept buying them, funneling them into old toe-shoe boxes until the storage room had a leaning tower of evidence that the DA seized in the eerie, dull moments of the raid. By then, other bars in other towns and counties and finally other states would call in their bets. By then, Loretta made her daily deposits to the NYRA folks, to a few unnamed participants at City Hall. The money flowed in, it flowed out, it flowered and withered, it had its sunny season and then eleven months of sleep, he didn't know and he didn't care.

He shouldn't be here. He wasn't supposed to be here. The days of bribing jockeys, the tellers not telling, altering the odds, Filthy Phil Weiss and the Four Sons, underestimating golden two-year-olds on purpose, all the tricks were played and gone. He'd gone from a stallion to a spit-the-bit, a worn-out old horse, and there wasn't a single place for this old man to stand in the whole of the Saratoga Racecourse. His town, his beautiful woman of a town, had spit him out like a piece of gristle. He stood for a long time under the wooden awning of the Big Red Spring; he waited until the sun was high in the sky and he was so hot and he labored out to the end of Union Avenue, thirstier than he'd ever been in his life.

* * *

He walked to the park entrance but he did not go in. He went around it, down Spring Street's big dip and up again to Broadway. He stood in front of the old library on the corner of Spring and Broadway, wondering where the new library was hidden. The brick building was now an arts center, hovering atop the fault line, the bottom floor of the library — what used to be the children's section — leaning against the hill and looking out onto the park. Once or twice he had led his pride of daughters through that tamed wilderness, past the duck pond and into the library, let them rub their greasy fingers along the hardcover books and sat with them in beanbag chairs to read them their selections in the late afternoon.

He crossed the street to the bus stop and stood in front of the ruined strip mall and across from his old bar, and a solution came to him, the answer to a problem he didn't even know he had. For five days he'd been followed by the Sha-Na-Na theme song, his daughters and parole officer and everyone he met telling him to Get a Job. All he had to do was walk two short blocks to Caroline Street, order up a shot of Jack and show up for Ms. Monroe with the stink of whiskey on his breath. That would be enough to send him back.

He stood at the bus stop and made a deal with God. He prayed, "If you send the bus here in the next five minutes, I will not go to Ruffian's." He had no watch so he prayed, "I will count to three hundred and if the bus is not here by then, I will go to Ruffian's."

He watched an old woman waiting under the glass awning, reading a Harlequin romance. She looked up and smiled at him, her face bloomed into a million wrinkles, and she revealed a mouth of missing teeth. He looked away, and kept counting.

The bus rounded the curve of Broadway at 179, and he felt a strange mixture of relief and anger circle inside him.

The doors of the bus blew open and he climbed into the air-conditioning. The driver was a fat man with bushy sideburns wearing a blue polyester uniform with stains along the collar. Belly nodded at him as he walked by.

"You gonna pay?" the driver asked.

"How much?"

"Eighty-five cents."

He felt in his pockets but all he had was the paper money. "You have change?"

The driver pointed to a sign that displayed the fares and read "Exact Change Only." Adults $1.15 and senior citizens eighty-five cents. The bus door remained open and the driver stared at him and one passenger called, "Let's go. Some of us have to get to work," and Belly wondered if the whole world knew.

He could get off now and drink instead. He could take this as a sign from God not to walk the straight path.

"Anybody have change?" he asked. No one answered. "You guys want to get going, give me some change."

The wrinkly woman with few teeth opened her purse and handed him three quarters and a dime. She said, "This is laundry money, you know."

He wanted to say thank you but his mouth was too dry. He took the change and held his hand out to the bus driver, who said, "Put it in the slot," and he dumped the coins in the machine and it whirred as it ate the change.

Belly sat down in a handicapped seat near the front and

braced himself as the bus jerked forward. He looked up at the sign again and thought to tell the driver that he'd underpaid and then he looked at the strange gray hue of his own skin, the way it was starting to slide off the bone, and said nothing.

Besides the Greyhound that had returned him home just a few days before, the last bus he was on brought him from the Circuit Court in Albany to Schuylkill, Pennsylvania, and though it was September and the rolling hills were green and the promise of fall was bleeding in the leaves, it had been a grueling ride, for he could see what surrounded the prison: nothing but strip malls and strip malls. There was nothing to escape to, the whole world was one endless series of fluorescent-lit aisles and he just wanted to get back to town so badly, he wanted to be back in his twenty-four-day town.

He turned to the wrinkly lady and said, "They undercharged me," and the lady smiled her blank, blooming smile and looked at her romance novel.

"Where does this bus go?" he asked the woman.

"To Ballston Spa," she said, not looking up.

"But the other way, in the other direction. Where does it go?"

"Out to the malls, and to Wal-Mart," she said.

He felt trapped — his choices were Ballston Spa or Wal-Mart, his choices were the parole officer or back to prison, some shit job or another shit job, and nothing in his future was bright, or open, no door portended light on the other side.

The bus rolled on down Route 50, past the park and the visitors' center and McDonald's and the Chinese restaurant constantly under new management, past the dance museum and the state park and everywhere he'd been in his five-day run as a tourist in his own town. He was going backwards.

They passed the back entrance to SPAC, where the parking

lot overflowed with tourist cars, and he heard someone say, "It's those Moody Blues in town tonight." They passed Geyser Crest, the first crummy development to spring up beyond the city limits, where Loretta and Darren used to live. They rolled through the little nontown of Malta, through the countryside, only there was no countryside. It was all gone. It was all strip malls. Bars and restaurants in strip malls, smoke shops and lingerie stores in strip malls, army-navy surplus and ammo supplies in strip malls, and the hills behind the strip malls rolled away as if they longed to escape.

Occasionally the bus stopped and someone got on or off, Belly didn't notice. He tried not to look at all these people who couldn't make enough money to buy their own cars. They were all of them white, a particular kind of pasty white, and everything about them looked poor: their hair, clothes, the way they smelled, how many teeth they were missing, and the things they carried. The nicest black people he'd ever met were not from Jefferson Terrace, the little embarrassment of a neighborhood on the East Side, but in prison. They were drug dealers, sure, but they were decent guys. He spent four years in perfect racial integration and now he was sealed on a bus full of white trash.

The bus stopped by the old mill at the end of Main Street in Ballston Spa, once abandoned and now remade into apartments, an "Apartments for Rent" sign permanently affixed to the newly repointed brick facade. Belly made a mental note of the phone number, though he knew what his daughters would say, or Loretta, or any of his old pals if they found he'd moved to Ballston Spa, the town they thought of as Saratoga's inbred cousin.

The wrinkly woman made her way to the front of the bus,

lifting her feet over Belly's splayed legs. She started to descend the steps and she turned and looked at Belly and said, "You're welcome," and he folded his knees up and stared at them.

He got off at the next stop, stood in front of the blob of beige stucco, smoking one last cigarette — thank God for his good friend the red lighter — before he had to report on his week of nothing, no job, no prospects, before he had to get his wrist slapped by a pretty woman young enough to be his kid.

"You're late," Ms. Monroe said. "Don't be late."

"Sorry." She led Belly back to her desk and he picked up a Plexiglas cube with pictures of kids on all six sides.

He picked it up and examined the photographs. "These yours?"

"Nope."

"They're not?"

She laughed. "I never had any kids. Those are just the pictures that came in the cube."

"That's weird."

"Oh, for crying out loud, it was a gift from my coworkers." She lowered her voice. "I'm just trying to be nice. I don't want the thing."

"You want pictures of mine? I have three grandkids." He reached for his wallet before he realized he carried no pictures of them.

"I don't like to surround myself with pictures of people I know," she said. "It creeps me out."

"What's your first name?" Belly asked.

"Does this have to do with your parole?"

"Why don't you have any kids?"

"Patty, and none of your business," she said. "Now, listen, what's going on with the job?"

"Do we have to talk about that?"

"Yes."

He said, "I am a senior citizen. Did you know that? I'm retired."

"No, you're not. The government seized your assets five years ago and you've got to start over."

Belly groaned.

"Listen, Mr. O'Leary, you should be grateful. Imagine being one of those guys who has to announce that he's coming, who has to see flyers with his mug shot plastered to every tree in the neighborhood. Imagine getting up every morning and having to face that. You're off easy, you've got the opposite problem, and you're complaining?" She shook her head. "Some of you guys are unbelievable."

"Those men are sex offenders."

"Yeah, but they're men. They're people. They're trying to cope with what they did just like you are."

"What did I do?"

"You want me to tell you?"

"Yes, I want you to tell me what I did wrong."

She read from his file. "Violation of New York State Penal Code 225.05 and Federal Penal Code 211.10, Promotion of Illegal Gambling in the second degree; 225.30, Possession of Illegal Gambling Records; 225.15, Profiting from Illegal Gambling. Advancing Gambling. Engaging in a Bookmaking Business. Gambling Across State Lines. I could go on."

"Yeah, but that's what I'm saying, I'm not a sex offender. Why should I feel sorry for those guys? I didn't do anything."

Patty the parole officer looked up from the file. "Let's see the sheet," she said, glancing at her watch.

"I forgot it."

"No, you didn't."

He took the crumpled paper with Margie's lone signature scrawled on the top line. He never even got Gene to sign, never went back to Wal-Mart to get their corporate check mark.

"Doesn't look like you tried too hard."

"Well, I did. I tried too hard."

She took a form from his folder and picked up a pencil covered in bite marks.

"Have you been actively looking for a job?"

"Yes."

"Have you been to any establishment where gambling is practiced?"

"No."

"Have you used any illegal drugs?"

"No."

"Have you used any alcohol?"

"No."

"Have you engaged in any illegal activity?"

"No."

She put her pencil down. "So what are we going to do about the job? I gave you a time limit. . . ." She ran her finger along the file. "Until Monday. That leaves you the weekend."

"There are no jobs in August. Everybody knows that. I have to wait till they all leave."

"Did you get your license?"

"Not yet."

"Why not?"

"I've been busy."

"Doing what?"

He rubbed the knuckle of one hand with the other and said, "Looking for a job."

"What'd you do in the can again?"

"I didn't."

"How'd you swing that?"

He patted the sides of his jeans. "Work release. Fake hips."

She looked up. "What for?"

"You wouldn't believe me if I told you," and she said, "Tell me," and he said, "Too much tango."

"No way."

"It's the truth," he said. "Plus, arthritis."

"Well, barring the possibility that you're going to open a dance school in the next two days, you've got to find something very soon."

"How long do I have?"

"How long do you need?"

"How long do I really have?"

"You have the rest of your goddamned life to screw up if that's what you want."

He felt married after this exchange, and he wanted to hold her hand as she walked him to the door.

"That's it?" he asked. "You're letting me go?"

"You're free," she said. "And listen, I mean this: have a good weekend."

He stood in the open doorway, his back frozen with air-conditioning, his front on fire from the heat wave, and he did not want to step into the sunshine.

When he got home Nora and the kids were gone, and she'd left a note on the table that read *Belly, we went swimming. Your statutory rape friend called.* Maybelline, it seemed, was still trying to make plans. Women never liked to hear, "Let's just wait and see."

He opened a beer and sat on the couch and was just about to drift off to sleep when he heard a knock. He lifted himself from the couch, rubbed his eyes as he went to the door. Maybelline.

"Hi," she said. "What are you doing?"

"What are you doing here?"

"Can you open the door?"

"I don't know. What are you doing here?" He kept his arms folded across his chest.

"Belly, for crying out loud. Open the door."

He swung the screen door open and stepped out before she could slip in.

"What do you want?"

"My car broke down. Can you give me a ride home?"

"I don't have a license."

"So? You always drive my car."

"I don't have a car."

"That's your truck, isn't it? You're always complaining about how you can't drive your own truck."

"Stop saying always."

"Please, Belly? I can't afford a cab. I took you out to dinner one too many times. I'm broke."

"You took me out for drinks once."

"I have no money."

He looked at the Bronco in the driveway, quiet and patient like an obedient dog, his loyal little truck. "Okay. Fine. Hold on."

Nora's keys hung on the hook by the sink. He could be there and back in an hour — it was 4:00 p.m. now, Nora usually started dinner around 5:30. She didn't even have to know.

He grabbed the keys, locked the door behind him, headed

to the truck. She was still on the porch. "Come on," he said. "Let's go."

He unlocked his door and climbed in. Maybelline knocked lightly on the passenger window. "It's locked," she said.

She climbed in, her little sparkly purse set on her lap.

He started the car and backed out of the driveway. Almost five years had passed since he'd driven his own automobile, and he felt like Apollo, mastering his metal chariot across the sky. He thought, I am an airplane. He could go anywhere he wanted. Florida. Mexico. New York City. Or Ballston Spa.

Maybelline sat staring at her fingernails for the duration of the trip.

"What's the matter with you?" he asked.

"I'm losing my job."

Belly laughed. "What'd you do, steal that big white celebrity cake? You getting fired?"

She shook her head. "It's not funny. They're selling it. It's going to be under new management. They're putting something else in there. I'm getting laid off."

"You're kidding. They're not going to shut down the Springway Diner." He banged his fist on the steering wheel, making it beep accidentally.

"Yes, they are," said Maybelline. "They're closing it."

"When?"

"Next month. Soon as the track's up."

He frowned the rest of the drive.

When he pulled up in front of her house, he leaned over her and unlocked her door, kept the car running.

"You're not coming in?"

He shook his head.

"Belly, come on. Come in. I have Piels in the fridge. Two six-packs."

"No, I've got to get back before Nora gets home."

She leaned over and down, unzipped his fly.

"Oh, okay," he said. "But just for a minute."

He hated her room when he was standing in it, her ugly cats. "What are their names?" he asked.

"Birdie and Par," she said. "I used to have Bogey and Eagle, too, but they got run over."

"You're a golfer? Bullshit."

"My grampa was," she said, but then she put her finger over his mouth to shush him. She pushed him down on her doll-house bed and straddled him, put her hand on his crotch.

"What's the matter?" She cocked her head to the side and pursed her painted lips.

"Where's the beer?"

She brought him a six-pack, and he chugged one beer down instantly and opened another. He kept drinking while she slipped off his jeans and his boxers, he drank all six beers till the room softened and swayed while she tried to get him hard. It never happened.

"Got to go," he said.

"No, Belly." She sat on his knees and put her hands on his shoulders. She said, "No," again and he pushed against her, she pushed down, they locked each other in a strange embrace, she leaned down and licked the scars that grinned along his hips and he pressed against the side of her face until she slid off the bed onto her back, her legs in the air like a baby waiting for a diaper change. He stood and put his clothes on.

Then she said, "Give me some money."

He laughed. "I don't have any."

"You have money," she said, and she started to cry. "You must. All that money from the bar, from the track."

And now he understood why the pretty, crazy girl wanted him. He said, "I'm broke, too. Flat broke."

He let her cry, let her pull on his arm with the might of a superhero, let her beg, and he watched her mascara run down her cheeks till she looked like the Joker, let her scratch him with those crazy nails, try to unzip his jeans and press her mouth into his crotch. He lit a cigarette with his circumcised lighter and watched her for a minute, took three puffs and threw it down next to her on the shaggy white carpet, twisted the fire out with his foot. He let her lie on the floor, where she pretended she was mourning something that had actually lived. He took her half-empty bottle of Old Grand-Dad and left.

He felt his legs wobbling beneath him a bit, it was still so hot, but he made it to the truck, started it up, he could go anywhere — Florida, Mexico, New York City. Saratoga Springs.

He couldn't go home yet, over the highway and through Burnt Hills to Spring Street where all his neighbors and daughters kept track of his coming and going. It was late now, and dark, he'd long ago missed dinner or the chance of slipping in before Nora could notice he'd stolen his own truck. So he kept driving, sipping hot whiskey from the bottle, another fifty-whiskey night.

The sky lingered between dusk and night, and as Belly drove he saw a girl walking along the road, swinging her arms as she walked. A young girl in a white sundress, and even though it was hot and the heat had seeped into the truck and surrounded him, the girl wore a pink sweater over her shoulders. A pink cardigan. He could just make it out in the last bit of dark blue gloaming light. She was barefoot, and carrying a tote bag, and walking quickly but not hurrying, walking past the grand old houses of Ballston Spa. She looked like a girl from a picture book, a Disney movie. He slowed, he slowed, he paced her in the big black truck.

What happened to the pink sweater, to his daughter's pink sweater? It was horrible to be old. Untenable. All these gaps of memory and information, retracing your steps, treading the same territory, just trying to recall. Only the things he wanted excised still remained: the painful irony of aging, the brain's big joke. He had not let them bury her in her favorite pink sweater. How he hated that stupid pink sweater. How he hated the way she insisted on dressing like a bag lady after watching those John Hughes movies with the martyred working-class girls, pretending to be poor. *You're not poor,* he would yell at her. *I was poor. You don't know what it's like to be poor.* And how she would ignore him in those moments, those times when he couldn't find his way back to an even temper, she would just walk right out the door and let him steam. He needed his third daughter, but she was not a normal child: she didn't need him.

There were rules to follow, conventions. A body should be buried in black, in a long black dress, a dress suitable for tango. He would not budge on this point, and now he remembered how Eliza wore that pink sweater, pink the color of little girl cheeks, over her black dress to the wake, how she tried to press the sweater into the open coffin and Belly had grabbed and slapped her right there in front of the guests. He remembered what would happen to his body in these moments, every muscle wakened, every synapse firing. It was how he imagined the experience of Scotty beaming you up, breaking you down to the tiniest molecules and then reforming: that was the physicality of rage. He could see himself, watch himself, grabbing Eliza, wrapping his big hand around the tiny twig of her emaciated arm, he could hear the crisp sound of palm on cheek and then feel his pointer finger frozen in the air just an inch from her nose, and all that crying, so much crying, weeping everywhere around him. He reopened a thousand wounds with that slap. He did that. That was him.

"Fuck," he said. If he were a superhero the power he'd want would be memory control — the ability to suppress or evoke any recollection he chose, to re-create his past as he saw fit.

The girl, now, on the road, in the pink sweater, now he knew: he remembered, after Myrna left, and they were packing the house, it was Ann who cleaned out her room, who boxed up her sister's toys and toe shoes and carted them off to the Salvation Army, sweater and all, the Salvation Army in Scotia, just down the road, and this girl, it must be the same sweater, a thrift-store shopper, a vagabond, a bum, a girl bum, a bumette.

He veered to the right, pulled into the breakdown lane, and screeched to a stop. The girl started like a deer, recoiled, covered her chest with her canvas tote bag. He jumped out of the truck and the landing stung his leg, and the girl raised her hands like he was sticking her up. She was not a bum, just a goddamned hippie, and she was listening to some god-awful Grateful Dead–type music on her Walkman, it bled out the tiny headphones, and what was he going to do with her? It was dark now, and there were no cars on the road, and she was terrified and trembling, the girl.

There were woods right nearby, and he could take her there. He could. He could press her face into pine needles, she could scream into the soil and the soil would soak it up; what was he thinking, now, where was he going with this? It was dark now, and she might not see his face in full, might not burn an imprint of his description. He could get away, he could get away with it.

He kept his eyes down, he did not look directly at her, because somewhere inside him he knew better than to let her view the dimple in his chin or the centipede scar above his left eye or his one dead tooth or the precise icy blue of his eyes.

"What do you want?" she asked, and her voice was so tiny. Hippie Minnie Mouse in his dead daughter's pink cardigan on the side of the road. He could rip off her white dress and fuck her into the ground, fuck her until she was covered, and this made his muscles contract in the same way, the same way, the same thing as slapping Eliza and he had to stop himself. "Please," said the girl, who was crying now. "I don't have any money. Nothing on me."

He imagined the headlines, the one way he could make headlines now, a holdup in Ballston Spa, a Route 50 mugging. The girl shook, harder now, shoulders bopping up and down like she was dancing to the crappy hippie music.

"Your sweater," he said.

"What?" Snot rolled down her upper lip and dripped off her chin.

"Give me your sweater," he said.

She shook her head and stared at him. "I don't understand."

"Give me that goddamned sweater," he said, and now he crossed the line, the white line on the side of the road, and he grabbed her. He grabbed her the same way he grabbed Eliza that day. He pressed on the back of the girl's neck to hold her and he unbuttoned the front of the cardigan, his knuckles pressing into her chest, he could feel her nipple underneath, her nipple was hard, why was her nipple hard, did she like this?, and he pulled off one sleeve, aggressively, and then he gently slipped the other sleeve off, and there was the girl in her white dress, bare shoulders and bare feet. Maybe he ruined her life, but it was his sweater now. He tucked the sweater to his chest and sniffed it — yes, it smelled like her, it was hers, it must be hers, he ignored the absence of the little green alligator on the front. The girl was crying, and he said, "Sorry," and got back in the truck.

He had a mission now. He would return the sweater to its rightful place.

The night his wife moved to Stillwater was the last time he saw her, ten or twelve or fifteen years ago, he couldn't remember. The town slept alongside a particularly calm stretch of the Hudson, and Myrna rented half of an old bungalow on the river. He had helped her move her things in the little blue Chevy Luv he had back then. She took her clothes and her telescope and what seemed like hundreds of pairs of shoes when she left.

Only one bar graced this town, undoubtedly one of the reasons Myrna moved there. She'd been to rehab and back three times by then, but she just couldn't kick the habit. Her role model was Betty Ford. *Betty Ford,* she used to say. *She can do it and look at the man she's married to.*

Belly didn't go inside that night when he'd dropped her off. He'd just lifted her things from the flatbed, hoisted up her suitcases and deposited them on the front porch, and watched her drag them in the door. She owned more shoes than anything else, walking shoes, running shoes (she'd never jogged a day in her life), sixteen different pairs of dancing shoes. Even when they were worn and scuffed and undanceable, she kept them as little leather memories of happier times.

When the flatbed was empty he'd said, "See you later," and drove off.

He thought now how he had never really wanted Myrna, never openly craved her in that Pavlovian way that keeps a man captive. He admired her, he even liked her, but he was frightened of her. She had so many personalities crammed into one tiny body, a body that swelled four times with the promise of some gift, some bend in the road up ahead that would bring them, maybe this time, to Paradise, maybe this time she would give him a boy, and each time she deflated and her skin sagged farther, her stomach a rippling pond of flesh, all that gravity pulling her down and he would find her some early mornings on the kitchen floor, that horrible stench of stale, watery beer emanating from her pores. She would pop open her eyes and smile at him, a stale, watery smile, the Busch beer of smiles, sharp and diffused at the same time like winter sunlight and her green eyes unfocused and panicked and blaming and calm all at once. These were the times he felt the faint twinge of love, in the aftermath of her drunkenness, but never before it, and certainly never during it. He would lift her up, sling her over his shoulders like Huck Finn with his bundle, and tote her up to bed. By the end these were the only instances that led them to share a mattress, a great sea of foam and metal springs, their pillow-topped ice floe there to rescue them.

It shocked him now to realize that though he had never lusted after Myrna, he had always loved her. He had always loved his wife, and he had failed her in every way a man can.

Since he'd last been to this town, a tornado had swept through it. He'd heard through Nora that the twister had ripped through a tiny piece of Myrna's house, torn the dormer window right off the top and left a hole in the roof that peeked right into her bedroom. He'd planned on going up there to help her, he really had, but Nora had said she had renter's insurance and the whole thing was covered. You could still see the line where the tornado had swung through, a squiggle of dead trees and destroyed land that curved along the river and the road.

The night curled around him now, in the truck, and he kept the brights on as he steered through town, the windows open and the AC on max just like he liked it, along the sleepy Hudson, searching for her house, refusing to think about what he had just done. He was his own superhero now. He was Captain Selective Memory. He drew heavily on his bottle of Old Grand-Dad.

He parked. He found her house, the short bungalow with no dormer on top and all its windows black, a round panel of glass where the dormer used to be, the butt of a telescope pressed against it. A low porch, empty of chairs, covered the front of the house, and he set the pink cardigan down there: a peace offering.

He looked at the moon, rising in the sky, and he thought about how his mother had taught Myrna things about the sun, how to tell the time from its angle in the sky. He could see her looking up at the sun, her pale skin all aglow from the light, the way she was before the Rudolph nose and deep, wavy lines cut into her face with alcohol. It was late and he was tired and he wanted to see his wife the way she used to be.

A small cross hung on the front door. He raised his hand to knock and then he let his hand fall back to his side.

He thought of Myrna, how Myrna had tried to take his babies away. Away to Stillwater, she had up and tried to slip them out in the night. In the night, he was with her that night he was unloading her boxes, he was backing the flatbed up to the porch. She had asked his baby girls to go with her and, this was the other part, the other side, that little jab of knowledge, he didn't want to know. Everything was unraveling now, and then reweaving, and this tapestry, he thought, this blanket will circle him, made of information he craved and dreaded. His wife had told them, all three of them, what? I'm leaving your father. I'm moving to a crummy school district west of here, want to come? That's why they stayed, yes. Who would want to change schools at the end like that? And their friends lived nearby, around the corner. That's what Eliza said. *We wanted to keep an eye on you.* And now he wondered, was it the drinking that worried them? The gambling? Their father without his favorite daughter? *We wanted to make sure you were all right.*

He had always seen the booking as illegal, but not *that* illegal. It seemed so harmless. Maybe somewhere up the chain there was real live danger, intrigue, the Mafia shit, murders, but day after August day the same people wandered in, same slipping the money under the coaster, same exultations and lamentations from watching the TV, same voices on the phone, all of it finessed and finagled by Loretta. The only time it changed was after that phone call, that warning, that tip-off from the DA, and then Loretta's disposition distorted. She wouldn't meet his eyes. She wouldn't kiss his lips. She wouldn't suck his dick. Not for that whole month between the phone call and the raid, and now, of course, now he realized how blind he had been and who had turned him in and he laughed.

To his children he told the same story, and to the cops, to the

judge and the jury. To all of them he said that the booking began after his third daughter died. He told that story over and
over again, of Loretta's fifty-dollar bill and the TV blaring behind him, of his dead daughter and Loretta's debilitated son,
told it so many times he'd believed it himself. But the booking
started well before that, started when all four of his daughters
were alive and well. Started in one of Myrna's dry spells, even,
when the house was clean and the children were properly fed
and the bar was doing fine, just fine, and he got greedy. He got
Loretta and he got greedy, and they cooked up a scheme to cul-
tivate more funds, and the scheme germinated, it grew, and
their plan had been to someday move together to one of those
big flowery places on Fifth Avenue, when the kids grew, Loretta
said, or when they had more money put away. She kept
putting it off, a little more, she said, a little longer, and then
their plans were foiled by the unexpected tragedy.

For a long time he wanted to go into her son's room in the
ICU at Albany Med and pull the plug on that kid, wanted to
rip the clear blue plastic breathing tube from his throat, like
cleaving a hook caught too low in a trout. Loretta's son swiped
him of his hope, and he wanted to kill that boy, and then for a
while he wanted to kill Loretta, and once he was so pissed that
his third daughter had died and fucked up his fantasy that he
wanted to kill her . . . but she was already dead. And then they
no longer talked of Fifth Avenue, and the booking bubbled
on, meting out the money, and Loretta counting the loot, the
drinks getting stronger and their sex-free stretches getting
longer and then the raid and then the trial and then the end.

And then for a while he thought his daughter's death was
some kind of punishment, but his list of sins was so long that
he could not pin it on any particular misdeed. For all his

wrongs, the booking was his only illegality, and he tried, he did, he really tried to put it away after her death. She died ten days before track season started, and that whole first week he wouldn't come to the phone, wouldn't take the cash slipped under the coasters. But a funny thing happened. He missed it. He missed holding his breath from the moment the starting gates opened till the horses finished their last lap. He missed the bugle song of *Call to the Post* and the jockeys in the paddock and the camaraderie among the bettors in War Bar. And when Loretta wandered in that night and slipped him her sweaty fifty, he took it, and he took it up again, and he didn't quit till it all came crashing down around him.

He laughed now because the woman he loved had ruined his life, because his daughters had stayed behind to look after him, because his wife had to leave him to keep from drinking herself to death, and because he was stranded in the middle of nowhere now, and his whole town was a mirage, the Queen of Spas, the Spa City façade.

He stepped down from the porch but there was no step and he tumbled and landed on his ankle. He looked up at the moon and the porch and the door and he said, "I'm all twisted up." He said to the closed door, "Untwist me."

The door did not answer. It did not swing open and unlock his wife from her almost ten-year silence, this ten-year night.

He pushed himself up from the ground and hobbled down to the river. He thought he might be sick, but he wasn't, and he took off one shoe and touched his toe to the tepid water and he remembered again: one foot in yesterday, one foot in tomorrow, and you're pissing all over today.

He unzipped his fly and relieved himself in the still Hudson River, his back turned to his wife's little house. He remembered the moment when his water phobia developed: they used to drive up north of here, where the Hudson River met the Sacandaga in class-two rapids, at the Hadley-Lucerne bridge. Steep cliffs jutted from the water, enticing young boys all summer long to jump from their slippery edges. And Belly was not afraid. He would scuttle up the rocks with the rest of his friends, leaping from the top and holding his nose as he plunged thirty endless feet into the bubbling river.

And then one day there was a boy with his retarded little brother — they still called them mongoloids in those days — and the retard had sat down next to Belly and his buddies, plunged his chubby hand right into their big bag of potato chips and crunched on them till a mustache of crumbs covered his upper lip. Belly had made fun of the boy endlessly, telling him to go home to Furness House, back to the funny farm. They razzed the little boy for not jumping, they harassed his older brother who stepped off the cliff and flew into the water without ever turning around, leaving his little retard brother to cry and yell and suffer at the hands of Belly and his terrible crew.

Then the boy stood and walked to the cliff's edge. Belly and his friends chanted at the boy, bullied him until he lifted one long foot trapped in Velcro sneakers and stepped off the rocks. Belly ran to watch him fall, just in time to see the boy twirl in mid-air and scrape his blond head on the rock, see blood squirt from the scalp, see the boy's mouth open as he splashed sideways into the water and did not rise above the river.

A search ensued, police and ambulance and fire truck, and Belly and his friends hiding their beers and joints and trying to flee but wanting so much to see the blond head bob above the rapids and be all right. They wanted the boy to live. But the boy's body was found, fifty miles down the river. It took two days to find him, and after that Belly never wanted to wade in the water again. He stuck to dry land.

So he stayed along the riverbank until he could forget what he'd just remembered, and then he climbed into the truck and drove back toward town, drinking his whiskey at the wheel, weaving in and out of the double line.

The car did it. The car veered itself toward the river, toward the Battlefield where the Revolutionary War was won, across the street to the sleepy, sweet graveyard where he had not been since the day he put his daughter in the ground.

He parked, and opened the door, fell out of the truck right onto his fake hip. "Fuck!" he yelled.

Then he wandered in the midnight heat through the graveyard, past all the Irish names, all the Italian names, all the kiddie graves with soccer balls in front, how strange, and a cell phone duct-taped to one. The victories of the dead etched, *Mother, Father, Husband, Wife, Son, Daughter, Teacher, Lover, Singer, Savior, Beloved, Missed, Called Back, There Is No Death.*

It was the hottest night in history, and the longest, and he watched the stars as he walked, he wanted to see something that could not move, could not change in his lifetime. He thought about the things Myrna told him about the stars, how it took so long for their light to travel to earth that they might not even be there anymore. They could have died days ago, years, she said, and he would never know. But he could see them. They hovered above him, lighting his way, and he knew they were real, they were alive and still glowing. It was all true.

He walked through all the withered flowers and all the shined-up stones until he saw O'Leary carved in marble. A new bouquet of daisies rested against her headstone, and he read her epitaph aloud. *God in his wisdom has recalled the boon, his love, too soon. The soul is safe in Heaven.*

"Who the hell agreed to that?" Belly shouted. "She would not have wanted that." He slid down to the dried-up ground and leaned against her grave. He took a daisy from the bouquet and pulled the petals out one by one, letting the flower decide whether he should live or die.

There was no reason left for Belly to live. There was no reason that his daughter had to die. It was God's sick sense of humor, it was God bored up there in heaven, fucking with him. Not God's will, but God's wrath, his punishment for Belly: adulterer, gambler, liar, abuser, lazy drunk that he was. His daughter had been gone fifteen years, and he could just hear what Nora would say if she were here right now. "Get over it. Come home, move on, get over it." He had tried, he had tried, but he could not forget that afternoon at the funeral home, could never forget what death looked like, the mean face of death, the dirty trick of the life he was forced to live out.

"Shannon," he whispered to the grave. "Please come back. Please come back. Shannon." But the grave was sleeping, it was silent. She was dead. And Belly was drunk. And Belly was alive. And Belly had to go home now. He rolled onto his knees and he kissed his daughter's name in the gravestone, and the gravestone was miraculously cool.

He wobbled back to the car. The monument from the Saratoga Battlefield — a miniature version of Washington's tower — glowed in the night, and he thought of Benedict Arnold, the traitor who saved America, and he thought, if you had only lost the war, I wouldn't have to be here now.

As he drove, he distanced himself from the foibles and failings of the night, but his knee and his ankle and his hip all reminded him of his crimes. He tried very hard to stop thinking.

Sometimes, when a memory came crashing back — a flash of his hand flat across Nora's face, his fist on Myrna's cheek, the slap of his fingertips staining red vines on Ann's back — he shook. He shuddered. Something he couldn't recognize, one of those goddamned feelings, surged through him, inhabited him for a minute and then fled, leaving him exhausted, sick, begging for alcohol. He drained the last hot sips of Old Grand-Dad and threw the bottle out the window.

Once it happened at the doctor's office, the *marriage counselor's* office. The *therapist's* office. Myrna had dragged him there twice, after Nora left, before Shannon died, when he stopped coming home for one, two, three days at a time. In that last year of her life, he was never around. "Put a space between the *e* and the *r* and you get 'the rapist,'" he'd protested, but he had to do something, one thing for Myrna. Because Myrna, well, she was a good woman. She was a drunk. She was a neglectful mother, that's what he thought when he came home in the mornings and saw the sandwiches she'd made the girls, soggy slices of white bread with wilty lettuce and one lame slip of pimento loaf. He felt sorry for his girls, a mother like that. When they were little, even when they were little she was drunk, dressing them in mismatched outfits, polka-dotted dresses and striped socks, their hair matted into rats' nests. On Sundays Belly sometimes would bathe his baby girls, wash their hair, joke with them about the first great lie of their lives on the Johnson & Johnson bottle, "No more tears, my ass," and he could be a real father if he wanted. So he agreed to the marriage counselor because maybe he could help Myrna be a better mother. She was a drunk, yes, but a nice drunk, a malleable one, a rag doll but not a rager. Not like him.

But then he quivered right there in front of that lady, that brown mouse of a woman with her fancy doctor glasses and her stupid framed art and her fountain and her big bookcase, and the woman had asked him what was wrong. He told her he remembered something, and she asked what, and he looked at Myrna, Myrna with her earnest loving look, her pretty green eyes, her skin gray and prematurely aged from cigarettes and booze, and probably from being married to him, and he refused to say what had caused that quake to erupt in him. It was the memory of Nora, just a few months earlier, all grown up and telling him she was quitting the business, she was going away from the booking and the bar, and how he battled her to the ground and she was so used to it, so inured, that she didn't even cry. He couldn't even make his oldest daughter cry by then, and he remembered the way she looked up at him from the scratchy wood floor with razors in her eyes, with pity, and, yes, then he shook, right there in front of the shrink.

The woman had told him when that happened to "shake off the shame" — literally. To rub his hand across his chest and simply wipe the feeling away. He told her to fuck off, and then he left, left Myrna in the office alone and never went back.

And now, in the thick black of summer night, with the street wobbling in front of him, a million of those goddamned feelings lit up around him like fireflies, taunting him *the girl in the pink sweater the girl in the pink sweater the girl in the pink sweater* and he took one hand off the wheel and tried to wipe them away, to fight them off, one by one, the bruised faces of his daughters and his wife, the time Loretta threatened to leave him if he didn't divorce Myrna and he fell to the floor and held on to the hem of her skirt, begging, begging, crying, even. The time Shannon came to War Bar asked if he was ever coming home again, and he'd said, "What do you mean? I live there," and she just shook her head and said, "Not really, you don't." The one time after Ann moved out that she appeared in the doorway of the bar, just looking at him, waiting to be invited in, and he called to the bouncer, "No underagers, Johnny." Eliza in the hospital bed, half-starved to death, Myrna in the hospital bed, holding Eliza in the minutes after she was born and Belly shaking his leg in impatience, leaving her five minutes later to meet Loretta. Myrna next to him at the morgue, crying, crying, crying so hard as they ID'd their daughter's body and then, no, he did not put his arm around her and hold her, he left her there and went to the bar and drank and fucked Loretta in the backroom next to his daughter's toe shoe boxes filled with illegal receipts *the girl in the pink sweater the girl in the pink sweater.* And the girl in the pink sweater.

It was too much. He had done too much wrong. He could not get a leg up, couldn't shake it off, couldn't erase it with a swipe of his hand across his sweat-dampened shirt. There was no way to recover from a lifetime of wrongdoing. He would rather go now — what was God waiting for?

The steering wheel fought him as he drove, as he tried to drive, back to town, and Route 29 still looked like a country lane here and there . . . minus the McDonald's. Back through Stillwater and Schuylerville and past Yaddo, he was almost home, he concentrated on staying right of the double yellow line, but he was over it, he seemed to be moving very slowly, spinning and opening like a big yawn or a tsunami or something and then: impact.

He stopped. His top and bottom teeth smashed, he tasted salt. Something dripped on his shirt, blood. He tumbled out of the truck. The whole front end bit into a tree, twisted up, the engine smoking, his head bleeding. He looked at his lap, his favorite jeans, and a dark red splash covered the thighs. He could only think of his favorite jeans, ruined by the night, by the women, his best pair of pants stained forever. He did not seem to be hurt, though drops of blood gurgled from his head down his shirt. Then he felt the throbbing, pulsing of blood rushing to escape through the opening in his scalp, and he wanted out like that, out of his own head. He felt crazy. He pressed his cuff to his skull to stop the bleeding.

He turned the key in the ignition and it started up. He said aloud, "I love this truck." And with the engine hissing and the smoke escorting him, he drove home, the truck cracked and rattling. He prayed the whole way home, please God, no cops, no cops, please God, if you keep the cops away, I'll be good, I'll be a good boy, and no cops followed him, and he turned the truck off and the back door was open and there was the couch and he was down.

CHAPTER

6

HE WOKE with ferocious sunlight attacking him. He was prostrate on the couch. The VCR clock read 11:11 and he remembered that he was supposed to make a wish when he saw that. He remembered Myrna had told him that he should always wish to have a good day and nothing more, a teardrop of wisdom so pure he sometimes still practiced it. He remembered in the days and weeks and months after Shannon was taken just wishing on everything he could — the clock numbers, white horses, bridges, graveyards, railroad tracks — that his family could have one good day, that Myrna could make it one day without drinking, that Nora could make it one day without her sneering sarcasm, that Eliza could have one day where she ate something, where Ann could emit the tiniest ray of warmth, that Loretta would love him again: that he could have one day, one good day, one day of peace. It never came.

When he lifted himself he saw a small mop of a dog, Eliza's mangy mutt, lying on a low pile of laundry — Belly's shirts and jeans. The dog raised its glossy black eyes and looked at Belly, cocked its head to one side in a question and Belly shook his head. "She left you," he said to the dog. "Just up and left you."

The dog stretched back on its hind legs and stood, and then Belly saw the pile of twenty-dollar bills clinging to the top of the clothes. He'd left them in the pocket of his jeans, left them for Nora to clean. He reached over and tucked them back into the pocket, and then flashes of the night attacked him. The girl and the sweater and the darkness of the road: he had committed a crime. She could be at the police station right now. A sketch artist could be capturing him in lead and paper, his likeness faxed to the cops, and then to bounty hunters, maybe, who would track him down and take him out and excuse him from the pointlessness of forward movement.

He was too tired this morning to raise his hips and practice his range-of-motion exercises, and his whole left side felt bruised and bullied. His release plan included a physical from Dr. Nielson, who'd written "68" under Life Expectancy on the form, and the gift of new body parts was a prediction that he would barely make it to his seventies. This morning he was glad of that. Sixty years of this life was plenty. Let the joints stiffen and halt, let them lead him into a corner and strand him there.

The light diffused. Nora stood in the doorway between the TV room and kitchen, arms folded like a straitjacket. It seemed like the first time he'd seen her without the baby straddling her ever-widening hip. He sat up on the couch, swooning, put a hand to his head and felt dried blood. He looked at the blood-stain on the knees of his favorite jeans. Nora sat down next to him. She had a warm, damp washcloth and she smoothed it over his temple.

"We have to get this checked out," she said.

"Anybody call for me?"

"No one."

She put a thumb and forefinger to his scalp.

"I was really looking forward to coming back to town," he said.

"I know you were."

"I thought it would be easy."

"Nothing is easy. You taught me that."

She raised herself from the couch. He heard the water running and she returned with the rinsed-out cloth and she put it to his forehead one more time.

"We're taking Margie's car to go to the emergency room. I had the Bronco towed to the shop."

"Nora —"

"I don't want to know," she said. "What happened, what you did, how you got home, who you were with, I don't care. Don't tell me. I don't want any information."

"You sound just like your mother."

"Mom's very wise sometimes." She put the cloth on her swollen belly and said, "Let's go. We'll just make sure you don't have a concussion. I've got a million things to do before tomorrow."

They both hoisted themselves from the couch, him with his fake hips and her with her big baby-to-be. They looked like a comedy routine, like father and daughter: the vaudeville act.

Margie's car was an ailing 1978 Dodge Dart. He remembered the car — the same one she had in high school, that Henry would borrow when he took Eliza out. "How is it possible she has the same car?" he asked.

"She never drives it. Ever. She walks, or if she's going somewhere far away she rides with other people."

He inspected the car. The rear end was covered in bumper stickers. *Keep Abortion Legal. El Salvador Is Spanish for Vietnam. Break All Ties with Apartheid. Capitalism Is Killing Music.*

"Jesus, we can't drive in this thing. We'll get shot. The Lord will strike us down." *Ratify the ERA. Impeach Nixon.* Some of these were older than the car itself. *I Believe You, Anita.*

"Get in."

The car started beautifully. "How does it work if she never drives it?"

"She starts it once a week and lets it run for fifteen minutes. She's very organized."

"She's a nut."

"That, too."

"Why did Eliza ever marry into that family?"

"They're a very nice family, they're just incredibly strange."

Nora drove down Broadway in the still sleepiness of a Saturday morning, and the town, for a minute, looked the way she did in his youth, and he loved her.

"Where are the children?" he asked.

"With Phil."

"No kidding."

"He took them to the Great Escape."

"What about the baby?"

"He took the baby, too."

"What can a baby do at an amusement park?"

She put one of her unlit cigarettes between her lips. "He took the kids as a favor so I could take you to the doctor."

She pulled into the hospital parking lot.

"Spending time with his own kids is a favor? Jesus."

"He did it as a favor to me, because if you'd woken up before he left he would have beaten the shit out of you."

"Oh."

They walked through revolving doors into the emergency room. He stopped.

"What?" she asked.

"I don't have any health insurance."

"Oh, don't worry about that. We've got it."

He said, "No. Let's just go." He tugged at her sleeve but she inched herself away.

"Sit down, Belly. I'll register you."

She came back with a form on a clipboard, made him fill out his Social Security number and a few other specifics. She'd written the number of her house down under "Permanent Address."

The emergency room ticked like a slow clock, a million years between every tick and every tock, no one in there but a teenage boy, scratching under his cast, and his overweight mother. He thought of all the times he'd been there before, for the birth of his four daughters and the death of one of them, but the hospital had expanded and changed, refurbished into one giant pink womb, Pepto-Bismol pink, Chinese restaurant pink, baby skin pink.

"I hate pink," he told Nora as she lowered herself back into the seat next to him.

"It won't be long. They're not busy, but you're not an emergency."

"Then why are we in the emergency room?"

"Because doctors don't see patients on Saturday." She picked up the *Saratogian*. He could be in there, a description of the accident, or the incident, an interview with the girl.

"Nora, you don't have to wait with me."

"Yes, I do."

"I can take care of myself," he said, but the look on her face silenced him into submission. He could see how outraged she was, and how sad, how much she hated him, and he thought maybe if he could keep pressing then she would set him free. If she would kick him out then he could voyage all the way to vagabond, like those women who let themselves get really fat, he could just give up or give in or give it all away, drink himself right back to jail, or right into the ground.

"Let me see the paper," he said, and he scanned the police reports but there was only news of a drunken hotwalker, an attempted break-in at the music shop, two teenagers — names omitted — caught throwing prunes at the windows of the new old-folks home. And with that absence of his offenses in ink, Belly began to wonder if it had happened at all, if the girl in the pink sweater was a drunken dream, a wake-up call, if that was Shannon's apparition sent to tell him something. No, it had never happened. He had not ruined the life of some helpless hippie girl. He would never hurt someone like that. He was a changed man.

He looked at Nora, reading a romance novel with one hand on her belly and her highlighted hair in a wave across her pretty, swollen face, and he put his hand on her forearm.

"What?" she said, refusing to look at him.

"Hand me that *People* magazine." And he took his hand away.

He read through the list of celebrity deaths, weddings, arrests, and divorces and thought about his three weeks of infamy. The raid came off like a sitcom, some fuzzy television flash-forward. He'd received an "anonymous" phone call from the DA's office a month before telling him to close up shop. But Loretta told him they were bluffing. Loretta told him they had bigger fish to catch and he kept the operation rolling, kept the bets coming and going from all directions, more like an orchestra conductor than a bookmaker. Then they showed up, a whole flock of eager officers, one little rookie just to carry the paperwork. They made a big show of reading him his Mirandas, formally announcing his long list of wrongdoings in front of the customers. The strangest thing about it was the lack of drama, the flat voices, the cloudy smoothness of the operation. In the end it was nothing like television, nothing worth selling the rights to like half of his podmates planned to do. His story was just too small.

I used to own this city, he thought, and now I don't even really live here.

Eventually they were seen by a triage nurse, who asked him if there was any deficiency in his vision or hearing, if he was nauseous or dizzy, confused or losing memory. He wanted to say yes, to all of it, but he simply shook his head. The nurse pronounced him fine, if hung over, slapped a little Neosporin on his scalp and sent them home.

Nora parked the Dart in the driveway, turned off the car, and faced him. "This is your last screw-up," she said. "One more stunt like that and you're out on the street. Am I clear?"

He nodded.

"I mean it, Belly. Stevie's confirmation is tomorrow and we're having something like sixty people over to the house and you are to be on your best behavior from this moment on. We were locked out of the house yesterday. You stole the keys, you stole the car." She swallowed hard, and the thought that she might cry launched Belly into a panic.

"Don't," he said. He put his hand on her shoulder.

"You stole money from me," she whispered.

His face erupted with heat.

"No more. No drinking, nothing. You're getting a job and saving some money to pay me back and you will behave yourself. Do you understand?"

"I'm not your child," he said.

"Well, stop acting like one then."

She waited for him to respond, and when he didn't she continued. "Mom told me that when she left us, even though she was only half an hour away, and even though she called every night and we saw her every weekend, she said she cried for three weeks after she moved out."

Belly didn't know that she called every night — he was at work, of course. How would he know? And he didn't know she was with them on the weekend. He was with Loretta.

"And after three weeks of just crying her eyes out every night and being so angry at how things had worked out. . . . She was so pissed at herself that she couldn't quit drinking and she couldn't make things work with you, and then she just hated crying so much, she was so sick of crying, you know, she was so bored of it." Nora cleared her throat. "And then she decided she would move on. That's her motto — that's what she always tells the kids when she watches them and they have tantrums. Move on." She looked at him but he did not meet her eyes.

Nora wedged herself from the car and pushed the door shut gently, walked up the back porch steps, and let the screen door slam behind her. Belly laid his head back on the bench seat. He was so tired. These women, they exhausted him. He closed his eyes, just for a moment, and gathered the energy to move on back to his oldest daughter's house.

He decided to fix the dining-room table. It was the least he could do. Nora was slaving away in the kitchen, then scrubbing the house from attic to basement, fielding phone calls and arranging for Stevie Ray's last-minute meeting with Father Keneally. He retrieved Phil's toolbox from the pantry and set about working on it.

It wobbled. The old thing, it had been his father's, a long slab of mahogany-stained pine, nothing that should last, but here it stood. One of the legs was loose. He could fix that.

He ducked under the table to examine the ailing leg. He had to lie on his side, his bruised-up hip burning against the carpet. He saw that the table had been repaired before, two metal L-brackets hanging from the wooden leg. Shoddy workmanship, that was the problem.

"What are you doing?" Nora's chubby legs appeared before him.

"I'm fixing it."

"You don't have to. Gene's coming over early tomorrow to do it."

Belly crawled out from under the table. "That's the problem right there. Gene."

"Not one word."

He was still on the floor. He had no idea how to raise himself up from that sunken-down plane of the carpet. Nora stood with her arms crossed and resting on her stomach.

"Why?" he asked. "Just explain it to me."

"It's none of your business."

"It is my business, Nora. People on the street are talking about it, and I'm, I don't know." He swallowed. "I'm worried about it, is all."

Nora took a deep breath and lowered herself to the carpet. She sat cross-legged in front of him, the big mound of her belly resting on her legs. The late-afternoon sun came streaming through the window, lighting Nora up, and Belly sat in shadow.

"Okay, Belly, we'll talk about this once more."

"Good."

"You remember when I went to Mexico right after high school?" He nodded. "Well, Gene and I were supposed to go together. We were going to elope. And then I told him I wanted to go alone, and I didn't tell him why, I just said I wanted to go by myself and be alone for a while, and I crushed him. I broke his heart."

"So now you have to adopt him? It's twenty years later. So you broke his heart, so what?"

Nora rubbed her stomach. "Just try and imagine what it would feel like to plan your future with someone, to expect someone to be with you till the end, and then have her disappear on you."

He knew exactly what that felt like. More women than one had walked out on him.

"And then she comes back and marries your best friend."

"Happens every day," he said, but he could see that she was shaken, that the other secret held her hostage. He knew she was pregnant when she went down there, and there was no baby when she came back. "Tell me," he said. "Confess."

Nora shook her head. "I never should have left. If I hadn't left, Shannon would still be with us."

Belly said nothing.

"I should never have left my sisters in the care of two mean drunks like you and mom."

He was sweating, and he said, "We're not talking about that. Not." He began to shake, it must be the DT's, already he had the DT's, after not even a week. He wondered if it was a world record, if he could finally make it into the Guinness Book.

"I'm responsible for two deaths," Nora said, and he did not try to dissuade her. "Gene never married anybody. He never even went out with anybody again, and we are not together, we are never together, but he's never giving up on me. He just waits, like he can make that baby come back from the grave."

Belly took the ring finger of her left hand and rubbed on the knuckle. She folded her palm against his and they held hands for a moment, in the heat, on the carpet. What could he say to her? This was his one chance to be a father to her, to reassure her, to erase twenty years of exponential Catholic guilt, to assuage the pain of killing her baby. He knew how hard it was to lose a child, even an unborn one. He could talk to her about that.

But he couldn't. He didn't. He only held her hand.

"Maybe I just married the wrong person. I just married the person who I didn't have to worry about hurting all the time, because I knew he didn't love me as much as Gene did. I didn't want to have that thing Eliza has, where her husband's like a child, where he's so dependent on her she has no room to breathe, and then she has to escape. Henry's so upset he can't take care of the dog, he had to bring the dog over here. He can't stop crying." Nora's upper lip trembled the tiniest bit. "Isn't it possible that we marry the wrong person sometimes, and we just have to figure out how to make it right?"

Belly nodded, slowly, one hand on the forehead bandage,

one hand awkwardly placed atop Nora's fingers, trying to figure out when and how hard to squeeze.

She said, "I can't get up. From the floor, I can't get up."

He pressed on the carpet but his hips were too heavy. "Me either."

"Turn around," she said.

"Why?"

"Just do it."

He scooted around so his back was facing her, and she did the same, she laid her back against his and told him, "Press with your back and your legs," and the two of them raised themselves like that, like an arch.

He said, "That worked," and Nora nodded and returned to her household chores.

Belly watched her working in the kitchen. "Do you remember that vacation? To Florida? To see the Mets?"

"God, yes."

"Why do you say it like that?"

She turned from the boiling pots on the stove and looked at him.

"It was horrible."

"What do you mean? It was the greatest."

"Are you kidding? All four of us kids got sunburned, terrible sunburns, and you made us go to the games every day in the sun with our blistered-up faces. We hated it."

"We cannot be talking about the same vacation."

"There were only two, and the other one was worse. Mom was plastered the whole time."

"Everybody loved it. You guys loved it. You all said you loved it. I remember."

"Belly," she said, and she walked over to him now, put her

hand on his shoulder, the other hand on her swollen tummy, and she looked him straight in the eye. "We liked it because you liked it. You were happy the whole time and that made us happy. Capisce?"

She just made him so tired. He could barely fill his lungs with air. He followed her to the never-used living room, where she polished a telescope pressed against a window.

"Where'd you get that?" he asked.

"Mom's giving it to Stevie for confirmation."

"We're supposed to get presents?"

"Jesus." Nora shook her fist at him. "What are we going to do with you?"

"Nothing," he said. "I'm a senior citizen, for God's sake."

"Your problem is you still want to be somebody big." She peered through the lens and adjusted the focus. "I heard this thing on the radio recently," she said. "This announcement that the average color of the universe, you know, the most common color, was turquoise, and then they had to take it back because it turns out the average color of the universe is beige."

"Your point is?"

"Belly," she said, and she turned away from the window and looked down at him. "If you don't get my point I can't help you."

He said, "Who asked you to?" and he left her there with her telescope and her stars. He took a six-pack from the refrigerator and trudged up the stairs to the overheated attic. He rifled through his things, looking for something he could give Stevie Ray as a present, but he had nothing, nothing to offer, nothing to give. He found yesterday's tip sheet. He found the pile of twenty-dollar bills and he skimmed one off the top and put the other five inside the tip sheet. He found the notebook Eliza had made and he stuck the tip sheet and the money inside, and he rewrapped it in the cellophane. He looked out at the dusky sky, the time of day when there is no depth, the tops of houses blending into endless firmament. He drank Piels and he turned on the fan and he lay on the single mattress with the sea of old belongings swimming around him: his daughter's paintings, his grandmother's artifacts, every possession Nora had saved over all these years, everything she thought deserved rescue keeping him company while he dreamed.

It was night when he woke. He peeked into the boys' bedroom, saw them both on their backs with open mouths, Jimi breathing heavily in the thick night air, no sheets on either of them, sweating. Downstairs Nora and Gene sat on the back porch, Gene with his mixed drink in a martini glass and Nora with her room-temperature can of Wink. He heard them when he took a beer from the fridge, laughter seeping through the windows. Dirty dishes from another dinner he'd missed towered in the sink.

He thought about bursting through the screen door and separating them, about lifting Nora from her chair and forcing her back inside. He thought about shaking his fist at Gene and telling him to get his own family, find his own wife and child, these were spoken for. But he listened to them chatter, listened to Nora's voice erupt into laughter, and he thought how lucky she was to have someone make her laugh like that, and he wouldn't touch it. He'd just leave it be.

He did not know what to do with himself. He looked around the kitchen, he peeked into the TV room, the silent living room, the sleeping front porch; no place was safe. He drank his Piels and he went to the sink. A picture window hovered above it and he could hear Nora and Gene, he could make out their diaphanous figures sloping gently toward each other on the porch. He filled one side of the sink with sudsy water and the other side with clear water and he washed the dishes and watched his daughter and let the night evaporate that way. He had passed four years waiting, every day some rocky hill to summit and roll down again in sleep, every morning the same unfriendly terrain to traverse, waiting waiting waiting to *get out,* and now he was out and he was still waiting, only he did not know why and for what. He had been waiting for Loretta, waiting to retrieve his woman and his wad of cash, and now neither would be returned to him. He looked out the window screen to the hazy night and he thought for the first time of the possibility that his life would not improve.

When he was done he took a bottle of Jameson's from the cupboard and he walked to the front of the house, unlocked the front door, and sat on the lonely porch. It was late, he did not know how late it was, but the street was quiet and no tourists walked by. He drank and he drank, there alone on the front porch, he drank until that horrible swollen feeling inside him loosened and seeped away, and when the world felt safe again he went to sleep.

Iɴ ᴛʜᴇ morning Belly climbed the stairs to the second-floor bathroom. He took off his clothes and inspected his head wound in the mirror. The temperature had already risen above ninety, and when he turned on the hot water in the faucet, steam obscured his image in the glass. He wiped a gash clean on the mirror, he shaved, he ran the shower spray over his hand until the temperature came out perfectly cool, and then he stepped inside the cave of water. He stayed under the spray for five, ten, fifteen minutes, until Nora called for him to save some hot water for the rest of them. He did not wash. He stood there under the spout with his eyes closed and the waterfall running over him until his fingertips withered, and then he stepped out.

Hanging in his closet was his one pair of khaki pants, with cuffed bottoms and pleats, his middle-class pants, his middle-aged pants, and next to those his good dress pants, the bottom half of his one suit. Nora had pressed them with heavy creases running down the legs, and woven a red tie with horses into the hooks of the hanger. He picked at the pleats, finding a tiny ball of pocket lint hiding inside. He left them hanging, slipped on a cleanish pair of jeans with his white shirt, then he climbed into his one navy blazer and ran his fingers through his hair.

A million electric sounds, razors and hair dryers, toasters, alarms, cell phones, everything was on, everything was going off. Belly had a miserable headache, and he longed to stay home and keep watching the continuing *Jeffersons* marathon on TV.

Instead he watched Nora milling around the kitchen like a hummingbird, moving so fast she looked still. He looked at her slicked-down brown hair with blond streaks and the pouch poking from her midriff and he felt like he was watching a reenactment of a daughter, that's how far away she seemed.

"Grampa's up," she said, giving Belly a little slap on his shoulder. He tried to put his arm around her but she was so big, and she was moving so fast. She was a mother on a mission: no stopping her. "What are you wearing?"

"A suit," he said.

"I put your good pants up there. Didn't you see them?"

"I saw them."

Jimi and Stevie Ray bent their heads over bowls of cereal, bracing for a fight.

"Don't give me a hard time today, Belly. Please."

"How am I giving you a hard time? By wearing jeans? How does that make your life hard?"

He poured himself a cup of coffee and sat at the table with the boys. They scooted an inch away from him.

"Go and put your good pants on. Just go upstairs and put them on."

"No."

"Yes."

"Nora, there's no reason why I should dress up for church. Jesus wore a toga, you think he cares? Denim is a good, strong, respectable fabric."

Stevie Ray was staring at him.

"What?"

"I'm wearing a suit," he said.

"I can see that. Very good for you. They'll let you right in up there in heaven someday."

Stevie Ray shook his head. "You're more immature than Jimi."

"Maybe I am," said Belly. "I like it that way."

Nora was standing with her arms crossed. He could see her making calculations, deciding whether or not to fight him on this, and he was prepared to stand his ground, to refuse to don those awful old-man pants. Nora shook her head and he saw her let it go.

"Let me tell you," she said, forcing a smile. "I can remember everybody's saint name in the whole family. Did you know that in Europe they celebrate your saint name day? Did you know that? You get presents and everything."

He shook his head.

"Mom's is Esther, the saint of stars. I bet you forgot that, Belly."

"I don't think I ever knew it in the first place."

"Eliza had Gamo, patron saint of the arts, even though it's a man's name. Ann had Bernadette — I remember just trying to spell that on the card — and that meant something like "bold as a bear." Do you remember all this, Belly?"

"Sure," he lied.

"And Shannon had Irene, saint of peace." Nora looked up now from her cookbook. "Do you remember mine?"

"Should I?" he asked, and Nora just glared at him.

"I know what it is," said Stevie Ray. "It's Josephine."

"Is that supposed to mean something to me?"

Stevie Ray leafed through his workbook. "Joseph is the saint of fathers," he said, closing his book. "Jeez, Grampa, you didn't remember that?"

Belly said, "Stevie, don't take the Lord's name in vain. And on a Sunday, for Chrissake."

"It's just about time," Nora said, closing up Stevie Ray's notebook and tousling his hair. Whatever war was between them had ceased for the day. Behind them, Phil appeared, six-foot-six and skinny as a street cat in his Sunday best.

Belly stood up. "I've managed to go a whole week without seeing my son-in-law." He extended a hand and Phil shook it, but loosely. Belly's palm was suddenly coated in sweat; he felt as if Phil were the father and he was a naughty little boy.

"Spell's broken, I guess," said Phil, and he served himself a cup of coffee but did not say more to Belly.

He watched his daughter's husband sit down and sip his coffee and read the paper, watched him keep still while his wife moved around him, watched his sons reach across him, spill orange juice on his paper, trying to get his attention, and the whole scene made some foreign feeling simmer up inside him, something he vaguely recognized as regret.

They wanted to all go to church together but Phil's pickup was a two-seater, so they tried to pile all three kids and three adults into Margie's borrowed Dodge Dart. Belly waited for them to smoosh in and then he said, "I'll walk."

"Oh, no you don't," said Nora. "I don't trust you to make it there on your own."

"It's six blocks away."

"There are, like, forty bars between here and the church. Get in."

"Just one minute," Belly said, and he walked up all those stairs to the attic. He changed into the dress pants and then he reached under the bed and pulled out the plastic Wal-Mart bag with the flask from Eliza, and downstairs he filled the flask with Jameson's and outside he squeezed into the car with the flask resting safely against his heart.

Eons had passed since Belly had been in this church, more moons than he could count. These last four years remained in sharp focus, his podmates and their fights over what to watch on television, the rare gift of a cigarette or square of chocolate when the guards were feeling generous. But the fifteen years before that were now as blank and beige as the universe.

The interior of St. Peter's was stern and bland, and a young priest had begun taking over for Father Keneally. But everything about the inside of this church was the same, even the parishioners. Mrs. Radcliffe and her girls, Phil's brothers and their wives, everyone coming up to him and asking, "How *are* you?" with faux Christian concern. He recognized a sea of regulars from War Bar and their families.

The question he'd been dreading all week now floated in the air around him: "What are you going to do now? What now? What lies ahead for you, buddy?" He followed Nora to a pew in the front and knelt, he tried to kneel but it was too hard on his knees and he sat back on the bench and looked up to the school of people on the stage, each of them wearing index cards with the names of their patron saints written in bold black ink.

Around Stevie Ray's neck hung a nametag that read "William."

Belly moved to the back of the church. He hid in a back pew and sipped from his flask, watching the parishioners and the clergy and his family all milling about in the unfriendly interior. There must be twenty people on the stage, up for confirmation, Stevie Ray obviously the youngest among them. There were two middle-aged sisters in matching outfits, garish green flowered things, fancy muumuus, and blond girls or ladies or whatever you called them when they were on the verge, thin pretty things with their hair done up just perfect, just in the way that calls for a man to take it down. Mostly they looked like high school students, pimply and awkward with dreamy eyes as they swayed to the lame-ass Christian band with piercing drums playing off to the side. In the apse, a girl with bobbed hair, wearing a bright, fifties shade of turquoise, sat next to a fresh-faced boy with a shiny, pomaded pompadour and sparkly eyes, such wholesome teenagers he wanted to shake them and say, Loosen up, have some fun, you are going to die. Go out and have some sex, for Chrissake. But they looked so peaceful, this blond boy and girl, holding hands in the wooden row.

A woman was singing with the band, the kind of old woman you saw in every church, in every elementary school office: big, pink, plastic glasses and a loose jumper in an unsightly shade of red hovering over her like a shroud. But then he realized the old woman was probably his age, and when they sang, when he heard the woman's high clear voice singing *I Am the Bread of Life,* then the old aching came back and it was all he could do not to leave.

The bishop wore a microphone so his words echoed off the concrete walls and found Belly in the back. When he was a kid the back of the church was for sleepers, and when your mother asked you what the sermon was about you legitimately answered, "I couldn't hear."

The bishop and the priest made their way down the long line of parishioners waiting to be confirmed. Asking, that's what the bishop said, they were asking to be confirmed. Could the church really say no? The confirmandi stood in front of their sponsors. Belly looked at the man standing with his hand on Belly's grandson's shoulder: it was Gene, big fat Gene with his chubby paw clutching Stevie Ray's clavicle. With relief he noticed they looked nothing alike. Gene would always be the avuncular family addendum and nothing more.

The ceremony began, the bishop asking the questions — "Do you believe all that the Catholic Church believes, teaches, and proclaims to be revealed by God?" — and the whole parish droning in response every time. He wanted to answer, Not so fast. Hold on. Let me think about it a minute. But he kept silent.

After the bishop and the priest had made their rounds, rubbing circles of holy water on the foreheads of the recently confirmed, they turned to the parish and beseeched, "Let us pray that all will proclaim Jesus as God." Belly wondered, Why? Why is that so important, that every single person should proclaim Jesus as God, even the Jews, or those Muslim types?

"What you doing back here, Grampa?" Jimi climbed next to him on the pew.

"Thinking," Belly said.

"You're not allowed," said Jimi. "We're supposed to go up front."

One by one the rows emptied as the parishioners walked up to take Communion, and Belly and Jimi sat in the back of the church and watched the lines of open-mouthed adults kneel and sip on a tasteless wafer and bad wine and Belly did not rise. "Get up, Grampa," Jimi said, but he did not rise. He watched the line move slowly like a sated snake and he thought of sneaking from row to row and rifling through the ladies' pocketbooks. What would the muumuu girls have in their bags? How much money did the red jumper lady keep? Were there condoms in the pockets of the fifties boy's suit?

He looked up and Jimi was not with him. The boy crouched by the big domed doors where the Bibles were kept, and Belly saw him reach for a little green New Testament and slip the book into his suit pants.

The priest told the story of when John baptized Jesus in the river Jordan and the sky opened and a dove came down from heaven and landed on Jesus, saying, "This is my Son, whom I love: with him I am well pleased." He watched Gene and Stevie Ray with identical gleaming grins on the stage, and Stevie Ray holding the nametag and peering out into the audience, looking for his Grampa, making sure that Belly saw. He wanted to stand and wave, there in the back of the church, wanted to jump on the wooden pew and cheer, but all the alcohol pinned him to the floor, gravity trapped him, and he had no recourse but to flee.

He pushed open the great oak doors and left his whole family there to witness his grandson's lifelong commitment to God and all his glory, he just turned his back on God the same way God had forsaken him. He stood outside and waited for his family to finish.

Mrs. Radcliffe came out first. "You didn't take communion," she said.

"I haven't gone to confession in about ten years."

"Oh, well, whoever lets that stop them?" She lit a cigarette and waited for her girls.

Jimi and Nora and Gene and Phil and Eliza's husband Henry and Stevie Ray and all the rest poured out the doors, flash photos and flowers and hugs and Belly tried to remember his own confirmation but it was a sober event as far as he could recall, and what was all this fuss for?

He approached his grandson, rested a hand on his shoulder as people swirled about him, congratulating, congratulating and Belly said, "Why'd you do it so young? You're the youngest one here, I bet." He tried to wipe something from Stevie Ray's starched white collar but the stain had set. "You've got some Christ blood on your shirt," he said.

Stevie Ray looked up with his big, sad blue eyes and said, "I want to be a priest."

"Oh, Jesus, you've got to be kidding me. That's the last thing you want to do."

Nora swooped in to separate them. "Let's head back to the house," she said, ushering them toward Margie's Dart.

They all piled in again, and as they headed home Belly said, "Why don't you just be gay and skip the whole priest thing?"

"Enough," Nora said. She was squished in the front seat between her husband and Stevie Ray and Belly smooshed in the back with King and Jimi and he watched out the window as if by looking he could make the town turn back into its former self.

Wʜat can I do?" Belly asked Nora when they returned from church. She was tidying furiously. "How can I help?"

"Stay out of the house."

"Don't be like that. Let me do something. I'll watch the baby."

"Right," was all she said.

"I cannot believe Eliza is not here for this. That is just so selfish."

"Don't start on that again."

"You're trying to tell me that it's okay if she misses her own niece's —"

"— nephew's —"

"— nephew's confirmation?"

"There'll be three more."

"But this is the first one."

"You missed all of their christenings."

"I was in jail."

"Only for King's."

He added up the numbers in his head, but it did not work out.

"That's not true."

"It is true."

"It isn't." He opened the liquor cupboard, hidden high above the microwave and pulled down the near-empty bottle of Jameson's.

"It's true."

"It can't be true."

"It is."

"Tell me it's not true." He opened the bottle and poured the last drops of alcohol into the flask. Nora never turned around, and he slipped the flask into his jacket pocket and put the bottle back in the cupboard, all this without her seeing.

She put down her spatula. "Belly, you didn't show up to Stevie Ray's christening or his first communion and you didn't come to Jimi's christening and today you sat in the back and left early and I don't know what to do with you, I really don't."

"Where was I?" he asked. "The other times."

"You were busy. You were booking. You were drunk." She rinsed the spatula and wiped her hands on her jeans. "Belly," she said. "You were a terrible father."

He opened the fridge and took out a beer.

"It's not even noon," she said and he said, "Who cares?"

She said, "I do."

He looked at Nora, and Nora was crying, and he needed beer and he needed a cigarette. He felt in his pockets but the lighter, his cherry-red lighter, was not there.

"You never did anything for us," she said, "not once. But now you can."

"Where's my lighter?" he asked, watching tears roll down Nora's cheeks.

She shook her head.

"I need my lighter, dammit," he yelled. He patted all of his pockets and he searched through the kitchen drawers while Nora's face turned red and blotchy, and the face of ten-year-old Nora with skinned knees broke through. "I can't live without my lighter," he said.

She opened her purse and pulled out a small white lighter, and she showed him how to pull back the childproof lever and light it, crying all the while. She said, "Eliza's gone and

Shannon's gone and Ann's not coming and you chased Mom off a long time ago." She was really crying now, steady tears, her shoulders jerking and Belly had never been so thirsty in his life.

"I did it for you. I did it all for you." But she kept shaking her head. "It was for you."

"We forgive you," she said. "So just, stop, you know? Stop. You don't have to be a terrible father anymore. You can just stop, that's what you can do for us." She moved toward him with one hand reaching out and he tried to root himself to the floor, he tried to make himself stay and open his arms to her, tried to summon some words of comfort.

"You know what I'll do for you?" He grabbed his suit coat from the back of the chair. "I'll go downtown and get drunk. Would that help?"

"That would be great, Dad," Nora said through her tears. "With my blessing."

He slammed the door behind him.

Downtown tourists swarmed. On Caroline Street the little bars looked like cells holding endless alcoholics captive. He put on his sunglasses, walked into Ruffian's, ordered a tequila with Sprite, "Just like in Mexico," though he'd never been, and then a Patron silver and a Guinness and a boilermaker and then he said, "One of everything."

The waitress, the little dark-haired waitress said, "You coming in every day?"

"I just might be. I might be here every day."

He drank in the midday heat until so many of his pilfered dollars dissolved and then he walked down Maple Street, wobbling south and into Congress Park.

The first thing he saw was Margie, sitting on a bench with a Café Newton coffee cup, reading the Sunday *Times*. He said, "Sipping with the enemy, I see."

"It was closest."

"Why aren't you at the house? You didn't get invited?"

"Of course I was invited. I just don't do religion."

"Jesus," he said. The world twisted and turned around him, and he had to focus on his shoes to slow it down.

Margie looked up at the darkening sky and said, "It's going to rain."

"A big rain or a little rain?"

"A big rain," she said. "Definitely a big rain."

A fat gray cloud covered the sky, and he said a little prayer that the heat wave would end, the tourist wave would end, that Labor Day would come a week early and give him his town back. He dripped sweat inside his Sunday suit.

Belly said, "Stevie Ray wants to be a priest." He slipped the flask from his jacket pocket and took a big swig.

"I know," she said. "Don't forget what you're doing is illegal."

He said, "I was getting too sober."

"However you want to justify it."

"How do you know?" he asked. "About Stevie?"

"Eliza told me."

He sat down next to her on the bench. "Why does it bother me so much?"

"I suppose you just want everyone in your family to be normal."

He said, "Fat chance of that happening," but he thought about them, his three girls, and he thought about their mother, and he tried to revisit the list of ways they'd wronged him but it was gone, melted in the heat or obscured by heavy clouds and suddenly they did not seem so strange.

"I don't know," Margie said. "I've seen some real freaks in my time and I'd say you lucked out."

"I've got a man-hater and a meat-hater."

"Count yourself lucky."

"What's lucky about that?"

"First of all, considering where they came from, I think your daughters are doing great. Amazingly, in fact." Margie looked up at the sky as it grew darker and she looked at Belly and she reached and put her hand on his shoulder, and he did not move away. "Second of all, you can't take that shit personally," she said. "Eliza's not a vegetarian because you force-fed her pork or anything."

"That's your influence," he interrupted.

"Maybe. My parents' influence, anyway. But Ann's not a lesbian to punish you. That's just who she is." Margie rubbed circles in the dirt with her foot. "Think about how it is for you. I highly doubt you ran a nationwide gambling ring just to disrupt your daughters. People just make mistakes or bad decisions or they can't help how they turn out."

He looked at his cowboy boots, scuffed on the side. His shirt stuck to his back, the humidity seeped into his brain, his bones, everything expanded and softened and all he wanted in the world was to lie down and look up and see the faces of his four daughters surrounding him.

He said, "She ruined my fantasy life forever, that Ann."

"You'll have to live in the real world like the rest of us."

He looked at Margie, big fat Margie in her hippie dress with her hairy pits and he asked, "How can you stand living here now? With all those big stores and everything all tidy — the whole downtown feels like a dental office. It was so much better before."

"Belly, you act like that all happened since you left town. Half that stuff was already here, the new library and the bookstore. And the plans to tear down the Woolworth's building were in place long before you left."

"That's not true. None of that stuff was here."

"The only thing that wasn't here before you left was Wal-Mart, and that's inevitable. There's not a town left in the U.S. without a Wal-Mart nearby. But everything you complained about — the chain stores and the coffee places and the whole makeover, all that was going on while you were still here." She paused. "You just didn't notice."

"No," he said.

Margie said, "Yes."

"Well, I guess there's good coffee now."

"That there is. And a bookstore. Good restaurants. It's not the same place, but it's not a bad place."

"I miss my town," he said. "This isn't my town."

"Yes, it is," she told him. "It's the same place underneath. You miss the seedy underbelly, but it's the same everywhere else. Same sewer system. Same streets. Same houses, just painted differently. It's going through a fancy phase. It won't last."

He stood up, he wobbled, he saluted her, and then he went searching for the tree he lost his virginity under, but they were all so tall now. He walked along the stripe of pavement where fifteen years before his Mustang had toppled over, taking Shannon away. He looked up at the canopy of leaves and the sky blackening behind him and the world morphed and swayed. He walked down the steep hill toward the war memorial and the duck pond, a cement gazebo where they'd played duck-duck-goose at Nora's fifth birthday party. The whole thing was covered in pigeon shit then, but now it sparkled. In fact, he hadn't seen any pigeon shit the whole week. The church on the corner of Spring and Regent, they used to call that the Pigeon Shit Church. The thing had been boarded up his whole life, but just before he got sent away some bazillionaire had bought it and turned it into condos. Really nice condos, not a speck of pigeon shit anywhere. They must hire people just to clean up pigeon shit now. There was a job for him: pigeon shit cleaner. He'd heard once that in Paris they hire people just to clean up dog shit. They wore orange jumpsuits or something, special uniforms just for the dog shit cleaners. He could do that, get an orange jumpsuit and a mop and a bottle of Windex and just scrub the sidewalks for money.

A raindrop brushed his cheek, just one, then two little tears of water and then it was pouring, raindrops dancing everywhere around him. He hated water, and he stood there in the rain, let it soak through the gabardine, let it seep into his cowboy boots, let it twirl around him like the women in his dreams, choreographing him into drowning.

He saw a gaggle of grown-ups galloping toward him, toward the cover of the war memorial, grown people with crazy strides bouncing along the soggy ground like giant toddlers. He moved closer, the water lapping at the leather edges of his cowboy boots, and saw that the group hiding under the cement awning were all retarded adults, all except one lucky Down Syndrome–less middle-aged lady who must have been their leader or caretaker or den mother or whatever you called them. All this time he'd been wondering where the retards had gone and here they were, at least a few of them, running through the rain in Congress Park on a hot Sunday August afternoon.

Belly shook the water off him like a wet dog. He stepped under the protective concrete of the ceiling and stood next to the retards, all seated in the center like big preschoolers.

"It's the retards!" he yelled. "Where have you guys been?"

The den mother had big gray poodle hair and big round red glasses that swallowed her face. She shushed her grown-up children and said to Belly, "Can I help you?"

"Where'd they all move to? What happened to all those retarded kids who lived at Furness House?"

"We call them mentally challenged adults, sir, and they dispersed them to smaller houses throughout the county," she said. "These guys live in Stillwater now."

He wanted to hug them. He wanted to twist their puerile bodies to face one another and dance around them, duck, duck, duck, and then he wanted to place his hand on the head of the girl who looked so close to normal, goose, with long blond hair and green eyes. Just a little twist of the genes and she could be regular, she could be real, she could be his grown third daughter, thirty-two years old she would be now and absolutely alive, this little inbred vision, this mangled version of Shannon. He placed his hand on her head and then the whole crowd erupted, the melted faces of the retards with their doughy skin and cross-eyes, harnessing all that innocent flesh to accuse him. The den mother said, "Sir, sir, please don't touch them," and Belly backed off, away, down the concrete ramp in the rain, up the hill, past the little creek they'd widened into a river, and the rain made circular eruptions in the water.

*   *   *

Belly climbed Nora's front porch and looked at the two ghost chairs. The railing was made of mud, it slipped in his hands. He set himself down in the chair and watched Spring Street on a Sunday afternoon. He missed the retards when they lived there in the giant extended family that he realized now he always felt part of. He missed Seaver, his old dog Seaver, who used to love to visit the retards, and the retards loved her. Half the time he'd go looking for her he could find her there, drooling demi-adults stroking her shiny black fur. The retards were allowed to walk themselves around the block once a day, and they'd come by in limping herds. He and Phillip Sr. used to offer them little sips of beer and puffs of Newports, and then Seaver would escort them home.

He turned to the empty chair. "Phillip Senior," he said. "Why did they go and break up the retard family?"

The chair did not answer.

He sang an old folk song Nora used to know. "Where have all the retards gone, long time passing?"

The chair did not answer.

"Should I go in now? Face the music?"

The chair remained defiantly silent.

He kicked it away.

"Why'd you have to go and die, Phillip?" he asked the chair. "We could have got an apartment together. We could pick up a couple of girls and go back to our bachelor pad and party all night. We're not too old."

Everything in his body ached.

"You're too old," the chair said. "Act your age."

He nodded at the chair. "You're right. You're right, you're right, you are so right." The rain died, his pants were dryish again, the air was soft and cool. He smoothed his hair, straightened his tie, sipped from his flask, and made his way down the front porch, along the driveway to the back door and into the kitchen.

The house was filled with women, teams of women with trays of pale carrots, dry cucumbers, mealy tomatoes.

Jimi sat at the kitchen table working on a big bowl of sugar cereal. "Somebody called for you, Grampa."

"Who?" asked Belly. He tried not to sway.

"I don't know. They said don't go back to the track."

"Who was it?"

"I don't know."

"Okay," he said. "Okay, okay, okay."

He stood in the kitchen doorway and watched the women pivot around the room, listened to the hums of chatter punctuated by an occasional high laugh. He walked through the TV room where some of Stevie Ray's friends played Nintendo. They called, "Old man, you wanna play? We'll let you win." He continued to the dining room. Bread, bread, I need some bread, he thought, something to sop up the whiskey and tequila and wishing.

He tried not to inventory the guests but he could see Gene and Phil on the couch with forties, and Eliza's poor Henry looking lonely and forlorn without her, his chubby hands leafing through the record collection. Nora stood over Stevie Ray, writing down what gifts and who gave them. Mrs. Radcliffe and her twin daughters stood in matching purple smocks, as promised.

Where was Ann? Which one was Ann? Would he even recognize her?

He planted himself next to the dining-room table and searched for something resembling food. Deviled eggs. Fruit

Jell-O. A dish of star mints. There was a giant white cake with strawberries on top.

Nora put her hand on his shoulder, and when he smiled at her, she recoiled at his breath.

"How much did you drink?"

"Not enough," he said. He wanted to ask her if Ann showed up, if Ann would speak to him, which one was Ann? But he said, "Listen, what a man needs at a time like this is a potato. I mean, we're Irish. Potatoes saved our people, and here we are in America and there's not one potato on this goddamned table." Nora escaped back to the couch. She sat next to Gene, smiled at him, and he smiled back, and Phil sat oblivious next to them, and he could see that they all had some kind of arrangement, something he could never understand. He could see some little wavelength of love stretching between Gene and Nora and Phil.

I'm hallucinating, he thought.

An oldish woman came and stood next to him, with another tray of crudités. The woman from church, with the fluorescent red muumuu and candy pink glasses, who was not so homely when he saw her up close. She wore a pink cardigan around her shoulders now. Something sad and familiar circled around her: he felt he could speak to her and she would understand.

"Why has the potato been so shafted in America?" Belly asked her. He was aware of himself as a spectacle, a stretched-out Dudley Moore in *Arthur*. "Look what's on here. Celery. I mean, celery." He put his face right up to this woman's — she had very dark green eyes that he recognized. "Celery is the worst-tasting vegetable ever made, but you've got a whole pile of it right here." He rifled through the celery sticks with his dirty fingers. "I hate celery."

The woman set the tray down on the dining-room table, her emerald eyes shining. She was littered with wrinkles, deep lines like hieroglyphics. He tried to read the message in those lines.

"I hate celery," the lady said. "I'm allergic to it, for gosh-sakes. Don't you remember?"

He looked closely at her, wobbling as he approached her face. Why, Shannon. She looked like Shannon. Old Shannon.

Belly put his hand over his mouth — to cover a scream or a laugh he didn't know. "Holy shit," he said. "You're my wife." He reached out to touch her face, "You look so beautiful," he said, and he felt himself tilt back in slow motion, like in outer space. He leaned back against the dining-room table. He felt the world shift beneath him, a hole opened in the earth and everything was falling in. He heard a shout and a few yelps around him, and he thought, the house is falling in. The world is falling in. Where are my grandchildren? Where are my daughters? I've got to save them. And he raised himself up, turned to look for them, saw he was covered in something, paint, or gravy, and he heard Nora yell, "Jesus, Belly, you knocked over the whole table," and he fell. He fell all the way to the floor and lay with his back against the tipped-over table like it was a lawn chair, and he saw the whole ocean moving toward him, the world has fallen in, the Florida ocean, the gulf coast, and his wife in the lawn chair next to him with her um-brella drink, and his three daughters burying the fourth up to her neck in sand. He saw all these faces before him and he reached up to Nora's shining face, put his hand on her cheek and asked, "Are you all right? Is everybody okay?" But the world went blank before he heard the answer.

*　　*　　*

When he woke on the couch the last sliver of daylight cut a line across the carpet. It reminded him of the slice of sky slipping into the pod, and he thought of the man a few cells down with all fifty-two glossy Sears portraits of his two daughters plastering the walls. The man once told Belly, "Every day I look at my girls and it's like I won the lottery."

One thought wandered across his eyes and plopped down next to him like an old friend. *I have three daughters.* He lay on the couch and had no idea how much time had passed. There were fewer people, but the house was still buzzing with strangers. He looked out the window. The trees flattened against the sky and the wind expired, and the soft air, the gloaming, swallowed all his fears. Dawn and dusk, those were the only times he felt the least bit hopeful.

Stevie Ray was standing over him. "Are you done ruining my party now?" he asked.

"I'm sorry," said Belly. And he was.

What should happen now, he thought, what would make this all so cinematic, is if he woke up tomorrow morning and he and Stevie Ray communed somehow, if during the night the weather and the words converged to form a pulmonary wind, to blow them safely to shore. Now he would have a little pal, a baby Belly, an ally. But he thought of the storkiness of the boy, his dogmatic faith, his sensitive skin and what he wanted to be when he grew up, and nothing in the past week would dull their glaring differences. He should summon some wisdom to bestow upon him now, some grandfatherly advice for his newly confirmed status. But the boy was going to be a priest, for Chrissakes. He would be coming to the boy for advice someday.

"Well, it can't get any worse," said Stevie Ray. "Get up, Grampa. Time to grow up." And he extended his hand toward Belly, and Belly let the boy pull him up to standing.

A beautiful song wafted into the TV room, an old Irish tune his grandma used to sing: "The Cliffs of Doneen." He followed it like a dog catching a scent. And there, next to the knocked-over dining room table, was Nora, Phil accompanying her on the guitar.

He walked right up to her, right up to her face, to make sure she wasn't faking. She used to love those lip-synching shows.

"Why, Nora, I didn't know you could sing."

All the women in the room glared at him. All of them, their faces melting into accusations.

"Belly, Phil and Gene and I had a band in high school."

"You did?"

She banged her fist on the knocked-down dining-room table. "We played out every weekend. We even played at War Bar. A bunch of times. You got a citation for having under-agers in there."

"You're making this up."

"I'm not."

He thought back, reached way back in his gray mind to the days before Shannon was taken, and saw Nora and Phil and Gene on the stage, some long-haired greasy fool behind them on the drums, his other three daughters perched atop the bar stools drinking Shirley Temples, and Myrna lacing up their shoes, his longtime regulars congratulating him on the talent of his oldest child, on how well she'd turned out.

"The Lawn Jockeys," he said.

"That's right."

His brain seemed to wake up then, he was using more than

the three percent of it Shannon said all humans had access to. "Keep going," he said. "Keep singing."

Gene stood next to him, awkward in his heavy Sunday suit over that lumbering frame. Belly nodded at him.

"She has the greatest voice," said Gene.

"Yeah, it's pretty good, I guess." He paused. "Gene, do me a favor, would you? I mean, let's fix the front porch. I really want to fix the front porch. Get some pallets up in there and make that thing nice again."

"We can do that."

Gene sipped his beer and stared at Nora. "Belly," he said. "You know you can't work for me now."

He said, "I've got something lined up. It's okay." All his life he thought he would come out above the bar, better than his father's life or his grandfather's. He wanted what every parent wanted: for his children to be happy, for their lives to be easier and more fluid than the bumpy ride he'd endured. He looked at his oldest daughter surrounded by friends and family, he thought of his youngest daughter sewing bindings in Alabama, of Ann and Bonnie and their cosmopolitan lives, and he thought of Shannon and her beautiful, sweet face, her eyes closed in the coffin.

He would never get his money back, never get Loretta, and he could never tell his daughters how he'd tried, for once in his life, to do something for them. He would live with his daughter for a little while and work for some crummy corporation, he would not be rich, and he would watch his grandsons grow into men. A small life, then, a small life of an old man near the end.

Stevie Ray stood next to them, and Belly tried something, just for an experiment. He put his arm around the boy's shoulders and squeezed, just a little, the tiniest pressure, and Stevie Ray let him stay there a minute before he ducked out of Belly's grasp and back to his friends.

Up to the attic one last time. They could make a museum out of this place, he thought. A life: in furniture. And he didn't want it, not any of it, not his recliner, his Piels sign, his tropical island wall-sized poster, not his great-grandma's spinning wheel, not his daughter's field hockey equipment, not the girls' beanbag chairs and that shaggy rug they used to call their pet doggie since he would not allow another animal in the house after Seaver passed. There was only one thing he would retrieve: a small, framed portrait, a goddamned Sears portrait with a creamy-blue background and the family posed awkwardly, a mannequin family with Belly at the head, Myrna next to him, wearing hangover eye shadow and orangey lipstick. All the colors faded till they were just reds and greens — a colorless Christmas family, and their four beautiful daughters: Nora, a tad overweight with a terrible feathery haircut, and Eliza sickly thin with a sallow smile, and Ann looking mean and glum and punk — he'd forgotten about her punk phase, that stupid spiked hair and gobs of black makeup around her eyes and all those black rubber bracelets. And Shannon, relaxed, smiling widely, in her homely thrift-store outfit. He looked at Nora's thick arms and broad shoulders in the picture, and around him now at her stacked-up tennis and field hockey trophies, and now he saw how she had tried her best to fulfill his wish for a son.

They had been, he realized now, a normal, unhappy family. Most men lost interest in their wives. Most wives had a vice like alcohol or cigarettes, television or the crossword puzzle; most gained weight, cooked poorly. Myrna had been kind to him, and she had done everything she could to quit drinking, until all she could do was leave him.

The attic was cool now, relieved by the rain, and he retrieved Eliza's homemade book and brought it back down to his grandson. Stevie Ray was surrounded by presents, and by flowery Hallmark cards filled with checks. A painting rested on the back of the couch. Belly felt it call to him, felt the colors beckoning. The whole world was a smear, but the painting remained sharp and clear: a portrait of Nora and Phil and the three kids. They all wore sneaky little smiles, didn't look happy or unhappy, just content, or resigned, or something else. Just real. They looked absolutely real. There was a signature on the bottom. Eliza O'Leary Kessel.

A card leaned on the gilded frame of the painting. On the front was the Irish blessing. *May the road rise to meet you.* And on the inside, though he knew he shouldn't read it, was a note from Ann. She loved him. She was sorry she couldn't be there for his big day. She would come to see him soon.

May the wind be always at your back. He lowered himself to the floor, next to the muck that had splayed from the crashed table, where the baby kneaded knuckles of cauliflower.

May the sun shine warm upon your face. That's what he would do. He would commission a painting. A painting of him and his wife and all four of his daughters, and he would move into his own place someday and put the painting right by the door where he could see it coming and going, *the rains fall soft upon your fields,* Eliza's initials winking at him from the bottom, happy to have them with him. He held the card in his hands, and recited to himself the words that graced the front of the card.

And, until we meet again, may God hold you in the palm of His hand.

Phil played a lamenting Spanish tune on the guitar, and Belly wobbled toward Nora with his bruised and aching hip and his dirty shirt, the stale liquor on his swollen tongue, and he offered her his hand. Long ago he had showed her how to tango, he had placed her tiny feet on his own and instructed her in the walk, the stroll, the chase, the beginning and the close, all the churning steps of tango he knew. And he curled her across the living room floor now, her grown-up feet on the ground, he guided her through the spilled crudités and appetizers that lay scattered across the rug like a massacre. They whirled through the living room till the onlookers blurred into the background. They stopped, they stood and stared at one another, and the room reeled around them, everything swirling except the faces of father and daughter, so much alike.

When all the guests had gone, and the boys were asleep, and Nora and Phil passed out on the couch in front of the soft purr of television, Belly clomped up to the attic and retrieved his belongings from the back. Then he made his way to the second floor, down the hall to the guest room, Bonnie's old room, Jimi's old room: now it would be his room. He set his clothes in Jimi's little blue-and-yellow-stenciled dresser, his khaki pants in the closet. He lay on the little bed and stared at the glow-in-the-dark stars on the ceiling. He felt his liver relax; no more alcohol surged in his veins and he could see clearly in the night, no spinning or blurring or twisting of the dark. Booze was like a baby blanket for him — he curled up with it to sleep, but now was as good a time as any to start this terrible sobriety. He closed his eyes, and sleep came fast to find him, sleep took him in and covered him so he did not have to dream.

ONE STRIPE of sun snuck in the window and rested in a band across Belly's face. He rolled his head from side to side. He swatted at it. It wouldn't go away. He opened his eyes and he knew where he was and how he got there. He knew how many daughters he had and he knew what he had to do. He looked at the wallpaper — dark blue with glowing planets and comets and meteors and gassy stars, and he looked at Jimi's astronomy books and his toys and his rug with the alphabet embroidered along the fringe, and he was not sure his daughters ever had such things, if he or his wife ever stopped to ask them what they wanted or showed them how to get it. He picked up a heavy hardcover book, *The Way Things Work*, and he opened it and read about the telescope, how it collects light to make faint objects visible.

The drawers of his new blue kid dresser slid open easily. The air was soft now, it was cooler and less humid; all that water had let him go. He leafed through his jeans, darker jeans and lighter jeans and jeans with holes and jeans with patches, his stained jeans and jeans from his heavier days and from when he was a little thinner. He shut the drawer and opened the closet and plucked from the wire hanger his one pair of khakis with a crease streaming down the center. He showered and then he slipped on the pants, the sleek polished cotton satiny against his shins, and they were an inch too big now, but he liked the way they hung, the way they hovered a little too low on his bones, the hint of hipbone sneaking out the top of the waistband. They looked like old-man pants, and it was a good look for him. He looked fine. He looked like a man who wouldn't have to hump someone half his age, who didn't have to invent witty drunken comebacks in the bar, who didn't have to chase women or drink too much or hunt down old enemies who had disappointed him. He looked like a man who could sit on the porch and sip beer and watch ballerinas waddle by in July, watch tourists cluck at the uneven bricks of the sidewalk and the sturdy tufts of green weeds poking through, watch where the retards used to wander and where Shannon used to wheel by on white rollerskates with pink wheels, watch all the ghosts float by and he wouldn't have to talk to any of them. He wouldn't have to move. He could stay put in this life for as long as it took, him and his family, his cheap beer and his shit job and his old-man pants.

Nora had left him a note on the kitchen table — the family had gone to Jatski's and he could join them if he wanted. The house remained in last night's postapocalyptic state, piles of dirty plates and dried-up appetizers crusting the edges of Nora's cut-glass serving bowls. He tiptoed through the downstairs, stepping around the mess and plucking from the surfaces cups and saucers and stray pieces of flatware, and he piled them in the sink. He swept through all the rooms, straightening the furniture, crumbing the couch, lifting the table and reattaching the lame leg until it stood upright again. He even straightened the maelstrom of magnets and photographs on the refrigerator door. Two wallet-sized photographs of his grandsons were tucked under a Cudney's Cleaners magnet, and he slipped them off the fridge and into his wallet.

When he was satisfied he helped himself to coffee, sat and read the *Saratogian,* scanning the real-estate ads for cheap studios in Ballston Spa. Then he read the society section. Mary Lou Whitney was in town, of course, and her whole socialite posse, unscathed by past racetrack scandals. The rich people in this town, the summer people, were untouchable, and what made them so? Just because Cornelius Vanderbilt hooked up with some crooked Tammany Hall boxer all those years ago to open the racetrack, now his distant relatives still reaped the benefits. It seemed so unfair, that your genes decided your fate, or sealed it, or just cleaned it up so no matter how you erred you could still find your face in the society section.

For a very brief moment, at the height of his bookmaking days, when Belly was welcomed at civic events and the Paddock Pavilion at the track and even once ushered into Jack White's fourth-floor box in the clubhouse, Belly thought he could jump ship. He thought someday he'd shake hands with Mary Lou Whitney, thought he'd be invited to her glamorous gatherings, thought he'd sneak his way into private parties at Siro's, thought he'd leave behind his bland Irish roots, his blue-collar ties, thought the working-class accent he couldn't even hear would erase and he would slip into Society. Loretta had done it, had married some money and floated away, but even with her new two-carat rock gleaming on her finger she was still a drunk, still slumming at a crummy bar on a Thursday night, and maybe no one could escape his fate.

Belly closed the paper. He thumbed through a jar of coins perched atop the microwave, and then he made his way out into the world.

He walked down Spring Street, and now he cut across the park, and it was the most beautiful day in the world, in his life, in his new life which was now a week old: he thought about when Nora turned six months old and they knew they'd passed the SIDS stage and they could breathe easily now. He was going to live.

As the opposite entrance of the park birthed him onto Broadway, construction crews were finishing the last big stretch of work on the new building by the bus stop. Somehow while he wasn't looking, brick walls were erected to make a nouveau strip-mall fortress. Tourists sat in front of Café Newton with their million-dollar cappuccinos and everyone seemed calmer today in the cooler air, everything seemed lighter. He sat at the bus stop, on the other side of the street this time, in front of the ex-library, and watched the tourists stroll through the park, down Broadway, hands clasped at their backs in perfect leisure pose, dreaming themselves back to the time when Saratoga was the Queen of Spas. If he closed his eyes and erased the construction site behind him, erased the fancy new cars, if he just looked at the women with their broad-brimmed hats and the men in their linen suits, Belly could believe he was back there, too; he was one of them.

The bus pulled up and today Belly had exact change. He had thirty-two dollars in his wallet and his expired driver's license and the photographs of his grandchildren, and he sat on the bus as it hobbled through town past all the rich people and the locals sucking their money and the teenagers with piercings and skateboards and cotton-candy shades of hair.

They rolled down the arterial, Vanderbilt Highway, and Belly felt that sweeping sort of wind blow through his stomach, the way he felt when he went over a bridge, or got near water, any road trip where the bad gets left behind and the future is blessedly blank. And there was the mall.

He got off at the old mall, a mere shadow of a big-box that shrank next to its new mall neighbor. Inside he found the DMV, the terrible DMV with a line snaking out the door. Here's where all the angry people were.

At the information desk he received a license renewal form. It cost a whopping twenty-eight dollars, and on the back was a little checklist: has your license ever been suspended, have you been convicted of DUI, and then, have you ever been convicted of a felony? He had to answer yes to every question posed.

He waited in the endless line, shifting his weight between the hips, fingering the waistband of his khakis. He was a man in costume: no one would know him in this old-man uniform. Belly inched forward in the line until a woman called his number and she scanned his form, took his money, he held his breath while she ran her finger down the form and didn't even pause over the boxes he had checked.

He had to stand for a photograph, the points of his cowboy

boots aligned with the strip of blue on scuffed linoleum tile. Only three minutes later they presented him with his new license, and the unsmiling man in the digital photograph was old; he was a senior citizen, but he was a handsome old fellow and Belly liked him.

He left the mall, left the stale air behind, and he walked over the bumpy highway and the sun smiled from the top of the sky and it was not too hot, not humid. Sun glinted off the tarmac. Belly wondered how yesterday had given birth to today. Yesterday he was ready for the Lord to take him and now he didn't mind so much that his time had not yet come. He minded, but not that much.

He dodged the trucks on the highway and then he was once again in the big ocean of the parking lot. He had his new and improved ID in his pocket and the crumpled application and Wal-Mart had a million people milling about in the lot, the kind of people he knew in high school, the kind of people he saw at War Bar, at Jatski's, at the East Side Rec, that poor man's park. No oversized wicker hats, no bowties and linen suits.

He stood for a long moment in front of that big-box shop, that horrendous block of concrete, and he thought of the very first time he jumped from the cliffs up at Hadley-Lucerne, long before the retarded boy fell to his death. All his buddies were already in the water; they'd survived the fall. And he stood on that cliff that looked so humble from the water, but from up there on the rock the river was miles away, miles below him, and his friends called to him, called him a sissy, egged him on till the bottoms of his feet burned on the hot rock, burned with the desire to jump. And he did. He jumped and he felt his heart swallow his stomach and it took so long to hit the water, and when he did he landed sort of sideways, on his hip. The water slapped him and he swallowed a big mouthful of river and the wind was knocked out of him and he sank too far down, under the rapids. It was all so slow. Bodies kicked above him and then someone grabbed the back of his shorts and dragged him to the surface and he coughed up lungfuls of liquid and they razzed him, those boys, they patted him on the back and laughed and renamed him Belly-Flop for the afternoon. He swam to the water's edge and caught his breath. Drank a beer. Let the sun warm his blue blood and melt his heart back into the right space, settle his stomach back down below his diaphragm. Then he climbed out of the water, climbed back up the cliff and jumped off again, this time holding himself upright so his feet splashed first into the river and the rest of him followed.

Now Belly buttoned up his white shirt and smoothed out his khakis, twisted his belt buckle back to the center. He looked at the eight automatic doors welcoming him to Wal-Mart and the distance between his feet and the entrance was as far as the top of the cliff and the water. And Belly took a deep breath. And he jumped.

ACKNOWLEDGMENTS

My mother, Helaine Selin, bought me a plane ticket to Mexico, where I hammered out the first draft of this book, and a new computer when I spilled cranberry juice all over mine. My Saratoga pals, Julie Natale-Dwyer and Amy Knippenberg, housed me during portions of the writing, and my friends Katie Capelli, Lisa Sanditz, Bonnie Nadzam, and Melissa Lohman did me the honor of reading and commenting on early drafts, as did my stepfather, Bob Rakoff. My friend Lisa Gutkin sat me down by the railroad tracks in Peekskill and helped me devise a plan for the writing life. My father, Peter, provided a lot of technical racetrack information (he's a musician, not a gambler, I swear) and was my gateway to Saratoga. And my brother Tim sat me down on his East Village roof one night in 1999 and said, "If you want to be a writer, why are you going to urban planning school?" I have two other siblings, Adrienne and Ben, who should be thanked just for being so swell.

My deepest thanks to Ron Carlson, greatest teacher ever, and to T. M. McNally, Jewel Parker Rhodes, and Beckian Fritz Goldberg for their feedback. Thanks to all the drunken poets at ASU, from whom I stole many a good line, and the MFA girls: Amy, Bonnie, Josie, and Kyla. Thanks also to the Muse coffee shop in Tempe and its wonderful oddball collection of regulars.

Also thanks to Mike Lapinski for dropping me off in the desert to do this, to Joe Stillman for not being surprised that I actually did it, and to Sean Sheridan for his endless patience, love, and support while I wrapped it all up. Thanks to my wonderful agent, Amy Williams, and to my equally wonderful editor, Reagan Arthur, for championing the book. Thanks to Ledig House for letting me hang out in bucolic paradise while I did the revisions, and special thanks to Josh Kendall, who sent me knocking on the right doors.

ABOUT THE AUTHOR

Lisa Selin Davis was born in Saratoga Springs, New York, and raised in Amherst, Massachusetts. She worked in the art department in the film and television industry for eight years, and studied urban planning and environmental psychology at the City University of New York. Her articles have appeared in many newspapers and magazines, including *New York, Metropolis,* and *Preservation.* Her fiction and poetry have been published in *The Literary Review, Hayden's Ferry Review, West Branch,* and the anthology *Women Behaving Badly.* She holds an MFA from Arizona State University and teaches writing at the Pratt Institute in Brooklyn.